HELLFIRE

SISTERS IN LAW

JOHN ELLSWORTH

PENNY LAWN PRESS

HELLFIRE: SISTERS IN LAW

by

John Ellsworth

1

The target was Arum al-Assad, the ISIS oil czar.

The place was Syria--a country gripped in a civil war and overrun by terrorists who called themselves Islamic State of Iraq and al-Sham: ISIS.

Riding lazy thermals at 20,000 feet, the Predator drone had followed Arum al-Assad to a stone house in Deir ez-Zor, eastern Syria. The purpose of the oil czar's trip from Damascus to Deir ez-Zor was unknown to the U.S. The U.S. authorities believed his movement had something to do with the sale of crude oil. So they followed him. Blackguard demanded no less.

The people al-Assad was meeting inside the stone house were likewise unknown to the U.S. What was known was that the drone operator in Reno, Nevada claimed a high-value target in Arum al-Assad. The "high-value" designation came from Blackguard. Blackguard wanted an immediate missile strike. The drone pilot was ready to pull the trigger but he lacked green authorization. So he keyed his data into Big Sister and waited. Five minutes later he received the call in his headset. "You are green to go, Black Cat. Repeat, green to go."

The drone pilot launched one Hellfire missile. As the missile tore free of the rails, a new optical tracking image flashed on his flat screen. Estimated close to target was less than four seconds.

The targeted stone house was a large two story. Gathered inside were Sevi al-Assad, who was the sister of Arum al-Assad, the target; their grandmother--who owned the house; their parents; and their extended family.

Sevi was marrying Mohammad al-Marri that evening. A wedding feast was cooking and long tables made ready for the thirty wedding guests. Under roof was also the groom's entire family. Then there were additional friends and business acquaintances and one low-level cabinet member from the Deir ez-Zor Governorate, whose job was water quality control for the Muslim community of 211,857.

As custom dictated, the bride and her entourage prepared on the second floor of the house while the groom and his fellows prepared on the first. Neither bride nor groom had seen the other for twenty-four hours now.

Sevi, the bride, was elated when her brother Arum arrived mid-day. They hadn't seen each other in a year, as he was the ISIS Oil Minister and always traveling on business. Neither had any idea he was an eyes-on target of the U.S. military, nor should they have. While he worked with ISIS oil planning, he preferred to think his role was discreet and his identity was unknown to the outside world.

Sevi had no ISIS zealotry running in her blood and, while she didn't relate to her brother's motives and methods, all those differences were shed at the door. This was a glorious time of five-thousand-year-old ritual and feasting and today's problems were left outside in the dust. Because Arum was not part of the wedding party, he was allowed upstairs to visit his sister.

They embraced and she cried, her cheek on his chest. He patted her and reassured her all was well and that he was always with her. The fight, he assured her, was going well and he was safe. Then they sat on the bed in her private bedroom and held hands and talked. She updated him on their father's business venture. Father had recently taken over a plant that manufactured automobile tires. She emphasized that father missed having his son assist him in the business. Arum studied the colorful bedspread and sadly shook his head. "I cannot," he said. "There is Syrian oil to sell and I am needed."

"Where will you sell it?"

"To the Chinese."

"Not to the Americans?"

"Never to the Americans."

"But is that safe? What if the Americans learn that Syrian oil is destined for the Chinese?"

"As Allah instructs, Muslim people are to prosper. The Chinese will pay double what the Americans are willing to pay."

"So that makes it an easy decision for you."

"Exactly."

As Sevi and Arum talked, the hurried preparation of female children continued within the next two bedrooms on the same floor. Hair was being combed out and fashioned into party coiffures, light blush was allowed for girls over ten, and perfumes misted the air as fragrances were tested on thin young wrists.

One floor beneath the junior girls' preparation, the boys were having their rust knocked off. Baths were made ready, all orifices scrubbed and inspected by fathers made wary by the boys' antipathy toward soap and predilection for wrestling in the sandy soil outside. Luxurious clothes, unpacked the day before and hung around the walls to lessen wrinkling, were now sorted and donned as males of all ages made ready. Sevi and Arum's two younger brothers were included in that male admixture, alternately rough-housing with other boys and being snatched upright by their father and made to stand still while they were dressed in their best.

The Lockheed-Martin Hellfire was an air-to-surface missile developed for precision strikes against individuals. The missile was developed under the name Helicopter Launched, Fire and Forget Missile, which led to the acronym "Hellfire" that became the missile's formal name. The thermobaric weapon was a type of explosive that utilized oxygen from the surrounding air to generate an intense, high-temperature explosion. In practice its blast wave was significantly longer in duration than a conventional condensed explosive--the better to kill you with. And it was the last thing on earth the wedding party imagined would be introduced into their dwelling.

The missile entered the bedroom two doors down from Sevi and Arum, instantly killing all thirteen occupants--four adult women, four girls under the age of twelve, and five early-teen girls. Continuing through the ceiling to the first floor, the missile exploded and sucked all oxygen out of the house and ignited lungs with flame that killed everyone except Sevi al-Assad. She was located furthest from the blast and was blown out of the second floor bedroom as the wall fell away. Then the house caved in on itself, marking the scene as a spent funeral pyre.

No cries were heard, no moans of pain, no tortured breathing.

Spread-eagled across the bed of a Toyota pickup truck where she had come to rest was Sevi, twenty-four years old. She lay unconscious, which was, in a desperate way, fortuitous because her back was broken, her left eardrum gone and her left kneecap torn loose and lying on her thigh. Had she been conscious she likely would have died from shock. Sirens sounded across the city of Deir ez-Zor. Pedestrians stopped in their tracks as their eyes searched the skies for the Predator responsible for the thick black smoke on the eastern end of the city. Many would be dead; the TV would broadcast accounts that night and another unfathomable tragedy would fashion a new population of West haters.

Before the EMTs arrived, a next-door neighbor discovered Sevi and stood watch over her broken body, discouraging those who would otherwise try to move her.

"Wait!" he told them. "She is injured and we don't know how badly. We'll wait for the EMTs!"

When the EMTs came, Sevi was expertly manipulated on a backboard and strapped in place for hospital transport.

At the hospital, it was determined she was alive.

But just barely.

2

Blackguard was ruthless in its pursuit of oil.

Sevi's brother, Arum al-Assad, had died because of his plan to sell crude oil to the Chinese instead of the Americans. Blackguard had come into this information through the use of paid informants. Blackguard belonged to the DuMont brothers; American oilmen who, in the end, believed all oil beneath the earth belonged to them.

It was all part of a much larger picture for the DuMont brothers.

They thought themselves patriots. They believed in the drastic reduction of corporate income taxes, the dramatic de-funding of services for the needy, and they opposed climate change activists on all fronts.

Their names were Wilfred and Edlund DuMont and they had inherited a two hundred billion dollar fortune from their wildcatter father, who was said to have drained off a trillion barrels of Texas crude for his five thousand service stations across North America.

The brothers were Massachusetts born and bred. They had graduated from Harvard Law two years apart, and were three years apart in age. Both had degrees from Yale in economics and both envisioned a return to the days before the EPA was formed with its regulations and restraints on drilling. They longed for the time when business had unfettered access to petroleum and coal reserves, and the clear-cutting of forests made good economic sense.

Wilfred was born in 1935 and Edlund in 1933. They were too young to serve in World War II and Korea, and sat out the Vietnam War, thanks to draft deferments handed out by John Kennedy not only to the unwashed but also to Libertarian elitists like the brothers. The whole Vietnam fiasco offended the brothers' economic sensibilities so they contributed twenty million dollars to Richard M. Nixon's campaign. It was thought President Nixon would immediately with-draw America's military. Vietnam possessed no oil; rice and bananas were the chief exports; so why make war there?

The wars of the Middle East were another matter altogether. Those wars were about oil and oil was to America what coal was to electricity. In 2009, when ISIS was struggling to arm its soldiers and feed the citizens of seized cities, the brothers boldly stepped forward. In return for Russian Kalashnikov AK-47 rifles, the leaders of ISIS entered into secret leases of Syrian oil fields with the brothers. The leases would take hold and the oil would begin flowing to DuMont oil tankers when the Syrian president was deposed and the flag of ISIS flew over the Syrian Desert. Arum al-Assad had gone back on the deal with his plan to sell Syrian oil to China. He died for that.

While these machinations were cloaked in secrecy, they didn't escape the notice of America's Fifth Estate in the person of one Althea Berenson, a freelancing journalist. She had blown the lid off things with a series of reports on the link between a certain vice-pres-ident during the Bush W years and a certain business owned by the DuMonts that masqueraded as a construction company. That company operated on a massive scale--erecting the Baghdad Green Zone in sixty days following the American victory over Saddam Hussein. The feat required forty thousand carpenters, plumbers, electricians, and engineers. It was said to have airlifted one hundred times the material delivered by Allied aircraft during the 1948 Berlin Airlift. The Berlin job was primarily the work of the DuMont broth-ers' sire, Colonel Edmund Hillary DuMont. The Green Zone was primarily the work of Blackguard, the brothers' global construction, acquisition, and vigilante arm.

When Althea Berenson discovered the link between the vice-president and Blackguard, her newspaper series was nominated for a Pulitzer. But then the vice president taught America what NFL running backs had long known: the virtues of misdirection. The VP's office exposed a CIA field agent, which obfuscated the appointment of a Special Prosecutor and the jailing of a minor talent among the VP's staff--a sentence later commuted by the president.

During the brouhaha that followed the CIA agent outing, the VP made his getaway to Montana, retiring there in near-seclusion while remaining "quaintly quotable"--his literary agent's words--when party politics required a hatchet job. But Althea Berenson wasn't finished with the story of the transfer of American treasure to Blackguard; rather than let the story die when the VP retired, she reversed field and went after Blackguard itself. The public's eye followed.

The war in Iraq earned Blackguard a half trillion dollars. Blackguard vice-presidents purchased island hideaways; Gulfstream jets were ordered by the hundreds; fabulous parties were thrown that began in Miami Beach and ended when the sun came up in Tokyo. One thousand Hollywood-ites were feted in Vancouver over a weekend that included, in the swag baskets, a three-carat diamond ring and a five thousand dollar marker for a posh Atlantic City casino. In the end it was said the U.S. Mint had established a Baghdad printing facility. Hundred dollar bills flew off the press 24/7 and truckloads of cash sallied forth to buy the allegiance of tribal heads and Blackguard soldiers. It was, Althea found, money in the extreme. It was, Althea wrote, the greatest transfer of public monies to a private company in American history. Of the five hundred billion dollars in question, Althea further reported the DuMont brothers had secretly pocketed--loosely speaking--one hundred billion for themselves.

Ten years later they were funding presidential campaigns to the tune of one hundred million dollars. So far their handpicked stooges had run unsuccessfully, but the brothers knew it was only a matter of time until they'd win. Before 2024 they expected to fund and thus own an American president. So Althea's reportage went. The only way to prevent this happening, she determined, was to break a story that revealed the brothers for what they were: Machiavellian puppeteers ready to recreate the United States as a Libertarian plutocracy. In short, the one percent would progress from ruling the country economically to ruling it politically as well. America would become a true dictatorship controlled by two brothers with oil coursing through their veins.

ALTHEA BERENSON WAS BLACK, thirty-five and remained hot on the trail of Blackguard's scent. Althea wore a size six and was mocha complected, like her friend Christine, but she wore her hair short while Christine wore hers long. Althea was a mother of four, and a two-time bride who was enjoying singularity now that the kids could babysit themselves and ex-husbands could be prevailed upon for weekend fathering. This new order freed up the journalist for her travels and restored her strength for her travails as she published widely and as she appeared on HBO's Real Time with Bill Maher.

Her public persona was forever argumentative and confrontational while her private persona was gentle and loving, especially with her children and her men. The kids were a given; the men came and went.

Friendships abounded among Chicago's greater and lesser lights. Althea worked South Side food drives as capably and gracefully as she worked North Shore charity auctions. During the social mix she became friends with Christine Susmann, the attorney defending the husband of Althea's college roommate on two counts of income tax evasion. A coffee was held to raise legal fees for the husband's defense fund. At the last minute Christine Susmann attended and proclaimed the coffee unnecessary as she was going to offer a free defense. Which she did. The husband served nine months in the same federal lockup where Martha Stewart had cleaned washrooms for lying to the FBI. That alone was enough for the husband to claim victory.

~

ALTHEA AND CHRISTINE began meeting for Wednesday lunch.

A few months later, Winona Lindsey joined them. She was a Chicago Police detective who had jumped ship and now worked as a full-time investigator for Christine's law firm. Where Althea was compact and cherubic around the face, Winona was tall, muscular, and capable of taking out a kneecap with a leg sweep. Her naturally blonde hair was often worn pulled back in a ponytail. And at night, when Winona was on the town, it would be worn down and brushed to a luster. Where Althea was an intrepid researcher and Winona was a fearless detective, Christine was both weight lifter and firearms expert who swore allegiance to the rule of law. But even while confirming her respect for the law, Christine would slam home a .40 caliber magazine. And of course Christine was a lawyer's lawyer; beginning as a JAG paralegal during her army days and then working as a paralegal for Thaddeus Murfee. Christine had come into her own after suing the president of Russia and paying for law school with his dollars.

Today they were meeting in Reynaldo's Bistro, an upscale Michigan Avenue eatery in Chicago on the North Loop. Reynaldo's was frequented by members of the local bar bent on keeping a low profile in a diner geographically removed from the Chicago legal system, which held court on the South Loop.

Althea arrived first, grabbed a table for four, and was systematically reviewing the menu a line at a time. So far, nothing had struck her fancy. A White Russian found its way to her and she took a mouthful and tilted her head back, allowing the chilled liquid to do its work on her alimentary canal while sparking her taste buds like Christmas tree lights. She was, in a word, happy with the world. White Russians and crowded menus did that to her yet never moved the needle on the size six ensembles.

Next came Christine straight from court where she had spent the morning arguing against a motion for summary judgment filed by the City of Chicago's attorneys in a case involving a highway lane-drop and a claim of negligent signage in a construction zone. Her client had been made a quadriplegic when a seven-foot drainage pipe abruptly halted his fifty-mile-per-hour Taurus.

"How are tricks, Chris?" Althea asked with another swallow of her drink.

"Starting early, Althea?" said Christine, referring to the alcoholic drink.

"Never quit so there's no early," Althea quipped.

"I hear that. Tricks are good. I'm suing all the right people and defending all the wrongly accused."

"And the kids?"

"Jamie is thriving. He's in advanced everything, his junior year. Janny is growing too fast and giving her third piano recital Saturday afternoon. Life is good."

"Men?"

"No. Still missing Sonny," said Christine, referring to her deceased husband who had been murdered by a hit man who was actually after Christine.

"That's too bad. But I understand, definitely."

At that point Winona Lindsey joined the two women. She wore a translucent skim of makeup like some Vogue goddess. She was beyond attractive even in middle age and turned heads as she passed through the restaurant.

"Hey, Toots," said Christine to Winona. "Glad you could make it."

Winona did a fake shudder. "Terrible case. Made me ill to hear about it."

"Like what?" asked Christine?

"Well, we got an email from some woman in Syria. An American missile wiped out her entire family. Girls, boys, brothers, parents, aunts and uncles--all buried under twenty feet of rubble."

"Sounds grisly," said Althea. "My guess is the DuMont brothers had something to do with it."

"Why would you say that?" asked Winona.

"I would say that because nothing horrible happens in the Middle East without the DuMonts' fingerprints all over."

"Why did she email us?" asked Christine.

Winona nodded. "She found our website. She liked what she read about you."

"And she's looking to us for what?"

"Something about suing the government."

"For what?" asked Althea. "Murder?"

"It was a drone strike. The only government I know of still killing off people with drones is the U.S. Stands to reason it was us."

Althea shuddered and took another sip of her drink. "DuMonts. Screw them."

The waiter materialized and took drink orders from Christine and Winona, who ordered coffee and iced tea, respectively.

"Seriously," said Christine to Althea, "what makes you connect the DuMonts to this particular drone strike?"

Althea shrugged. "Their next stop is Syria. There're ten trillion barrels of sweet crude under Syrian sand. How could they not be involved in removing obstacles in the way of DuMont oil tankers?"

"Gives me pause," said Christine. "We'll need to follow up on that," Christine said to Winona. "Let's see where it goes."

"Hey, you're talking to the wrong lady there," said Althea. "How about hiring me to investigate? It's only one more rock on a huge pile I already have stacked up against the DuMonts. With me having ninety-nine percent of the research already done on my laptop, I can get back to you on it inside of thirty days."

"Interesting," said Christine. "How are your resources?"

"Intact. I've got people everywhere in the Middle East."

"CIA?"

"Some. Some Mossad. Some Iraqi. Some even Syrian army. You need it, I've got it. Why, are you thinking about suing for this lady?"

"I'm thinking we should give it a hard look," said Christine. "I'm thinking I definitely want to follow up with her. What's her name, Win?"

"Sevi. Her name is Sevi al-Assad and the wedding party was in Deir ez-Zor. Which is eastern Syria, to you."

Christine nodded and spoke thoughtfully. "Sevi. *Sevi al-Assad versus Blackguard, Inc., Defendant, and United States of America, Defendant*. Has a good ring to it."

"It does," agreed Winona. "I told her we were interested."

"You did? Without talking to me?"

"You said when I came over from the PD that I would work independently. Well, this is an exercise of my independence."

"Got me there," said Christine. "I wasn't challenging you. Or maybe I was. Sorry about that."

"Forget it. This case has legs. A huge upside."

"How many people died in the drone strike?"

"Get ready. She said forty-two lost their lives."

"OMG," said Althea. "I'm definitely in."

"Yes, so am I," said Christine. "When can I talk to her?"

"I told her you could come to Turkey next week. That too soon?"

"Depends on my calendar."

"Covered. I moved some staff around so you could take the Gulfstream to Turkey."

"We're serious today, aren't we?"

Winona smiled and accepted her iced tea from the waiter. "That's what you hired me for. Just doing my job, Boss."

"And rocking my world," said Christine.

"So what about me?" asked Althea. "Am I onboard?"

"You are," said Christine. "I want a smoking gun linking the DuMonts to the drone attack. Plain and simple."

"I can do that," said Althea. "It'll be the best money you spend this year."

"What, you're charging me for this?"

Althea smiled. "You're lucky to get me. I'm worth every penny."

"You are, Girl," said Christine. "Definitely that."

3

Five months passed.

Microsurgery repaired the fractured spine. The knee was reconstructed. Four surgeries later and Sevi began physical therapy. It was at first thought she wouldn't walk again, but in her determination she managed to develop a limping gait. Hearing loss was 100% and 50%. She was fitted with a hearing device and managed to again converse.

All her family was gone. Her father and mother, brothers, aunts, uncles, and in-laws-to-be were lost in the destruction leveled at them by the Americans. The fiancée she planned to build her life with would never become the husband she had dreamed of so often. She missed her people and cried dozens of times a day. She saw no reason to recover and live on, but her therapists demanded she start her life all over.

She returned to her home in a small village outside Deir ez-Zor and eventually found a job as an Internet-based computer programmer. Her undergraduate degree was in computer science and she had most of a master's done in software engineering through an online school in California.

While her body had been restored, her emotional state was anger from one end to the other. She hated Americans, hated America and hated everything Western. She came to understand that her oldest brother had been the target that wedding day and that the rest of those present were merely collateral damage in the Americans' quest for "high-value" targets. With every day that passed, she loathed the West for its dispassionate genocide. She yearned to hit back, to destroy something--anything--and so displace her pain outside herself.

At night she studied maps and articles about America. She wondered how one might smuggle a bomb there--anywhere inside the country would do--and avenge her family's death. She imagined herself as a suicide bomber for ISIS and carrying forward her brother's work.

One night, as she scanned the Internet and sought her revenge, she came upon a website. It was the website of an American lawyer, a woman who claimed she practiced public policy law.

In a flash, Sevi recognized what needed to be done. She sent an email to the woman's website. In it she asked, "Would you sue the U.S. government for the death of my family?"

The woman's staff immediately wrote back and the conversation began. They wanted to talk. They wondered if Sevi could get to Ankara, Turkey. Sevi had never in her life considered traveling to Turkey. But she began to study the route and began to realize how that might be done. For if she made it there, the American lawyer would come to Turkey and they would talk.

Sevi wrote back and said she would find a way to meet the lawyer in Turkey.

Then she studied the woman's Internet page.

Her name was Christine Susmann.

"Well, Christine," said Sevi to the night sky, "while you are busy making the lawsuit, I will be busy making the bomb. Just get me to America."

With no other surviving heirs, her father's business ventures defaulted to Sevi. This included the plant that manufactured tires.

Having inherited from her father the adaptive business gene as well, she put the tire enterprise up for sale. After outstanding balances and tax owed to the governorate, she netted 2,833,931 SYP--about $15,000 USD. She gave away her TV, refrigerator and computer to the family living in the flat directly below her.

Relieved of all worldly goods, she purchased a seat on a train that took her to the Syrian border with Turkey. At the border, she then walked to the bus station with her backpack and traveled into Turkey.

It was a long, crowded, dusty ride that provided only intermittent times of relief from the overcrowding whenever the driver managed to kick the AC unit with the proper force, causing it to roar to life and circulate air back down the aisle to where Sevi sat reclined, a damp handkerchief over her face, as she tried to find a moment alone.

Then she was in Ankara, where she checked into a hotel.

Now to notify the American lawyer she was waiting.

Then it would begin.

4
—————

Christine located her window seat on the Turkish Airlines' Boeing B777-3. It was a wide-bodied plane with ample legroom and a seat three inches wider than business class.

She buckled in and stared out the Plexiglas. Her reflection stared back: thick black hair parted severely down the middle and jaw-length on the sides, chocolate eyes gleaming with anticipation, eyes that interpreted her world carefully and courageously, a thin but attractively flat nose with a white scar across the bridge from a training accident suffered in the Army's SERE school in Fort Bragg, and a firm mouth capable of holding its own in any dispute. She liked her face and, knowing she was totally alone, she winked at her reflection. It was childish and a bit coquettish, but it balanced out all the serious in her life.

Stowed in the overhead was her backpack. It was her only piece of luggage. The topmost pocket contained her iPhone and mini-iPad, both of which had been carefully scrubbed of all IP addresses that would indicate she was American, then loaded with browser bookmarks and histories that proved she was a Pakistani. An unopened juice bottle of Pakistani origin lay secured in the water loop on the other side of the pack. Inside the large zipper on the front of the bag were Pakistani cigarettes and blue jeans and colored T-shirts, as well as American Teva sandals with an Amazon purchase receipt stored on the iPad's memory chip, which showed a conversion of currency from Pakistani rupees to American dollars. And down below, in the lower pocket, she had carefully stowed her passport and driver's license, also Pakistani, both several years old, both carefully forged at a cost of $12,500. Everything she carried and all traces and electronic bytes proved--and, more importantly, didn't disprove--her claim of Pakistani citizenship.

SHE FLEW Turkish Airlines from Chicago to Istanbul with a four-hour layover in Berlin. A change of planes allowed onboard a dark man. When first stepping inside the aircraft, his quarry was immediately picked out from the three hundred faces aboard the 777 in a quick glance down the aisle. He had received a half-dozen photographs to memorize and he had been a careful student. He took his seat directly behind hers. He carefully avoided looking at her.

They landed at 7:15 p.m. Istanbul time, jarring her awake from a light, restless sleep. She stood in her row and waited for it to clear, then reached up and found her backpack in the overhead. She swung the backpack out and down and worked the straps up over her shoulders. She hadn't changed out of her sweatshirt, though she thought the outside temperature would be stifling and that she would need to shed the sweatshirt before leaving the terminal.

The dark, seemingly oblivious man behind her, timed his own standing and gathering of his backpack so that he would be able to slip in behind her and follow her from the plane. He was shiny and dark, a Baghdad native and a Muslim. A hex-wrench shaped scar traveled from his right eyebrow straight back for an inch then down his cheek for three inches. The suture line was pink against his skin and fresh and angry. Tortoise shell eyeglasses were perched atop his head. He fingered them absently once the backpack was in place. He was dressed in black khaki pants and a black Polo shirt. He appeared almost careless as he tinkered with his pack and glasses. More than anything, he was patient.

As Christine fought to shrug into her backpack straps over the bulky sweatshirt, the dark man leaned back against his seat and allowed two travelers to pass by and join the line standing in the aisle. He pretended to be busy with his own pack but actually was not; he was simply waiting for Christine. When he had boarded her flight in Berlin, he brought with him her flight particulars courtesy of the hacked Turkish Airline reservation system. He knew her only as Ama Gloq. That was the name given to him. Not much of a challenge, he thought of her stature, as he sized her up. The rest of it promised to be simple, for an inveterate plant like him.

The Iraqi followed her up the Jetway and into the terminal. There she found a light-skinned woman wearing a headscarf and holding a simple hand-lettered sign that said, "Ama." Christine approached the woman and identified herself.

"I'm Ama Gloq."

"Say it."

"When it rains it pours."

"When it's raining it's pouring."

Christine nodded and accepted the straw-colored bag the woman held out to her.

Without another word they parted.

Christine headed for the restroom. She found an empty booth and opened the bag. Perfect: Glock 19 with IWB (In Waist Band) holster and extra clip for the belt.

She shrugged out of the backpack, pulled up the sweatshirt, worked it over her head, and stuffed it into the large pocket. She pulled at the waistband of her blue jeans and inserted the holstered gun inside on the right. The extra clip snapped over her two-inch-wide black belt. She pulled her white T-shirt hem down over the holster. The T-shirt was two sizes too big, and hid the print of the IWB carry. Quickly she finger-brushed her hair back on both sides and stood upright. Everything fit, the gun felt familiar, so she unlocked the stall and stepped out.

She managed one step before a forearm came smashing around the corner of the stall and caught her directly in the throat. She was thrown back, staggered, gasping for air, and raising her hands defensively as her tae kwon do reflex took over. A woman followed the forearm and stepped directly in front of Christine, pointing a small revolver in a two-handed grip. Christine appeared to faint and as she dropped, she swept her right leg against the woman's shin, dropping her to the tile floor. As the woman fell, Christine rolled into her, seizing the pistol and slamming it hard against the woman's nose. Blood spurted from the gaping wound and Ama knew the woman's own tears would momentarily blind her, giving Ama at best three seconds to end it. She raised up to her knees and struck again, this time with the butt of the pistol, fracturing the skull. Instantly the woman's eyes fluttered and closed and she limply sprawled across the tile. Christine stood and wiped the gun quickly. Then she dropped it on the floor, and stepped over her assailant, exiting the restroom while assuming the relaxed face of a passenger who just woke up and stepped off a long flight. She didn't notice the dark man standing across the passageway, outside the men's restroom, studying a street map and moving his lips as if reading.

Nor did she notice him toss aside the map and follow when she headed outside for the taxi stand.

A ten-year-old Volvo cab was next in line. The driver motioned her to climb in. She pulled open the back door. Tossing her backpack across the seat, she stepped in and was lowering herself to the seat when she felt a hand push her shoulder. The dark man looked into her eyes and she raised her legs as if to kick at him, when he said, simply, "When it rains it pours."

She froze, then lowered her feet to the floor of the cab.

"You are?" she asked.

"I am Swarmi Reddiz. I am your bodyguard."

"You are early. You were to wait until I met the woman."

"I know. Move over, please."

Christine slid across the seat and the man sat down beside her.

"Winona Lindsey sent me."

"Show me your ID, please."

He smiled. "Ama, I'm not carrying ID any more than you are. The last thing we want here is ID."

"How do I know you're who you say you are?"

"Respond, please, so I can be sure you are who I think you are."

She sat back hard against the seat and stared out her window for several seconds. The man had the passkey--the word quintet that proved authorization. She turned back around.

"When it's raining it's pouring," she said.

"Thank you," said the man named Reddiz.

The cab driver raised his hands and shrugged and said in Arabic, "Where to?"

Christine answered in Arabic. "Pendik Station, please."

The cabbie nodded and smiled. It was a welcome fare, as Pendik Station was twenty-five kilometers east of Istanbul. He wheeled the old Volvo into the moving traffic lane and beamed in the rearview. "Please relax and enjoy."

"We'll talk at the station," said Reddiz to Christine, with a nod at the driver. "Ears."

Christine stared out the window to her left.

Istanbul was a modern city, the freeway was smooth and freshly topped, and the evening air not nearly as hot as she had expected. In fact, it was even pleasant. She cracked her window and inhaled. The air was pure and clean with a hint of plowed earth and new plants pushing through the soil of the fields that were opening up as they left the city behind. Ahead of them was an eighteen-wheeler with the omnipresent mud flaps of the nude woman in silver silhouette and for a brief instant she imagined she was back in Chicago, rolling eastbound on the Kennedy, headed for the office. She thought of Sonny, her husband of ten years, now deceased, and her two children, Jamie and Janny, probably huddled around the TV since Christine was away and their nanny was known to snooze.

A pang of regret pierced her; what in God's name had she been thinking, taking on this assignment? Had she totally lost her mind?

She gasped at the cool air but then caught herself and forced her mind to empty itself of thoughts of home and family and focus instead on the Now, where she was traveling ninety kilometers per hour on the outskirts of Istanbul next to a man whom she neither expected nor trusted but who seemed to know her. Her mind raced off in a new direction and again she forced calm down through her body and up into her brain. It was partly from her military training; the SERE school at Fort Bragg where she had learned Survival, Evasion, Resistance, and Escape. It was her innate ability since birth to control her thoughts and feelings and steady herself even in moments of danger. At last she smiled and stared ahead through the windshield.

Suddenly she was all-in.

No regrets, no looking back; let's get underway and see about suing Uncle.

The last ten kilometers were a blur. She could almost feel the luxury of the overstuffed seats on the high-speed train to Ankara. The man sitting next to her was silent. Was he her bodyguard? If so, he was early to the game. Or was he a plant? But who would know about her mission? She knew the answer to that, of course. The NSA monitored all communications between Americans and foreigners. She had no doubt they knew she was meeting with the Syrian woman. She had no doubt they knew the topic of the meeting. She glanced sideways at the man. She wondered if he knew about the meeting too and had come to protect the government. Or was he simply there as her protection?

She wondered if he knew he might breathe his last in the next fifteen minutes.

She just hadn't decided.

5

Sevi was waiting in Ankara for the meeting with Christine. She was at once both excited and sad, as she considered taking her revenge against the Americans. Excited because her time had finally come around; sad because of her loss.

She was lying on the made bed, a four-poster, when the alarm on her iPhone beeped. It was almost time.

She rolled upright on the bed and crossed to the window of the JW Marriott Hotel. The room was richly constructed with wainscoting all around. Mirrors festooned all six walls and reflected the indirect and direct lighting that had been expertly installed so that the mirrors all represented eye-catching points of light. Expensive, soft bedclothes and a luxurious bathroom with recessed lighting and whirlpool tub enhanced the ambiance. Room service that would bring any food from its five star restaurant in under thirty minutes, no matter the food, country represented, or difficulty in preparation, was an almost unimaginable benefit. The room had been reserved by the American lawyer's office and impressed Sevi no end.

Earlier that evening, she had been reflecting on the things she would say to the lawyer and the things she wouldn't say. There were much more of the latter than the former. For example, she wouldn't mention that ISIS activists in a camp near her home had schooled her in the gathering of materials for making a bomb. She also wouldn't mention that she knew the chemistry and physics of plastique explosives or that she knew the mechanics and electronics of timing devices and detonation plugs. The schooling had been quick and she had been a most willing student, as she allowed her mind to consider revenge and the bombing of an American grade school in payback for all the young people murdered on her own wedding day. Among the dead were over twenty-five children--all related to her, or who soon would have been, by marriage. The twenty-five were all under the age of fourteen and were total innocents in the struggles among oil-seeking nations in the Middle East. They had been children who knew only that there was going to be a wonderful party after the mandatory wedding ceremony.

Crossing to the window and its drawn curtains, she was wearing the comfortable Turkish bloomers called ÅŸalvar, a top with sleeves to the elbows, and a headscarf, as she would be venturing downstairs to the hotel restaurant and one always wore the headscarf in public.

She passed her hand through the curtain closure seam and peered out at the traffic below. In the distance she could make out the buildings on the campus of Bilkent University and a mile or two closer the low profile of the campus of Hacettepe University. She knew these things because she had been encamped in the hotel for two days and had purchased a guidebook in the hotel gift shop as a way of passing time. Almost at her feet below was the Armada Shopping Center, where she had spent a long, leisurely afternoon window-shopping and tasting coffees from America at the bazaar there. She had with her the clothes on her back and a small suitcase containing all her other worldly goods remaining after what she called the great selloff. She had transformed her world from one of property ownership to one of a small sum of money in the Bank of America and a willingness to travel lightly to America where she would start over.

The lawyer would be arriving at Ankara (ESB-Esenboga) Airport any moment and would settle into the room next to Sevi's--all reservations obtained and paid for by the lawyer.

Sevi watched the traffic below as it crawled along the boulevard. At a level with her thirtieth floor room, and in the distance, a continuous stream of winking aircraft lights passed from left to right as incoming flights arrived and disgorged their customers in Turkey's capital city on this particular Friday night.

She considered her temporary circumstances. She knew that Turkey was bordered by eight countries: Bulgaria to the northwest; Greece to the west; Georgia to the northeast; Armenia, Iran and the Azerbaijani exclave of Nakhchivan to the east; and Iraq and Syria to the south. On the other side of the hotel from where she stood, the Mediterranean Sea was to the south; the Aegean Sea to the west; and the Black Sea to the north. Her guidebook, while instructive enough, had been carelessly deposited in the bathroom waste paper bin that afternoon. It was a final gesture by Sevi, a way of saying goodbye to the Middle East, and she was anxious to strike out for the West, anxious to learn about her new home. She was bravely resigned to the fact that she would be totally starting over there. None of what she knew would matter anymore. Life as she had known it was over and done. For her, a new day was coming.

She withdrew her hand from the curtains, allowing them to reseal along the seam, and went to the marble desk with its gold telephone and array of in-hotel buttons that could be pressed and instantly summon everything from food to facials, from massages to flowers. It was nearing the time for her meeting with Christine so she reconsidered going downstairs to eat. She selected the room service line and lifted the phone.

"I would like American food," she told the attendant. "What do you recommend?"

"We have beefsteak dinners, chicken, and fish."

"Something with fish."

"May I suggest our sautéed salmon? It comes with spring potatoes and steamed vegetables. And perhaps a cocktail or wine?"

"That would be fine. But no alcohol. American coffee, instead."

"American dining at your service. We will be at your door in thirty minutes or less. Always our promise to you at the JW Marriott, Ankara."

"Thank you."

She sat back in the desk chair and considered herself in the mirror. She was young looking despite the horrors of the last year, but still moved with a limp, had difficulty with conversations and couldn't hear at all without her behind-the-ear hearing aid worn hidden beneath her long hair. They had left her quite a mess, the Americans. She was always in pain somewhere in her body, especially along the spine where she had suffered massive trauma. Sleep was difficult and restless and she doubted she would ever be able to receive a man in the missionary position. But that was beside the point. She had lost the only man she would ever consider marrying and there would be no looking for another to replace him. That part of her life--the romance of youth--had been amputated away from her psyche as carefully as the damaged bone and cartilage of her physical injuries had been removed. No, she was alone and she had come to be satisfied with that. Not happy, certainly, but satisfied. And though there was a major difference between the two, it was a difference she had learned to live with.

The Americans had taught her that.

Now it was their turn. She would teach them what that loss felt like.

Then, maybe in the future they would be less careless with their missiles. Her explosive device and the message it would send would save Syrian lives.

Maybe.

She could only hope. It was all she had left.

6

Althea Berenson had wasted no time in buying an insider. She had traveled from Chicago to Washington and was meeting the man at three o'clock on the benches directly south of the Capitol Rotunda.

It was cold in the nation's capital that day, as a late-winter storm front had entered the area, and a soggy snow was forecast, one that wouldn't stick. Althea had dressed accordingly, and was wearing navy slacks with a pale pink shirt and a Fog overcoat with the liner zipped inside. Large sunglasses hid her chocolate eyes and her hair was pulled back and loosely captured in a ponytail with a gold clasp. A camera hung from her neck and, as she approached the rotunda, she appeared to be snapping pictures of the tourist vistas offered by the Capitol and its environs. She approached the row of green benches and sat at the far left end. Now to wait. He had said he would be wearing a red vest beneath his top coat so she vaguely recognized the cue when a man approached. He was in his mid-forties with a high forehead, wearing a heavy overcoat with a red vest beneath. He also wore deerskin gloves and a checkered brown and white muffler. He sat on her bench at the far end. He stared straight ahead, as did Althea.

His code name was Agreeable. That's all she knew about him, although a "real" name had been provided in the two phone calls she had had with him on secure phones. He was a high-level employee of Blackguard, the world-wide black arts/construction company belonging to the DuMont brothers, and it was said he had, one, become disenchanted with the company's policies, and, two, was open to the idea of accepting a large sum of money for information. With Christine's full blessing and support, the money had been provided out of a special fund kept offshore by the lawyer for just such purposes as this. One million USD now reposed in a Swiss bank in a numbered account accessible only by the man known as Agreeable.

Now it was up to him to earn the final four digits of the account's access code. Was he prepared to give up the information Althea desired? She would know the answer to this in the next several minutes.

"I am Agreeable," he said through a plume of frosty breath. He neither looked at Althea nor away from her, instead staring straight ahead as he spoke clearly and confidently.

"And I'm Willing," said Althea. "You're late."

"We can't take enough precautions in this city to make sure we're not being followed. While I am ten minutes late, I can assure you I haven't been followed."

"Then my wait was worth it," said Althea.

"Do you have my digits?" he asked.

"I do. Do you have my data stick?"

"Yes. It is inside my left glove. I will leave it on the bench when I walk away."

"And it contains the communication between the drone team in Reno and Edlund DuMont, as you have represented?"

"It does. And more."

"More? Such as?"

"I have given you all Syrian drone strikes over the last thirty days. A freebie, you could say."

Althea's pulse quickened. The additional data was more, much more, than she could have hoped for.

"Why would you be so generous?"

"You are paying me a large sum of money. I want you to know that not only do I have access to the messaging you want, I can also supply it at a quantity you probably never imagined possible. I can give you a year's worth of evidence. There could even be other cases for the lawyer."

"For the right price, of course."

"Of course. So take my glove with you, study the data stick, and do what you will with the information. When you decide you're ready for more of the same, notify me as before."

The man stood to leave. Both gloves now remained where he had been sitting.

"My digits, please."

"We've made it easy for you."

"Then go slowly, so I won't forget."

"One-one-one-one. Enjoy your money."

Without another word, the man turned and headed for the Capitol Rotunda itself. Althea waited until he had disappeared inside the building, and then she stood and retrieved the deerskin gloves, stuffing them inside her left and right pockets. As she walked off, she felt inside the left glove, the one in her left pocket. Her fingers touched the data stick--the thumb drive. A smile played briefly on her lips, then she abruptly forced it from her face.

She headed for Union Station. Upon arriving there, she was shown to an enclosed seating area at the East Street Cafe. She ordered hot chocolate and a cream cheese pastry and, while she waited, fingered the thumb drive inside the pocket of her coat. Her refreshments arrived and she dawdled over her drink and pastry, watching the other customers coming and going, all the while making sure she hadn't been followed and wasn't being observed. Thirty minutes crept past. At last satisfied that her assignation had gone unnoticed, she paid her check and left by taxi for her hotel in Arlington.

The hotel room was as she had left it except the queen bed was made and fresh flowers were now centered on the small dining table.

Althea tore off her overcoat and flung it carelessly across the bed, then hurried, all but running, to the laptop she had left on the dining table.

She flipped up the lid and waited while the computer sprang to life. Then she inserted the thumb drive. Carefully she first copied all data to the cloud drive accessible by her and Christine only. Then came the acid test: a review of the communications transcript between Reno and Edlund DuMont the day of the wedding.

She studied the data for a good half hour before she finally leaned back and smiled.

There was no doubt. None other than Edlund DuMont himself had signed off on the drone attack that had killed the family of Sevi al-Assad. It was unmistakable and undeniable.

The Sisters in Law had their smoking gun.

Now the real work could begin.

7

The man in the red vest hurried back to Blackguard's headquarters in the Watergate Complex after his meeting with Althea. Waiting in his office was Randall C. Maxwelle, a Naval Academy graduate and navy commander (retired), who now headed up Blackguard's military-commercial liaison team. Maxwelle's undergraduate degree was in computer science and his Ph.D. from Georgetown was in computer engineering.

Maxwelle's role in the data sale had been to prepare the transcripts turned over to Althea Berenson and, by extension, Christine Susmann, the lawyer looking into their oil dealings in Syria. Maxwelle was a no-nonsense type whose authority included the early termination of parties adverse to Blackguard in those instances where the adverse party refused to get on-board with the massive company. That day, Maxwelle was spinning his keychain in his hand, winding and unwinding it on his index finger, as he awaited the return of the man in the red vest.

At long last the field agent walked into his office and found Maxwelle sitting in the field agent's desk chair. This was standard protocol by Maxwelle and his underlings knew it, so the field agent took one of the visitors' chairs after he had hung his topcoat behind the office door.

"Well?" said Maxwelle. "Don't keep me guessing here, Kerr."

Kerr shrugged. "It went exactly as we expected. It was Althea Berenson herself. I left the thumb drive in my glove on the bench, as directed."

"And we've checked your Zurich account. We found the numbers on your thumb drive. The one million has been paid."

Kerr smiled tightly. "Any chance that money could find its way to me personally? A kind of bonus?"

Maxwelle frowned. "It gives me pause that you would even suggest it. You know that's not how we do business here. But there is hope for you. I'm coming to that."

Kerr raised a hand. "Forgive me. It's been a stressful morning. Okay, so what's my next move?"

Maxwelle grasped one hand in the other, elbows on the desk, and leaned forward confidentially.

"You have no next move."

"But I spent weeks preparing the data. I'd like to be told when they discover they've been duped."

"Here's what I'd like you to do. I'd like you to go back over the data you made up and prepare responses. This would be denials that Blackguard has ever seen those portions of the communiqué this Susmann woman will be quoting in her requests for admission."

"Afraid I don't follow. I'm not a lawyer, Mr. M."

Maxwelle nodded and an agreeable look came over his face.

"Fair enough. Let me give you a little background. In most lawsuits, there will come a time when the injured party asks the defendant--that's us--to admit that certain statements have been made by us. In this case, that would be the orders to go-ahead with the missile strike against the Sevi woman's brother. The data you just turned over contains those orders. However, when we are asked to admit those orders were given, we will deny that. That will be your job."

"And we're doing that because they have no recourse."

"Exactly. They have no recourse because they can't go crying to the judge that they illegally bribed one of our employees for data. That's a huge show-stopper for them."

"So I'm basically giving them some bad news."

"Right. You're telling them that we've never seen those orders before and we don't know what they're talking about. Then they'll know they paid a million bucks for some made-up B.S."

Kerr shook his head nervously. "But where does that leave us when they ask for the real data, the real conversations about the drone strike?"

Maxwelle made as if he was flicking a flea from the cuff of his suit coat. "Simple. We deny the existence of any such conversations. We weren't involved, we tell them. They're barking up the wrong tree."

Kerr felt a certain discomfort. He couldn't see how all the pieces of the puzzle fit together at that point.

"And that's the extent of my role," Kerr said. "That's it?"

"Not exactly. We then plan to expose you as an employee who engaged in espionage against Blackguard and who was paid one million dollars by the Susmann woman for corporate secrets. We have her million-dollar wire transfer that's easily traced back to her. We have your recording from your meeting today."

Kerr pulled at his collar. "Wait! You're saying I'm to be given up as a corporate spy against Blackguard?"

"Well, aren't you?" Maxwelle said with a sly smile. "Isn't that what you've been doing here?"

"So am I--will I be--"

"Terminated? You will lose your job. That's the extent of it."

"But I won't be able to find another job."

"Don't worry. You'll be provided for. We have one million dollars that will connect with you on down the road."

"So I'm being thrown under the bus--"

"Thrown under the bus with a million dollars in your bank account. That's right. It's not a bad end to a less-than-exemplary corporate career. I mean, Kerr, you've never exactly been a shooting star in your work here. Let's say that's why you were selected to be sacrificed."

"So my role is to embarrass the Susmann woman and ruin her lawsuit."

"Bingo! Now you're getting it straight, Kerr. I'm so proud of you, my boy!"

"The judge will throw her out of court."

"With sanctions. We'll ask for a huge fine for her theft of our data."

"I think I understand. It's beautiful in its simplicity."

Maxwelle raised a finger. "Simple always outperforms complex. Trust me on that, Kerr."

"I do. I do trust you." He didn't; he was buying time. But it didn't help him, as Maxwelle continued on.

Maxwelle smiled. "Now, then. While you were attending your meeting with Ms. Berenson, Security was busy. You are no longer able to log into our network."

"My God. I'm being pushed out."

"Only the beginning. We need to be able to say that once we became aware of your espionage we took steps to protect ourselves. Locking you out of our network is only a first step."

Kerr blinked hard. "What else will you do?"

Maxwelle smiled. "Patience, Kerr. Patience, my boy."

"I don't think I'm going to like this."

"No, but what are your options at this point? You're like the hand-fed pheasant raised from birth to be released from its pen and dodge buckshot. You're a target, Kerr. An expendable commodity. You, my boy, have met your maker and it is me. Now go home and prepare to work from your kitchen table until we're finished with you. You will use your own laptop and your own email account. Prepare the lawsuit answers. You no longer work here, Kerr."

"How will I live? How do I pay my bills?"

Maxwelle wagged a finger at Kerr.

"You should have thought about that before you committed these crimes against your employer, Kerr. Your theft of company data is a serious crime. You're lucky we don't plan to prosecute you. If you resist, you could find yourself on the wrong end of a criminal indict-ment. Don't go there, Kerr. Like the kids say, resistance is futile. Now leave us be."

Kerr stood and retrieved his coat from behind the door.

"All right."

"Leave the micro-recorder with my office on your way out. My secretary will log it in from you, so make sure you stop by."

"I can do that."

"Of course you can, Kerr. Of course you can, my boy."

8

Sevi punched ten digits into her burner phone and waited. On the fifth ring the man answered.

"Moustafa, it's Sevi."

"I have told you--no names!"

"Yes, I apologize. Should I call back?"

"Yes."

She ended the call and then dialed the same ten numbers.

"It is I," she said this time into the phone.

"Go."

"The lawyer is arriving by plane any minute."

"Ankara?"

"Yes."

"Has our friend put men there?"

"He has."

"Good. She will be followed and they will report back to me. If she's traveling alone, you will be safe. If she's in the company of another, we will take our precautions. So you may or may not see her tonight. Stay where you are."

"Got it. Goodbye."

Without another word, the call was ended.

Sevi sat on her bed with her cell phone in her hand. She stared wistfully at the phone, trying to think of who else she might call. She felt a need to explain her life to someone--preferably her own mother, but she had perished in the drone attack. She yearned for buy-in to what she was about to do, a stamp of approval from someone who knew her and who cared about her life. But all in all she knew that such yearning was not healthy and definitely was not safe. The worst thing she could do now would be to call someone up and tell them about her plan to bomb an American grade school. She feared she would be found out and terminated by the American forces. More often than not, that's what happened to terrorists who were planning attacks against the Great White Shark across the Atlantic: they were murdered in place. There wasn't a trial, they weren't arrested; they were terminated without a second thought. It was very American: quick, final, and without warning. You had only to have witnessed the drone strike that had nearly killed her to know that. Sudden, irreversible, and without regard to innocent lives that might be sacrificed in killing off an ISIS official. Sevi shuddered and tossed the phone on her bed pillow.

She had never felt more alone. She had never been more frightened.

The end of her life was about to begin when the American lawyer entered in.

WHILE SHE HAD reservations on Turkish Air from Istanbul to Ankara, Christine had let the plane fly on without her. It was all part of her plan to avoid being followed by someone who had obtained the flight manifest.

Now she sat on the high-speed train, watching the blur out the window as Turkey passed by at more than 100 frames per second. Or so she calculated. Beside her, in the aisle seat, was the man who had shared the cab ride with her. He claimed to be from the bodyguard group that operated along the Turkish-Syrian border whose primary work was to protect journalists and TV crews seeking and preparing their news stories on the activities of the Islamic State in Syria and the response of the Syrian government to ISIS's war-making.

But Christine needed more. She needed certainty, because if the man wasn't who he said he was, she needed to take steps before they reached Ankara. Elude or assassinate--it was all the same to Christine, as he was the actor and she was the mark, in the vocabulary of covert action, and his end was his problem, not Christine's. If he had to be eliminated, she would act. Alternatively, if he could prove his legitimacy, then he was a needful assign, meaning she could use him.

She nudged him with her left elbow.

"So tell me who sent you."

The dark man glanced over.

"So. It is time to talk?"

"It is time. What is your name?"

"Does that matter?"

She smiled. "Only in the sense that I need to know what you would like me to call you."

"Call me Hussein."

"Very well. Hussein. I'm sure there aren't many Hussein's out there," she said and indicated the direction of Syria and the greater Middle East.

The briefest smile played over his lips. "You might be wrong about that."

"Trust me. It was sarcasm. You and I both know Hussein is not your real name."

"Not any more than Ama Gloq is yours."

"Ama Gloq is my name. That's who you've been paid to accompany, if you are who you say you are."

"Ama Gloq is who I was told."

"You knew the sign and the countersign. That was a good start. But where were you told to join me?"

"I was told to join you in Istanbul. The deceit was that you would be traveling from Istanbul to Ankara by plane."

"But I wasn't traveling that leg by plane. You knew that?"

The man smiled. For the first time, she realized he was hand-some: clean black hair, arching eyebrows over dark eyes, dimples when his mouth formed certain words, and a strong jawline with a hint of shadow. He could have leapt from the pages of GQ, she thought. Except he hadn't, she reminded herself. He had come from that hell that called itself No Man's Land and that existed in the mile-wide swath between the Syrian and Turkish border, where hundreds of thousands of Syrian refugees clamored and cried for food and water and for entry into Turkey. Turkey had responded with help, but still the displaced were dying by the thousands daily. Dysentery was rampant; starvation was a problem. And diseases such as diphtheria--eradicated by the civilized world a hundred years before--were begin-ning to reappear and harvest the weak and the young from among the bodies pressed up against the border fences crying out. Yes, he was handsome, but she also knew he would be desperate. One more reason not to trust him. "I knew you weren't traveling that leg by plane," he replied to her question. "Before you ask, let me just say that I have my methods."

"But only two people knew I wouldn't fly. And those two are in the U.S. You wouldn't have had access to them. So what do you say, come clean or we part ways now. And you won't like how that happens, I promise you."

This last was said with a strong hint of violence in Christine's voice. He had to take her seriously or it was no use.

His next answer proved that he took her seriously.

He said, "NSA data is accessible to me. Three days ago you told a woman named Althea certain information. It was recorded in from a cell call intercepted by the NSA. In it you said that you would be taking the train from Istanbul. Which was enough for me to act on. Thus, I knew better than to remain on the airplane flight from Istanbul to Ankara. Satisfied?"

Christine shook her head and glanced out her window.

"Who else has this NSA data?" she mused.

While she wasn't speaking to him, Hussein answered. "Only the entire world."

"Holy hell."

"Yes. Americans have traded their privacy to a world that gives nothing in return--certainly not the safety that the Patriot Act pretends to promise the citizens."

"That's politics. I don't go there."

"No, that's your reality, if you're American. You can hardly have a dream over there without someone knowing."

Christine smiled faintly. She nodded. "As you say."

His gaze wandered beyond her, out her window. The exterior light caused a glaze on his eyes and she could no longer peer within.

"Back to your mission," she said. "How do I know you're not here to assassinate me?"

He laughed. "If that were the case, we wouldn't be having this conversation."

"From my side, that might be the case. And your next words might be your last. So careful how you answer me now."

"Fair enough."

"Who am I traveling to see? If anyone?"

"Sevi al-Assad."

Christine's eyes narrowed. "And who is Sevi al-Assad?"

"She's a Syrian. The victim of an American drone strike."

"Why on earth would I be coming to Turkey to see her?"

"She wants to sue the American government. This is what I was told by the person who contacted my group."

"And that person's name?"

"She works in your office. Her name is Althea Berenson."

Christine didn't respond. She only looked ahead.

Then, "Let me tell you, Hussein. I'm willing to take a chance on you. Why? Because I need backup. Plus, you seem to know your way around the facts of what's going on here."

"Thanks for that."

"But if I find you're not who or what you say you are, you will die. Suddenly and without warning. Now, knowing this, do you still wish to accompany me to Ankara?"

Hussein settled deeper into his seat. "I have been committed to you. In my country that stands for something."

"Yes, and what country would that be?"

"Not America."

"So. We can leave it at that. Now, would you like to accompany me to the dining car? I'm starved."

"I would. I can introduce you to local dishes."

"I was raised in a Pakistani household," said Christine. "There's probably nothing new."

"You might be surprised. Turks don't eat like Pakistanis. Nowhere even close."

At just that moment, she decided to wait and see about the man. More information was needed.

With her elbow she pressed the gun inside her waistband.

Never mind the differences in food or anything else. Adjustments would be made as the day and night unfolded.

But first, she needed to know more about her companion. She needed to go through his bag and his clothing. Which meant she might have to undress him.

Which would happen that night.

She was ready for anything.

9

His name was Lugo Zettler and he was from a small town in California where he had surfed and lifted weights in his early days, attended USC on a track scholarship, and eventually found his way into the Special Forces and a second tour in Iraq, where he lost his right leg below the knee and now ran his laps with a blade foot. He was Blackguard's trouble-shooter in Eastern Turkey and tonight he was preparing to intercept an American lawyer flying in from Chicago with stops in Berlin and Istanbul.

Lugo was six feet tall, thin in the upper body, with massive thighs that had once propelled him through one hundred meters in record time for Pac 10 athletes. He was light complected, which meant he stood out to no end in Turkey, and his blonde hair was beginning to show grey tints on the sides and in his too long sideburns. He spoke four languages and read seven and gave Blackguard courses in Syrian geopolitics at Dallas whenever he was unwillingly dragged back and made to perform for new recruits.

Blackguard's Ankara Station consisted of four field agents and six support staff. Chief among the field officers were two Turks who sometimes operated undercover with ISIS and assassinated key militants as necessary. They were fearless, Zettler and his field operatives, and tonight they were poised around the Ankara airport awaiting the flight from Istanbul that would deliver the American lawyer into their hands.

"Your role will be to take her into custody and bring her to our rooms. We will proceed to ask her nicely to return to the States and forget about this al-Assad woman."

"Dallas expects her to cooperate?" said Amman el-Shadda. "Seriously?"

Lugo brushed a lock of blond hair off his forehead. "Who knows what Dallas expects, Ammie?"

"What do we know about her?"

"She's an American lawyer. At one time she undertook a mission for the CIA but her flight was skyjacked to Russia and it went off the rails from there. We know that she's a difficult case. She will almost certainly ignore our request that she leave Turkey."

"And if she does?"

"If she does, we escalate. We'll cross that bridge when we come to it. Now, I want Ammie at the gate. Jordan, I want you at the luggage carousel. You have her photo-set on your phones already. She is comely and diminutive in stature, but don't let that fool you. This one is capable of taking care of herself."

The man named Jordan lifted his hand to high-five Amman. Amman ignored him.

"So we are to ask her politely to accompany us?"

"Yes. If she refuses, we'll collect her at the hotel."

"What hotel?" asked Jordan. He was a small man with a wrinkled forehead and ever-widening bald spot, across which he spread long strands of hair that normally belonged elsewhere. But he was deadly with small arms and was the one Lugo would normally ask to walk point in a situation where a firefight was likely.

Lugo nodded. "She is registered at the Marriott Hotel. Under the name of Ama Gloq."

"What," questioned Amman, "is that some kind of joke?"

"The CIA Director himself gave her the name on the aborted

mission she was to run for them. Evidently she liked it enough to use it again."

The conversation continued as the threesome spread through the airport. They checked their comms and took their places exactly fifteen minutes before the Istanbul flight was due. Lugo stationed himself at the main entrance and the other two melted into the milling passengers and companions as assigned.

10

Christine checked into the Marriott under the name of Ama Gloq. She then unlocked the door and waited until Hussein came up to the room ten minutes later.

They sat at the dining table and ordered two coffees with fruit and cheese. When the food and drink arrived, they chewed silently for five minutes and then Christine broke the silence.

"I'm meeting Sevi. It's all arranged. I'd rather you didn't wait here while I'm out."

He gazed the windows beyond the gently moving sheer curtains. It was dark outside but the city was ablaze with fixed lights and moving headlights. He turned back to her.

"You need to trust me. You have nothing to fear from me."

"Trust is earned, Hussein. So far there has been nothing earned. Nor should there have been. So I'm not faulting you. I'm saying it's premature. No, I would like you to wait elsewhere while I'm out. Please try to understand."

He smiled and collected a slice of cheese with apple, which he thrust into his mouth and chomped. "No harm, no foul. You have a meeting; you don't know me. I'll do whatever you say. But let me ask one thing. Would you agree my time would be best used watching the room while you're out?"

She stopped herself with a coffee cup between the table and her lips. It was the most sensible thing she had heard all day.

"Absolutely," she said. "That would be helpful."

"Assuming you can trust me at all," he smiled.

"Yes, assuming."

Which was when she decided to put him to the test. It was getting close to her meeting with Sevi and she found herself in the position of half-trusting and half-fearing her companion of that day. It was time to stop weighing it in her mind and start taking steps instead.

"I'm going to jump in the shower and get refreshed," she said. She wasn't normally a seductress, but she was down to the wire and needed more information. "Would you join me?"

He dropped a slice of cheese into his lap.

"Join you? In the shower?"

"Sure, why not? I'm hot and tired and would like to relax. But only if you want."

"Of course I want. You're extremely desirable. Not to mention dangerous. I've noticed the print of the gun through your slacks."

She smiled. "I thought my top covered that."

"Only to the uninitiated eye. I happened to be looking. You're well armed."

She stood and raised her shirt. She pulled the IWB holster and gun from her slacks.

"Glock. Forty caliber. It's enough. What about you?"

He spread his arms. "Search me. I have no weapon."

She laughed. "Join me in the shower. We'll see about that."

"Please. You first. Then I'll come in."

She stopped removing her shoes. She didn't want to take the gun into the bathroom with her and she wasn't about to leave it with him. He would have to undress and get under the water first.

"No, you go ahead. Then I'll come in."

He shrugged and stood and began removing his shirt. It was white and slightly billowy at the waist. He removed it and looked into her eyes. She dropped her gaze to his belly. She was glad to see his stomach was flat and tightly muscled. Her pulse picked up. It had been forever since she'd last held Sonny in her arms. There had been no other man since then. A quick breath snapped in her throat. She stepped to him and held out her arms. He opened his own arms and drew her to him. She placed her face flat against his chest and felt, for the first time in months, just a little safe.

He finished undressing down to his underwear and modestly headed for the bathroom. He went inside and shut the door halfway. Christine stripped off her clothes and followed him inside. Then they were both under the water, nude, bodies pressing together, mouths seeking and hungrily searching.

AT THE AIRPORT, Lugo summoned Amman and Jordan to join him back at the main entrance. They stepped on the sidewalk and held a brief conference. The gist of it was that Christine's announced flight had landed and she was nowhere to be found. Somehow she had escaped notice at the other end when she hadn't boarded, as their intel had her boarding and among the passengers making the flight.

"Where do we begin?" asked Jordan, the small arms expert. His face was dark and he was clearly upset with how it was playing out.

"Even now our office agents are reviewing hotel check-ins by lone women. In ten minutes we will have a list to begin working."

"How did we miss her?" asked Amman. "Everything I've seen had her onboard."

Lugo nodded vigorously. "I agree. Someone is definitely playing loose with the surveillance. We've been duped."

"How do we even know she came to Ankara?" said Jordan.

"We don't, I suppose," said Lugo, "which leads me to our next point. We need to backtrack to Istanbul and begin reviewing film. One or more house cameras will have her."

"Which, I assume, is ongoing even as we speak."

"Yes," said Lugo, "even as we speak."

They talked on until their earphones crackled with new updates. They learned that the woman had indeed been found on two airport cameras, one inside and one curbside, and both indicated she had in fact departed the airport not by plane but by taxi. Hussein had been with her.

"So I assume cameras at train and bus stations are being reviewed," Jordan said to the caller. He was assured that was in fact the case.

"Where do we start?" Lugo asked rhetorically. "We start at both ends. Our Istanbul team is already arriving at the train station to review data and others are headed for bus stations around the city. For now, we will begin with the Marriott where Sevi al-Assad is lodged. The odds are excellent that our target is there to meet with her."

"Or at least close by," said Amman.

"My guess, too," said Lugo. "Gentlemen, we're about to turn over the right rock. So my gut tells me."

With that, they walked along curbside parking to where they had left their Blackguard vehicle parked in the no-parking zone. It had been left there unmolested, of course, once the plates had been run by airport security.

En route they called ahead to the Marriott desk. There had been two check-ins by women traveling alone. One was named Ama Gloq.

"She's there and she's checked in," Lugo smiled to his companions.

"Where does that leave us?"

"Leave us?" said Lugo from the passenger seat. "We grab her. What else would we do with her?"

The two junior agents nodded. Grab her, of course.

DINNERS WERE SERVED from the dreck of the garbage dumps. There were no landfills in Iraq, only surface-level dumps where human detritus was laid down in horizontal sediments and creases that were endless in design, an insane tapestry of garbage woven by the howling gods of Saddam Hussein's not-so-benign neglect.

Hussein was four when he first found his way to the dump. He followed his half-naked older brother Nasser beyond the city limits to the Place of the Birds. The dump earned its name for the thousands of seagull scavengers that lazed and floated and fluttered and beat a pattern of hungry wings over the mess. "We eat with the birds," his older brother told him, and Hussein understood the teaching. It was their lot in life. A few more years and he would learn that it was his lot to change.

When the boy was nine he witnessed his first killing. The gang had followed an old man home from the chicken fights. A group of older boys set the pace, twisting and turning a block behind the mark as he shuffled along, oblivious to the pursuit. They rolled him at the intersection of a black alley and an unlighted street where windows shed no light. Across the street was the city cemetery; Hussein's own father and his younger brother were buried there side-by-side, victims of the same malaise that visited their village every five years, like clockwork. It was actually a virulent form of the Avian Flu, though no one called it that; no one knew what to call it or even that it should be called something. It was just The Death.

Of the five young men who set upon the old man--whose only crime was flashing a roll of bank notes in the open market that after-noon--three were orphans. Off to the side stood Hussein, shaking and wetting his pants at the unspeakable violence that issued from his older friends as they systematically surrounded the man and began beating him with heavy sticks. When at last he collapsed they turned his pockets inside out, divvied up his bank notes, and turned to go. At that moment the most ferocious of the gang turned to Hussein and asked him if he wanted a share. Shaken and unable to speak, Hussein remembered sticking out his hand, whereupon the killer laid two perfect bank notes in his palm. That was the first money he had ever held and the first time he knew the feeling of being someone who could acquire something at the market without stealing it. He never visited the garbage dump ever again after that night and it was the beginning of wealth in his life.

At sixteen, a Western do-gooder organization brought Hussein to Turkey to study engineering.

His jumping off point was Istanbul, where he studied, received his undergraduate degree and an advanced degree and then went to work for the Turkish intelligence service. Following a meritorious ten years of service for his government, Hussein retired to go to work for an American corporation.

Its name was Blackguard.

And its oil tankers were offshore, awaiting Syrian oil by the millions of gallons.

11

Before dawn, Althea reviewed the trio of snapshots texted to her by Christine. She studied the man.

He had been asleep when the pictures were taken, so the full eye color and features weren't revealed in the pictures. Still, Althea compared the pictures to the known actors in the database she had compiled on Blackguard and its agents. This guy was new--if he was in fact one of them--and was untraceable. But one thing was certain: the man who introduced himself to Christine as Hussein had been renounced by XFBI, the group Althea had hired to protect Christine in Turkey.

Althea had forwarded the snapshot to XFBI just after five in the morning.

XFBI reviewed the Hussein photo and immediately got back to her.

"He's no one we've ever seen before," Michael Hammit, the Overseas Liaison of XFBI told Althea by phone. "Where did the pictures come from?"

"They were taken last night by Christine as the man was sleeping."

"Where was this?"

"Hotel in Ankara, I assume. She didn't actually say as the only message with the text was one line."

"Which was?"

"'ID. XFBI? Knows about rain.' She asked for an ID on the guy. She knew I'd come straight to you."

"Meaning he says he's working for XFBI?"

"Apparently he claims to be working for XFBI. That's what's so confusing: he knew the keyword to the response. When it rains--"

"When it rains, it pours. That was the sign/countersign for the contact at the airport."

"Exactly. Chris says he knows about rain. So she let him get close to her, I'm guessing. That's how she got the picture. But now you're telling me he's not one of yours."

"Definitely not," said Hammit. "In fact, we were notified just after four that our man lost Christine in Istanbul during the plane change. Then there had been a disturbance. A dead body was found in a restroom. He was afraid that might somehow be connected to Christine, and left his post to go investigate. Evidently she slipped out of the airport during the confusion."

"You're seriously telling us your man lost her?"

"He was fired as soon as I heard. Not ten minutes ago, by me personally. We're terribly sorry and we've called up all Turkey resources to locate Chris and bring her to safety. They are headed for the Ankara Marriott hotel as we speak."

"Did they call to track reservations?"

"Yes, she's reserved at the Marriott. That was the conditional plan before she left the U.S."

"She was traveling as Ama Gloq."

"We know all about her cover, Althea. We helped her prepare it."

"I know. My sarcasm. I'm just stunned this could happen, that your man could lose her and now she's with someone we can't ID."

"It should never have happened. But it did, thanks to the uproar at the airport."

"Okay. So how do I get word to Christine? How do I tell her the man in the photo is not XFBI?"

"Let us do that, please. Right now we're staying off her cell and avoiding texts and emails. We don't know what's safe to use and what isn't."

"I understand."

"I shouldn't have to tell you not to respond to her text?"

"No, that's why I called you guys first, Michael."

"Oh wait--"

"What?"

"Wait, I'm getting a Sat call. I'll be back in two ticks."

The phone went silent as Althea was put on hold. She nervously began drumming her fingers on her desk. She tried not to imagine the worst but deep down was terrified for Christine. And she was furious at XFBI for dropping the ball.

Then Hammit came back.

"Front desk confirmed her reservation under Gloq. She was seen by the desk clerk leaving the hotel with another woman within the past half hour."

"What about the man? Anything about him?"

"Hotel security is headed to the al-Assad room right now. We should know any minute if there's any sign of him. Okay, wait one."

Again the line went silent.

Then, "Housekeeping reports a man was in the Gloq room and just left."

"What about the al-Assad woman's room? Anything there?"

"They're saying no and they're saying she's not in. No one can say for sure whether it was Sevi al-Assad with Christine or not because we have no pictures of the woman to flash around."

"So Christine was seen leaving the hotel with a woman. Nothing in her room shows anything unusual. Do we know how long ago she left the hotel?"

"They're saying it was in the last half hour. Something like that."

"What about any men leaving soon after?"

"Our people asked. Front desk has no idea about that. Evidently this is a busy hotel since it's near the airport in a rather large city. The hotel is a popular destination for business people and comings and goings at all hours of the day and night are the norm. Nobody would have noticed a single man entering or leaving."

"Why was Christine noticed? Any comments about how she got their attention?"

"Yes. The woman with Christine was limping and appeared to move only with great pain. In fact, she was using a cane and having difficulty walking. One of the clerks asked if she could call someone for help but Christine waved her off."

"Good heavens. What the hell was that all about, I wonder?"

"Unknown. But it was enough to get the attention of the front desk."

"And then they matched the picture your people showed them of Christine with the woman they saw leaving."

"Exactly."

"Okay. Now, what about the airlines and trains and buses? Do you have eyes on them?"

"We do. All public transportation is covered. We're turning Ankara upside-down looking for Chris."

"Okay. Stay on that, Michael. We're counting on you."

"I can project that we'll have eyes on her in the next thirty to sixty minutes. There's only so many ways she can move around. We are fairly confident she's bringing the woman back to the U.S., which means we're especially interested in airline manifests."

"My guess is, the al-Assad woman will be traveling under her own name. Christine is probably traveling as Ama Gloq. But she has other ID with her as well."

"Names?"

"I couldn't say. She has several passports with her wherever she goes. They change with her."

"We figured as much. Well, the plan called for her to fly Turkey Air to Germany. Perhaps that's still on the table. It could be as simple as that."

"Probably depends on what happened to the sleeping man."

"Yes, that's confusing. No bodies, no signs of a struggle or other evidence of anything untoward."

"Exactly."

"We'll have the airline manifests in the next few minutes, Althea. I'll get right back to you on that."

"You damn well better, Michael. And there damn well better be no further problems."

"There won't be. We're all over it."

"Stay all over it. I need to know what's happened to my employer."

"We'll be back to you within the next half hour."

Without another word, Michael Hammit hung up. Althea replaced the phone in its cradle. Then she thought better of it and dialed Winona's cell.

"Win? Althea. Are you in line?"

"I'm at O'Hare waiting in the international line. The flight's on time and I'll be in London in about seven hours, give or take."

"Have you heard from her?"

Win's phone crackled with a boarding call at the airport. Then she continued. "Haven't heard from her but I assume the plan is still for me to meet her at Heathrow and cover her six while she makes her way home."

"Well, I haven't heard anything either."

"I know. I'm a little concerned because she was going to call in from Istanbul once she had the girl with her. Have you made calls to XFBI?"

"Yes, and incredibly enough they lost her at Istanbul airport. It's a long story, but the upshot is that Chris didn't fly from Istanbul to Ankara. The consensus is that she went there by train instead."

Winona was silent for several beats. Then, "She wouldn't have done that without a good reason. How did XFBI lose her? I thought you guys were the best."

"Evidently there was some disturbance at the airport and Chris departed while eyes were diverted."

"Great. So I'm going to London and we don't even know whether she has the al-Assad woman with her?"

"We think she does. She was seen leaving the hotel with a woman in tow. A limping woman in lots of pain."

"Limping woman? What's that about? What's with these guys that they can't run her down anyway? Seems clear to me she'd be at the airport flying out of Ankara. Duh, how dumb are these people?"

"They're following up on that as we speak. My guess is they'll locate her fairly quickly."

"So should I call her myself?"

"Negative. We don't want her cell used to locate her. If she's on the run that cell will be turned off and she knows better than to turn it on anyway."

"Agreed. So I should go ahead to Heathrow and try to connect up with her there. Right?"

"Right. We need you there to get on her six and make sure she isn't being hunted."

"I'm on my way. Oops, I'm next in line. Gotta go."

"Call me when you touch down."

"Will do. Hang tough, Althea."

"You too."

SEATED onboard the British Airways 777 in first class, Winona accepted a serving of pre-flight champagne. She swallowed it down and accepted another. The sparkly liquid began to settle her nerves, the result of husband Gorman's announcement that morning that he was in love with someone else and was moving out. That someone else came as no surprise; Winona had been sharing her husband with Gorman's twit assistant for almost a year now. Where Winona was tall and lithe and moved like a runway model, Gorman's assistant Washida was short and stacked like a Playboy bunny. Winona glanced outside the window when the tow truck began moving it backward. That was the problem, the Playboy bod. Washida was fifteen years younger than husband and wife and represented a chance for Gorman to recapture his youth--a desire he had verbalized to Winona that morning when he told her he was not only moving out but also that Washida was pregnant. Expecting. And that the

child was Gorman's. "Are you sure it's yours?" Winona had asked, ever
the cynical detective.

"Oh, yes," said Gorman as he twisted his club tie into a Windsor
knot. "She hasn't been with anyone else but me."

"And you know that how?"

"I know that because she said so. Unlike you, I'm not so jaded that
I immediately reject everything anyone tells me."

"I don't reject everything. I just reserve judgment until I evaluate
agendas. Huge difference."

"Well, Wash has no agenda."

Winona had grimaced. "No, other than stealing my husband away
from me and the kids, she has no agenda."

"The kids hate us both anyway," he'd said, referring to their twin
boys, now fourteen, who were in that peculiar stage all teens must go
through where confidants are required to be less than twenty years
old. They had stopped speaking to their parents months ago. The
parents now felt rejected and could only hope and pray there would
be an end to the stony silence at some point. But the rejection hadn't
been without effect; each parent secretly thought the other responsible for the impasse. Which made Gorman's reaching out to
Washida all the more predictable.

Winona settled back in the plush first class seat and closed her
eyes. She tried to empty her mind of all thoughts of hearth and
home. She tried to resist wondering what Gorman was doing just
then and who he might be doing it with. She pushed her back hard
against the seat, uncomfortable. That was it, the unknowing. If he
had already moved out and taken up housekeeping with Washida it
would feel much different. There would be no reason to hold out any
hope that he might come to his senses and give her up. But having
him still at home--even given that morning's announcement--made
her feel as if she still had some ties to him. Didn't those ties give her
some ownership rights in him? She wondered, even feeling she was
thinking foolishly. Maybe the marriage could yet be salvaged if only
he could be made to wake up and see how the twit was using him.
God, some men could be dense, especially when the little head was

doing the thinking for the big head, Winona thought with a smile. She wondered if the big head ever regained control after the teen years. If only.

Almost without thinking she opened her purse and withdrew her cell phone. There was still time to call him and try to reason with him before--

She stopped herself. Words weren't going to be enough. Gorman's future was decided the minute he first laid hands on the bunny. Hungry hands, her bedroom eyes--Winona had met her at a party last Christmas Eve at the big box store Gorman managed--it was a done deal. Slipping the cell back inside the bag, she motioned the steward over. Another glass of bubbly, she told him. Might as well get good and oiled and sleep it off over the Atlantic. Which was totally out of character for Winona, who was ordinarily first cousin to the teetotalers of the world. She drank little and she had never done drugs, even in college; she had majored in criminal justice, and CJ majors didn't drop acid or snort coke. It just wasn't who she was. But right now, on this huge jetliner, with her husband moving out and two kids who had forgotten her name, she was losing control, it seemed.

Winona tasted the third offering of champagne and the steward waited while she swallowed it all down so he could collect the plastic ware before the plane began its takeoff roll. Her head lolled to the side as she offered the empty plastic to him. She closed her eyes. The alcohol was already relaxing her and a feeling of warmth was spreading through her body. She smiled. It was the first peaceful moment she'd had in months. And it came at the expense of her high standards where mood-altering substances were involved.

Wouldn't you just know it?

Even her own feelings had become artificial.

How sick was that?

12

C hristine had tapped on Sevi's door three times. Then a count of five followed by two quick taps. The code they'd agreed on. Sevi limped to the door and placed her hand on the handle. She waited. Then there it was again: three--five--two. Now she was sure.

She pressed down the handle and pulled. The woman whose picture she'd seen on the Internet hurried into the room. She closed the door behind her, quickly, as if she was being followed.

Christine hurried through the room, pulling the curtains away from the wall and looking behind, then placing her hand on her waistband gun as she crept into the bathroom and threw on the light in there. Satisfied the room was empty except for Sevi, her upper body relaxed and she approached Sevi with both hands out. She received Sevi's outstretched hands and gazed into the Syrian woman's dark eyes.

"Sisters," Christine said. "Caught up in God-knows-what."

"I'm Sevi."

"Yes, you are. Now let me see your passport, please."

Christine arranged herself at the small dining table while Sevi retrieved her bag and dug out her passport. She placed it before Christine.

It was a Syrian passport and the picture clearly matched the bearer sitting across from her.

"Order some tea," said Christine, studying the passport front to back. "And rolls with butter. I'm famished."

"Was there trouble coming here?"

Christine gave the woman's passport back to her.

"Let's say it was interesting. There are people who don't want us to meet."

"That would be the government?"

Christine slowly nodded. "Could be. And there are others, companies in America that make unbelievable profits from war."

"And from stolen oil."

"That's right."

"They start wars so they can steal oil. Those are the ones I want to sue."

"Those are the ones I want to sue for you. They are the rot at the tree roots. That's why I came here."

"Will you take me to the U.S.?"

"Yes. I have a plane waiting."

"A plane is waiting. For us?"

Christine nodded.

Sevi held up one finger and picked up the phone. She dialed room service.

"My plane will be here within the hour. No one knows except the pilots and me. And now you."

"Are you being followed? Is that it?"

Christine stretched her arms and arched her back. She was tired, not having slept at all last night, and her mind was exhausted after the last two days of cat and mouse and constant movement from the U.S. to Ankara. She closed her eyes and allowed her racing mind to calm. As she did this, Sevi saw the lawyer's need and gave her space. Christine shook her head as if coming to and smiled at Sevi.

"Yes, I've been followed."

"Who is it?"

"There's a man. He's looking for me now."

"Who is it?"

"He goes by Hussein, though that's not his real name. I'll never know his real name, most likely. I left him back in my room."

"He let you leave without following?"

Christine smiled and shook her head. "He didn't have any choice. I drugged him. He'll be unconscious for several more hours. In the meantime, we'll leave for the airport."

"Should we hurry?"

"No need. The drug I used is powerful enough to stop a mule for twelve hours. This man has met his match."

"Then we should hurry."

Christine raised her hand. The woman studied the hand with the missing fingers. She realized she wasn't alone in her suffering; this woman had suffered too at some time.

Sevi pulled herself to her feet, with the use of her cane, and wobbled to the room door. Christine followed close behind and stepped behind the door as it opened, out of sight. Her hand was on her waistband as she waited to see who had knocked. Satisfied it was their refreshments and nothing more, she then stepped around, received the room service tray from the man in the green coat, and allowed the door to close on its own.

They made their way back to the table and took the same seats as before.

Sevi poured tea while Christine hungrily buttered a bun. She pushed the plate toward Sevi and nodded.

"Forgive me," she said, chewing in double-time. "Sex with strange men always makes me ravenous."

Sevi's hand paused between the butter dish and bun.

"Did you just say you had sex with the man?"

"I did, didn't I." It wasn't a question. "Well, there you have it. Now you know the extent of my dedication to your cause. Any questions?"

Sevi appeared to be thrown off. "No--no--""Good, then eat up. It's a long way from here to the airport."

"No, it's only a few miles. I have watched the planes landing."

Christine smiled and wiped her hands on her linen napkin.

"It's a small trip for normal people. Sister, that no longer includes you. Welcome to my world."

"Oh."

"Things--" Christine said as she took a sip of the strong tea, "are no longer as they appear. You can make bank on that."

Sevi shook her head. She had no idea what her lawyer meant.

But she was ready. One step closer to American soil and high explosives.

An airplane ride away.

13

——————

Winona had been a cop long enough to immediately discern when someone was following her. And someone was.

That someone followed Winona off the plane and waited in the second circle of passengers at the luggage carousel. Winona didn't actually have luggage to pick up, she was simply using the location to study those around her. Eventually all passengers had taken their luggage and departed the area. All except Winona and her overseer.

She stepped around the woman and watched over her shoulder as the last three pieces of unclaimed luggage rode the metal merry-go-round. The woman grew uncomfortable with Winona behind her and abruptly departed. Winona waited until she was totally alone, then went back along the hallway at the end of the luggage claim and located the bank of elevators.

It was time to meet Christine. She had Christine's flight number from Istanbul--stopover one from Ankara--as well as gate number, and she began punching buttons and walking through passenger areas toward the numbered gate.

Heathrow Airport is a huge enclave of terminals. The Heathrow Express, a passenger tube, connects them. From Terminal 1 Winona rode the express to Terminal 5 where she would meet the incoming flight from Istanbul.

Would the woman follow her?

She turned after stepping from the car; the woman followed her off. Winona fought down the impulse to walk up to the tail and confront her. That would solve nothing and certainly would result in the woman being replaced by yet another, unknown, pursuer. So she did nothing and instead casually approached Christine's gate. There she sat in the long row of waiting chairs closest to the jetway exit, where Christine would, within the next half hour, appear in Terminal 5. As expected, her tail sat just behind her and two seats to her right.

Winona selected the mirror app on her phone and studied the woman over her shoulder. What she saw told her little: dark-complected, probably Middle Eastern though maybe Far Eastern; short hair and high forehead; small gold bar in her left earlobe; ring-less hands; and some kind of e-reader that was having trouble keeping her interest, as the woman repeatedly stared across at Winona who, she failed to realize, was watching her.

Winona soon tired of the sport and took to reading an eBook on her phone. As she did, her thoughts wandered time and again to Gorman and the twit and she admitted, finally, that his words yesterday advising her that he was moving out still played hard upon her. She loved Gorman despite his frailties and dalliances. She thought their relationship more one of the tried and comfortable type rather than one of the heart-fluttering romance newly acquired type. He was her old shoe and she had wanted him to stay on. But he hadn't and now she would be alone.

Sitting there, in Terminal 5, with a deranged person on her tail (who else would perform such a chore except someone deranged?), she was lonely and not just a little sad. In fact, she felt tears come to her eyes and she dabbed at them with two fingers and a wisp of tissue.

"F-ing men," she whispered under her breath, and tossed her head back with new resolve to keep her mind on the present and off the old. She had a job to do and she steeled herself against what was to come.

Thirty minutes later Christine appeared with the other passengers, one of the first off the plane.

Except it wasn't Christine, she realized when she stepped within three feet of the woman. Winona was shocked and a little unnerved: the woman was Christine's height, wore Christine's hair color and hairstyle, bore the same complexion, and was sturdy across the shoulders and back like Christine. Plus she was lugging along the exact same backpack Christine was so often seen traveling with. Winona froze.

But the new Christine came right up to her. She held out her hand and gave Winona a note, which the detective took without thinking. She pulled it open and read:

Win: This is an actress my plane flew in from Chicago. She is dressed and made up to look like me. I have used her before and she's quite good at being me. She is flying on my real passport and on my real commercial flight from Istanbul. Fly back to the U.S with her and interact with her as if she were me. Chris.

P.S., sorry I couldn't tell you all this beforehand. I'll make it up to you and buy your lunch at Sisters In Law.

Without missing a beat, Winona swept the new Christine up in her arms and hugged her. She leaned forward and whispered into the new Christine's ear and both women smiled and drew apart.

"She's the dark woman with the short hair," said Winona.

"Got her," said the new Christine, whose name, she whispered to Winona, was actually Rae. "So she's our companion back across the pond?"

"Evidently. Her or someone just like her. Whatever, our Brit Airways flight back to New York doesn't leave for ninety minutes. What say we grab a brunch and fill our bellies? You must be starved."

Said Rae with a huge smile--two old friends reuniting--"You know, no airline serves a full meal anymore. Welcome to the new air travel where you lose weight as you go."

"That's beautiful. And so true."

The women left the gate area and began making their way back toward the Express, where they would travel to Terminal 1. Neither carried luggage; their bags were backpacks that hung from their shoulders. Not quite what one would expect from women traveling internationally.

But, then, who knew what to expect from women anymore anyway?

HUSSEIN AWOKE AT NOON. Just barely noon. He awoke to the sound of the housemaid rapping her keys against the door and announcing she was there to clean. He stood up from the bed and immediately fell back down with a thump. The room swirled around him as the dizziness coursed through his body, disorienting him and causing him to blink hard against the daylight. He sat on the side of the bed for several minutes and, as he slowed his pulse and forced the dizziness away, the housemaid let herself into the room. She was startled to find him sitting there, looking up at her with his best effort at a smile under such circumstances. She backed away and said in Turkish that she could come back later. No need, he told her, he was about to dress and leave, would she just give him five minutes alone?

She shut the bedroom door behind her and he stood once again. Locating his trousers and underwear, shoes and socks, he assembled the lower half of his outfit. He found his white shirt flung across the back of a chair in the other room and discovered his passport and wallet were missing. He half-smiled. She didn't need the money; she had taken his ID to slow him up. It would work and it wouldn't. He seized the phone, got an outside line, and called the Ankara Blackguard desk. New papers would be delivered to the front desk in fifteen minutes with enough U.S. currency to keep him for two weeks. He would need a sizable chunk to set up shop in Chicago and begin the hunt. They asked, could they do anything else? He told them thank you but no. He would contact the company from Chicago.

He was about to hang up when Lugo came on the line.

"She fucked you and put you out, eh?" said Lugo in his most cynical tone.

"She drugged me. Whatever else happened, I have no memory."

"How about the lawyer? You're just going to let her go?"

Hussein grimaced. "How can you say that? Haven't you people learned anything about Hussein yet?"

"Whatever, I just know Randall C. Maxwelle in Washington is going to turn on you if you fail again."

"You tell Mr. Maxwelle the plan is proceeding just as I made it up. There will be no lawsuit filed. That is what I was hired to prevent and, by all that is holy, it will be done."

"I'll tell him that. He will be calling any moment now."

"Good. And tell him I will be in touch from Chicago. The women will be erased by tomorrow night. Tell him that."

"He'll send the hounds of hell after you if it's not done as you say."

"There will be no need. I'm just getting started."

They said their goodbyes and Hussein finished dressing.

At the front desk he was given a folder containing a new passport, ID, American dollars, and Chicago addresses belonging to Christine Susmann, both office and home. Plus there was a dossier on the lawyer, complete with comments and recommendations for taking her down. He was interested to find she was the mother of two children, a boy and a girl. Evidently the boy suffered from some kind of handicap that kept him on crutches. Just the sort of lad Hussein might like to meet. What else was in there, he wondered, and he turned more pages.

On the flight out of Ankara to Istanbul, Hussein devoured the file. He declined the offer of food and drink and sat scanning page after page. Then he watched the clouds passing by below. Had she just flown through these same clouds? He wondered at that, for he knew he wasn't that far behind.

Once he changed planes in Istanbul he settled in for the long flight to London. It was time to sleep. He ordered a small pillow and blanket and tucked the dossier under his leg for safekeeping. As he drifted off he remembered the American lawyer embracing him in the shower, water beating down on their heads.

Then they had ordered room service with coffee. He had excused himself after dinner to use the restroom. Which was when she doped his drink. He was sure of it.

He smiled as he drifted off to sleep.

The favor would be returned tenfold with a bomb they would never forget.

14

T he hiring officer at Blackguard believed everything Althea had to say. She believed Althea's ID was legitimate, believed her Social Security card was real, took photos of her driver's license and put those in the file marked Applicant, and studied the W-9 IRS form before sliding it into the file as well. The position was officially titled "Administrative Assistant" and her role would be assisting a pool of thirty-some data analysts in the overseas arm of Blackguard. Exactly the spot Althea wanted to land.

Althea finger-combed her short black hair as the woman reviewed the application a third time. African-American, thirty-five years of age, ten years of experience as clerk in the Cook County Circuit Clerk's Office--complete with a letter of recommendation from the clerk herself, and a junior college transcript that reported a 3.8 GPA in business administration in her Associate of Arts degree.

"Assuming my supervisor signs off," said the woman, closing the file folder and smoothing its seam with two fingers, "when could you start?"

"Well, today is Thursday. How does Monday work?"

The woman's brown eyes widened. "Oh, that would be perfect. I was thinking you might have to give two weeks at the Clerk's office."

"No, I left there. See--" Althea reaching and opening the Applicant file and pointing at the Circuit Clerk's letter--"I left there two weeks ago. I'm ready to start immediately."

"We should talk salary."

"Is it salary or hourly?"

"Salary. It's an exempt position."

"Oh, impressive. This is definitely a step up for me."

The woman nodded and turned to her keyboard. "Let me memo my supervisor. I'll see if I can expedite your app. Hang on, please, Ms. Andersen."

"Sure."

Althea sat back in the gray visitor's chair and glanced around the small HR conference room. Like everything else she'd seen so far of Blackguard, the room was gray, the door molding gray, and even the industrial carpet was gray. The HR rep's orange earrings stood out like two small suns, Althea thought as her mind took in this new world. She had come here knowing that the information she needed to link Blackguard to the Arum al-Assad missile strike was insufficient. She needed a smoking gun, so to speak, because she expected the transcript already turned over to her was bogus--an attempt to entrap Christine and her lawsuit in an industrial espionage web. It was an old ploy, one Blackguard was known for, and Althea had obtained the transcript to lull Blackguard into thinking it had a one-up on Christine before the lawsuit was even filed.

She had discussed it two nights ago with Christine when she had dropped by her boss's home after hours. Christine had just served dinner to her two children and was puttering around in the kitchen, cleaning and straightening, and then poured Althea a small glass of white wine. They sat together, then, at the large glass kitchen table and Althea watched Christine turn her own stemware in her fingers as she contemplated.

Then Christine said, "I've read the transcript ostensibly between Reno Air and Edlund DuMont the day of the missile strike."

"It sounds good, doesn't it?"

Christine pursed her lips. "That's just it. It sounds too good. If the transcript is to be believed, Edlund DuMont himself ordered the missile strike that killed Sevi's family."

"Yes, it leaves no doubt."

"Except it leaves me with a lot of doubt. I admire that you acquired the thing from Blackguard, but I'm not buying it. Frankly, I smell a rat."

"How so?"

"Well, let's give credit where credit is due. Blackguard is a world-class black arts operator. They are smarter than the norm and the games they play are usually very sophisticated."

"Agreed."

Christine took a small sip of wine. She pinched the corners of her mouth with the second finger and thumb of her right hand.

"So it wouldn't surprise me if the entire transcript is simply created out of thin air. It wouldn't surprise me if it's all imaginary."

"But why?"

"So we rely on it. Use it at some point in the litigation. If the transcript were to officially come to light--somehow be made known to a judge--Blackguard would then have us in a position where we're holding stolen company documents. Being the transcript. If they can do that, they likely would get sanctions that would include having the lawsuit dismissed."

"Smart."

"Oh, yes. These people are inordinately smart."

"And you wouldn't put it past them to play these games?"

"That's why I went along with paying the courier so damn much money. I want them to think we've bought their ruse. Now the next thing is to get you on the inside."

"Inside of Blackguard? How would I do that?"

"We'll obtain ID for you. We'll have you apply for a position there."

"How does that help?"

"It gets you inside their computer network. At least to some degree. We can work from there in obtaining the real transcripts or other company communications about this particular missile strike.

Then we'll--how should I delicately say this--steal the damn stuff. Frankly, I'm pissed. We paid them a bunch of dollars for real records and they've screwed us. But it's not done yet, not if we can get you inside their firewall."

"I'm game," said Althea. "Just tell me what you want."

"I've obtained a security analysis from XFBI."

"What's that? About their network?"

"Exactly. We need to know where you can do the most damage before we send you in. Turns out there's an administrative assistant opening in one of Blackguard's overseas data wings. It might be exactly what we're looking for. At least that's what Michael Hammit over at XFBI thinks."

"Just point me where you want me. I'm game."

"Okay, here's what I'm thinking."

They spent another hour discussing Althea's application at the company and her role in hacking the overseas databases. Documents would be lodged inside those servers and, once Althea passed her background check and proved herself trustworthy, she would have complete access to those documents. XFBI had already created an entire background and history for Althea, Christine explained. Blackguard would be led down the primrose path in checking Althea's background and they would definitely like what they found. Girl scouts, college, military service, two responsible jobs since, including the Circuit Clerk's office--plus the credit report was firmed up, there was no history of any kind of illegal activity--not even a parking ticket, and on paper Althea was married, happily, the mother of two honor roll students.

Althea was drawn back to reality as the Blackguard HR employee spoke.

"All right," the woman said, "my supervisor has signed off on a Monday start for you. Keeping in mind this is all subject to your background and credit check--which you've already agreed to let us on do on one of the forms you signed."

"That sounds fair. I think your security department will be impressed with my background."

"I'm sure they will be. Now, can I expect you here, in my office, at eight o'clock Monday morning?"

"Definitely," said Althea. "How exciting!"

The woman turned back to her keyboard. "Then I'm going to pull the opening out of our online jobs board. There we are--filled. Okay, Ms. Andersen. Monday morning it is."

"Thank you. I'm excited."

"I'm so glad."

ALTHEA HAD HEARD all about Christine's son, the computer virtuoso. So...she called him up, unbeknownst to anyone, including his mother.

"Jamie, this is Althea Berenson. I work with your mom."

"Hello, Ms. Berenson. I've heard mom talk about you."

"Yes, you probably have."

"What I'm calling you about is computer networks."

"Sure."

"And how to--how to hack them."

"You don't want to do that. It's illegal and if you get caught you're hosed."

"I know that. But this time it's ultra-important to your mom's case and Sevi's case that I peek inside a computer network and get away without getting seen. Can you help me do something like that?"

"Sure I can."

"My question, then, is, will you?"

"I'd have to ask my mom."

"No--no--no, I don't want to implicate your mom in this. This is just between you and me."

"I don't know. She'd be pissed if I did something like that and didn't tell her."

"I realize that. So I'll tell you what. I'll take full responsibility and talk to her myself. Fair enough?"

"Sure, if you wanna do it that way, that's fine. Keep me outta that part of it."

"Okay. Here's what I need from you to help me. We're going to hack Blackguard's computer system."

"Network."

"Network. And we're going to take documents from them and put them on another server."

"Federal crime. I'm in."

"Good. Now let me tell you what I know."

The conversation went on for another hour. Jamie outlined a battle plan and implementation was discussed. At last, she was sure she knew what she was doing and Althea thanked Jamie and reminded him not to speak a word of their conversation to anyone.

Jamie swore he would keep silent no matter what.

15

They landed at Chicago's Midway Airport just after midnight. As the front hatch on the Gulfstream opened, Christine, standing in the door, felt the cool night air race up her skin. She turned to Sevi, waiting at her elbow.

"It's much cooler here. I've got a car waiting and we'll get you out of this."

She then turned to her client and stepped backwards down the stairway, helping Sevi make her way down the steps, which was quite difficult, thanks to the frozen knee. Still, the Syrian woman gamely came down, and Christine was pierced with deep respect for her new friend.

At the bottom was the waiting Mercedes, black in the black night, diesel engine putting, and Christine's XFBI driver behind the wheel. They opened doors and quickly slid inside. Bags were loaded into the trunk of the car and Christine sat back and closed her eyes. She said to Sevi, "All set?"

"As much as I will be," said Sevi. "I'm still trying to grasp that I'm actually here."

"I'm taking you to my house. Much safer there than a hotel. We have armed security and this man Hussein and his fellow travelers will remain at a distance. They know better than to cross my bodyguards."

"I'd feel safer, frankly, if they hadn't crossed your bodyguard in Istanbul. When you told me about Hussein stepping in, that frightened me, to tell the truth."

"I only told you so that you'd understand my need to hustle you out of the hotel and onto my private jet. Shit happens," Christine muttered, and turned to stare out her darkened window.

"Indeed," said Sevi. "So. Tell me about Chicago."

"Not much to tell. Population-wise, I think Chicagoland is America's third largest city. Behind L.A and New York. Lots of sports teams, some culture, tons of great shopping. If you're into that sort of thing."

"How will I support myself? Where will I live?"

"I think, until we get this sorted out, I'm keeping you close by. You're going to be staying with me at first. As far as working, with your computer programming skills you'll have no problem there. I already have one of my office staff scouting jobs. We'll help you there."

"That's all quite generous. However, I don't want to be a burden."

Christine smiled. "You'll be with me only for a short while. Then we'll get you your own place and get you settled in. You're probably looking at two weeks, max, until then."

"Oh, that would be wonderful."

"Sure. By the way...let me think out loud for a minute."

The car had exited the airport and they were making their way north, skirting east around Chicago downtown.

"Think out loud. Please do."

"Well, I've got a son, Jamie. Jamie is a precocious young man who lives and breathes computers. I'm wondering. Would you be interested in tutoring him in some of the stuff you know?"

"I don't know that I could help all that much. Software programming can be largely self-taught."

"With Jamie that's probably true. But I always want him to get a more classic view of the discipline--you know, history, industry standards, that kind of stuff."

JOHN ELLSWORTH

"Sure, I could try."

"Let's talk more about that. I think we might find you have a heck of a lot in common with Jamie."

Sevi turned and looked at the lights passing in the oncoming lane. The glazed look on her face didn't say much, near as Christine could tell. Christine hoped she hadn't insulted the woman by suggesting she work with a beginner like Jamie. But Jamie was pretty far down the road when it came to computers and programming. Maybe her guest would find she did, in fact, have a lot to offer the young man without being an academic pedant. Jamie had a cowboy bent when it came to computers and perhaps Sevi could let him have his head while still backfilling the engineering standards he wouldn't have learned. There could be a real symbiosis between them. For now, everyone was tired and looking forward to a meal and bed. Enough said.

"We'll be home in about twenty minutes from here," said Christine, as they followed along Lake Michigan's western shore.

"So tired. Some food would be nice."

Christine nodded. She caught the driver's eyes in the rearview. He shook his head ever so slightly. Good, that meant they weren't being followed.

The young lawyer sat back against the seat and deeply exhaled.

Maybe this was going to work out just fine for everyone.

CHRISTINE SPENT the next morning in her home office, with Sevi, getting down the details that would be fashioned into the lawsuit. Name, address (Christine's, for now), marital status (single, sadly), children (none), education level (bachelor's degree plus one), employer, family (deceased), DOB, place of birth, citizenship and so on. Christine had called in paralegal Billy Tattinger from her office, and Billy took over the complaint-drafting chore.

By two o'clock, Billy was ready to present a draft complaint for Christine's review. The caption of the lawsuit put the venue in the

U.S. District Court, Northern District of Illinois--Chicago. The sole plaintiff was Sevi al-Assad. The defendants included the United States of America, the President of the United States of America, the Defense Department, Blackguard, and the DuMont brothers. Billy had Christine's signature on the original and was headed for the District Court Clerk's Office to get the case filed before five o'clock. Christine in the meantime called a press conference in her office, and all the major news outlets were represented. The conference began at three o'clock--time enough for the news of the new case to hit that evening's news.

"Today," she told the assembled reporters in her conference room downtown, "my office is filing on behalf of a woman named Sevi al-Assad a lawsuit against the U.S. Government and against the Blackguard Company and the DuMont brothers. The complaint alleges that this woman lost her entire family in a Predator drone strike several months ago in Syria. The strike was carried out by the United States with the aid of Blackguard and the DuMont brothers. The target that day was one Arum al-Assad, the ISIS oil minister who, in fact, was killed in the strike. But was it necessary to kill over forty other innocents--mostly children--to kill one member of ISIS that the government had its heart set on killing? This lawsuit challenges the authority of the president to authorize such a strike and seeks monetary damages for the wrongful death of Ms. al-Assad's family."

"Where is this woman?" asked the reporter from CNN.

Christine nodded. "She's staying with me temporarily until we can find her suitable lodging."

"Is she here legally?"

"She's here on a visa with her passport. All signed, sealed, and delivered by the U.S. Government."

"How much is she asking?"

"Ten million dollars per family member. A total of two hundred fifty million dollars. Remember, the strike occurred right before a wedding celebration was to begin. Sevi's entire family and her fiancée's entire family were all under one roof when the heavens fell in on them."

"What do the DuMonts have to do with this?" asked the *Chicago Tribune* national news chief.

Christine smiled at the woman. "C'mon, Angela, you know better than that. The United States doesn't install an outdoor toilet in the Middle East without the DuMonts signing off on it. Blackguard is their front man but they're also behind the curtain pulling all the strings."

The woman from the *Tribune* made a note on her pad. "I stand admonished," she said.

Christine quipped, "I'm not here to admonish anyone. But let's keep it real, shall we?"

Several others smiled, which the twin TV cameras picked up. It was no secret, what Christine had just said. The DuMonts did run the Middle East for the U.S. Plain and simple.

Another voice spoke up. "So if your client is seeking two-hundred and fifty million in monetary damages for the deaths, who does she expect to pay that?"

"Whoever the jury says must pay. That's the jury's job to decide, not my client's job."

"How did the law office of Christine Susmann get involved?"

"She found me on the Internet. My client is a software engineer and so it's no surprise she would find me there."

"Where is she from?"

"A small city in eastern Syria."

"Was she injured in the attack?"

"Yes, Sevi was seriously injured. All over her body. Her recovery-- meaning she can now walk with the assistance of a cane--has taken the better part of six months."

"Is she asking for money for her own injuries?"

"Yes. You'll each be given a copy of the lawsuit as you leave here today. Most of your questions about the details of the case will be answered there, I believe."

The elderly gentleman from the Associated Press waved from the far end of the table. "Do you fear for your own safety for filing this case? Does your client?"

Christine saw an opening and took it. "Fear what?"

"Fear some kind of retribution from the defendants."

"You're asking are we afraid of physical harm for bringing this case?"

"Yes."

"Well, a good part of the reason for this lawsuit is to put the defendants and their agents on notice that the press is now involved and watching. If any harm should come to Sevi or me while the case is pending I would expect the press to chase down the responsible party or parties and demand that justice be done."

"So we've got your back now?"

"In a manner of speaking, yes, you do. I'm counting on the press to keep the playing field level."

The man from the AP wasn't finished. "What precautions have you taken?"

"We're under armed guard twenty-four-seven. My family is surrounded by bodyguards, as is my staff."

"You're taking this seriously."

"Wouldn't you? I mean, any group that would fire a Hellfire missile into a civilian wedding party could be expected to use the same kind of insanity against the lawyers who sue them for it. Frankly, I don't trust any of these bastards. Least of all the government."

"And the DuMont brothers."

"You've got me there. Maybe I should have placed them at the head of the line. So everyone, thanks for coming. We'll keep you updated with press releases as the case progresses."

"And we'll watch your back," said Angela from the *Tribune.*

"Thank you for that."

~

IN WASHINGTON, D.C., a terse conversation was held just minutes after the press conference concluded.

Gathered around the desk of Edlund Dumont were his brother

Wilfred and Randall C. Maxwelle, their military-commercial inter-face guru. The DuMonts were steaming and Maxwelle was trying to play down the damage inflicted moments before by Christine Susmann.

"Bitch named us in her lawsuit and named us on live TV," said the rage-filled Edlund. His fist slammed down on his desk and papers jumped and pens rattled. "Damn her! How did we miss our opportu-nity to silence her before the lawsuit was filed?" He looked dead ahead at Maxwelle as he said this, his eyes accusing and threatening.

Maxwelle swallowed hard. Always the Naval Academy cool head in most situations, he was feeling the heat. "I don't think the damage is that severe at all," he said, struggling within himself to find a reason for his words. "I mean--I mean-"

"You mean, hell!" Edlund shouted. "Your team missed her and Wilfred's team killed the Syrian woman's family. What kind of huge damn mess have you given me here? I'm up to my eyeballs with both of you."

"That's not fair," said Wilfred evenly. He was the older brother and his tone was meant to remind Edlund of that important fact. "My group was protecting American oil interests when the strike occurred. Now as for Randall, I don't--"

"Now wait," said Randall, breaking in where few if any ever dared break in, "For my part, I've hired the best out there. Granted the results were less than expected, but that wasn't through any fault attributable to me. I hired the right people; they let us down. It's that simple."

"I was going to say," said Wilfred, "before I was interrupted--" looking hard at Maxwelle, "that we've spent a ton of money to fix this mess. Why didn't someone just pay off this woman and the collateral family members still alive? Isn't that our usual take on these things?"

"Right enough," said Edlund, still fuming. "Why didn't we just spread some money around? Randall?"

"The Syrian woman was in fact approached. Three times. Two times in the hospital and again after she first called the American lawyer. She was offered ten million to let it go. We even offered to move her anywhere in the world she wanted to go and help her start over."

"And?"

"Basically she told us to go screw ourselves. Nicer words, of course."

"Of course. She's Middle Eastern and proper."

"Wouldn't want to anger the gods," said Edlund.

"Or the Prophet," said Maxwelle.

"Careful there," said Wilfred. "We might be being recorded in here."

The men shared a laugh, finally, once the brutal posturing and finger-pointing was done.

Beneath the desk where they sat, piggybacking on a bolt was a tiny listening device, placed there by Althea Berenson, whose new duties at Blackguard gave her access to the brothers' offices. Edlund's office was bugged; Wilfred's office was bugged as well. Maxwelle's soon would be. Plus she had untraceable no-bread-crumbs access to the top-secret computer network that ran between the military, the White House, and Blackguard. Data packets were being intercepted and analyzed by the hour.

Jokes about the gods, about the Prophet, and questions about the life expectancy of Sevi al-Assad were ill conceived, as far as Althea Berenson was concerned, as she listened from two floors below in the Watergate Complex.

The hard drives recording it would convince others of the same.

16

They had first met one month ago in Syria.

Hussein came into the physical rehab compound in Aleppo to introduce himself to Sevi and inquire whether their interests might align.

She said she knew nothing about him. He tried to explain.

"I appear to be working for a company called Blackguard. In truth, I am a jihadist who wants only to see terrorist attacks carried out against the United States."

Sevi nodded. Their interests just might align, she thought. She leaned against the wall and pushed away, extending her frozen knee behind. It was an exercise meant to limber up the knee all but destroyed in the missile attack. The timing of the exercise with this man's appearance in the room wasn't lost on her: he wanted to attack the U.S. So did she.

"A jihadist? As am I," said Sevi, grimacing as she pushed herself away from the wall. "But how did you find me?"

"Everyone knows about you. In ISIS your name is a rallying cry. The drone strike against your wedding celebration has caused our ranks to swell. Recruitment is up over a thousand percent, thanks to the stupid Americans and their ignorant Blackguard ally."

"Then I am glad," said Sevi. "Our interests might align at that. I am in touch with an American lawyer who will sue the government for me. Is there an opening there for you? I think there is for me."

"Are you going to America? Or is she coming here?"

"Both," said Sevi. "She's coming here to talk. If she likes what she hears, she'll be taking me to America with her. The lawsuit will progress. At the end of it, I expect to strike a school full of children. With a bomb."

"I would join you in doing that, if you wish."

"What can you offer me?"

"For one thing, both Blackguard and the government of the U.S. will be out to prevent your lawyer's trip here and back. I can help make her journey here to visit you a safe one."

"You would do that how?"

"Act as her bodyguard."

"Why would she let you help her?"

"She will have protection when she comes here. I will take that over myself."

"That will work?"

"Oh, yes."

"What about in the U.S.? What can you offer there?"

"My idea is about notoriety. Bombing a school is one thing. But bombing a school in the name of your murdered family is quite another. You have the chance for a huge public relations coup among the Arab world. I would like to be part of that. I can help organize the attack on the school. I can provide the ingredients for your bomb. I can even plant it for you. But you will send a video to the press and take credit for the attack in the name of your loved ones who were killed by the government. ISIS recruitments will soar after that."

"So you would like to use me?" She changed legs and now extended her left leg behind her as she pushed away from the wall. A bead of sweat broke out on her forehead as she bore weight on the injured limb. It was excruciating to load it with full body weight. Something she would forever loathe the Americans for doing to her.

"Yes, we would like to use you."

"That can't be all bad. From my perspective, I still get my revenge and ISIS sees its numbers swell. I like that."

Hussein shifted his weight from leg to leg as he watched the woman perform the painful exercises. At just that moment a therapist came by and massaged the injured leg. "How's that?" she asked the Syrian woman.

"Hurts."

"Good," said the therapist. "Recovery is painful. No pain--"

"I know, no pain no gain. Thank you."

The therapist wandered off to the next patient. Sevi glanced at Hussein and rolled her eyes. "Do you see what they've left me with?"

"Pain. Loneliness from the loss of your loved ones and pain from the loss of your body functions."

"If you only knew. The spinal pain is only controlled with large doses of narcotics every day."

"I am sorry."

"It's not your place to be sorry. You didn't cause this."

"What do you say we meet after you're finished here? We can discuss this in more detail." He checked from side to side around the room. No one was listening, however, and his shoulders relaxed.

"I can do that. I will meet you downstairs in one hour. That gives me time for the rubdown and the therapy pool. Fair enough?"

An hour later they were downstairs on the sidewalk. They walked a block south to a small cafe and ordered coffee and pastries. At the front of the shop, just beside the large window, was an empty table just then vacated. Sevi headed for it and claimed the closest chair.

"Now," she said to Hussein as he took the opposite chair. "Let's talk about how we kill American school children."

"And let's talk about how we trigger a rise in ISIS numbers."

Sevi tasted her pastry and licked the fingers of her eating hand. She nodded at the pastry and held it up.

"Sometimes we are left with life's smallest pleasures. Sugar where there is only the taste of death."

"So it is," said Hussein. He took a bite of his own pastry. "Now let me tell you my story. Let me tell you what the Americans did to me and to my wife."

Sevi's eyes fixed him with great interest. "A missile? You too?"

"Just as bad. Remember George Bush's 'Shock and Awe' the night he attacked Baghdad?"

"I do. It was on CNN."

"Right. Well, my wife and I were working late in the Defense building. A Cruise missile buried her under six floors of debris while I was out at our car retrieving a thermos of coffee."

"No."

"Yes."

"So they made you a soldier."

He nodded violently. "Just like you, Sevi al-Assad. Our stories are the same."

"So you work with ISIS but you also have skin in the game, as the Americans say."

"I also have skin in the game, as the Americans say."

"So it is. Then we shall work together, you and me."

"Yes," he said, finishing off his pastry. "Yes, we shall."

17

The Sisters in Law met for Wednesday lunch the week after Christine returned from Turkey with Sevi. This time the meeting was in Martha's Grillet, an upscale Lakeshore hideout featuring a menu without prices. Christine said she was paying, so no one minded that they had no clue how much their orders would cost. Least of all Christine. Winona arrived first. She was wearing a silver gray suit with pink shirt and black tie. Her lithe frame carried the ensemble well and, as usual, she turned heads as she was shown to their table. Christine arrived next. She was loaded with a leather briefcase she couldn't leave in the Mercedes out in valet parking lest someone make off with her bag and, indirectly, her entire lawsuit. Then came Althea, who had come into town on an overnight pass from Blackguard with the excuse she needed to connect with her kids.

They had barely been seated and were making drink orders when, to the surprise of Winona and Althea, Sevi al-Assad joined them. She was supporting herself with a new black enamel cane with an ivory grip and she wore blue jeans and a blue Ralph Lauren shirt with the horse and rider on the shirt breast. Her limp was noticeable and Christine recognized the grimace on Sevi's face--which was always there when she walked around.

"Sevi," cried Christine, "you did come. Thank you for that. Everyone, this is Sevi al-Assad, our newest client."

Hands were shaken all around and Christine stood while Sevi took the fourth chair. Her back was to the large domino of plate glass windows that opened onto the lake. She pulled her chair in and checked around the room. The restaurant was jammed; it was half past noon and Winona had made the reservation last week to secure the table they now were gathered around. Sevi squeezed the lemon wedge into her water glass and inserted the lemon into her mouth. She started chewing.

"So," said Sevi, "Christine told me I would meet my team. You are all going to be working on my lawsuit? I'm impressed!"

Winona smiled. "We are. I'll be doing witness workups and field investigations."

Althea said, "And I'll be providing adverse statements and documents. You might call me the smoking gun lady."

"Smoking gun lady. I like that," said Christine. Then, to Sevi, "And I'm heading up the team and preparing the case for trial. With Ed Mitchell, I'll be actually taking the case to trial."

"What's that mean, taking the case to trial?" asked Sevi.

"Appearing in court. We have filed your case in the District Court and one day--maybe in five or six months, we will go to court and have a jury listen to the evidence. I will ask witness questions and communicate with the judge and jury."

"And what will I do?"

"You will testify. You will sit in a chair and look at the jury and tell them your story."

"Will you help me get ready to do that?"

"Of course," said Christine.

"We'll all help you," Winona added. "It's a team effort to present your story in the best light possible."

"Speaking of which," said Althea, then she stopped and looked at Christine. "Can I speak freely here?"

"You mean is Sevi in our inner circle?" said Christine. "Yes, she is. We have no secrets from her."

"Well," said Althea, "I have tiny microphones planted in the offices of Blackguard's owners, Sevi. Anyway, the brothers have been wondering why no one made an effort just to buy your silence."

"Which begs the question," said Christine. "Should we go to the brothers with a pre-trial settlement demand this early in the case?"

"Would that be good?" asked Sevi.

Christine shrugged. "We never know. Actually, we don't know anything, not without asking. But in a case like this you can bet there's lots of information the DuMont brothers don't want to see the light of day. So maybe settlement is a possibility at this stage. I believe it very well could be."

"What do you mean, 'don't want to see the light of day'?"

"I mean, they might want to buy your silence rather than allow company secrets to become public."

"So my story wouldn't be told?"

"That, and so their complicity wouldn't become known to the world. They would rather have no one know how close they are to the American drone attacks."

"So the world wouldn't know the DuMonts gave the order to kill my family if I settled?"

"Pretty much," said Winona as she accepted her iced tea from the drinks waiter. The others received theirs. "If you accept money at this stage the volume gets turned off. No one hears your story."

"Then I won't do that," said Sevi. "I want the world to know about my family and about the DuMont brothers. I want the world to know how the U.S. government murdered my loved ones."

"Of course you do, sweetheart," said Althea. "No one can blame you for that."

"How much would they offer me?" asked Sevi, more out of curiosity than anything else, as she had made it clear she wouldn't entertain settlement talks.

"Maybe five million. Maybe twenty," said Christine. "Somewhere in there. Not enough."

Sevi smiled and touched Christine's hand. "I am glad to hear you say that. Not enough. It won't bring back my loved ones, no matter how much I get."

Said Althea, playing devil's advocate, "Then why go after them at all? Is this only about publicity? Because if it is, I'm a journalist. I can do your story and get worldwide syndication. The whole world will know, if that's your angle."

"Would that be a good idea?" Sevi asked Christine. "Why not just do a story?"

"Because stories are news one day and gone the next. A trial moves at a snail's pace and lingers and lingers. The story is told day after day. It can go on for a month. The impact is increased a hundredfold by a trial."

"Makes sense. We'll have a trial. No news story."

"Good on you, girl," said Althea. "I wasn't trying to talk you out of a trial."

"I know. You were only explaining my options. That I can appreciate."

The talk then turned to local gossip. Through it all, Sevi paid close attention. Christine got the feeling the young woman had come to learn about America in general and about Chicago in particular. She listened to every word, missing nothing.

A lull in the conversation prompted Winona to blurt out, as much a surprise to her as anyone at the table, "Gorman is leaving me."

"What?" exclaimed Christine. "Girlfriend!" said Althea.

Winona swallowed hard. "He told me the day I flew to London."

"The twit?" questioned Althea.

"The twit," said Winona. "It was bound to happen."

"Your husband is with another woman?" asked Sevi.

"My husband has been having affairs with one woman after another for years. This time is different. This time he says he's in love and he's leaving me for her."

"I am sorry," said Christine. "The bastard. Will you want me to nail him for you?"

"Divorce case? Not yet. I think I'll make him file if he's serious. It will make both families hate him all the more."

"That's right," said Althea, "his mother likes you better than she likes her own son."

"That's what she's told me. At least a jillion times. Everyone knows he's a two-timer. Not that I've told them anything, because I haven't."

"What will you do?" said Sevi. "In my country it is customary for men to have several wives. Not so here?"

"No, darling girl," said Althea, "Not so here. And if some asshole tries to convince you otherwise, please remind him you're no longer living in the Stone Age. We have Arabs in America who are just looking for naive Arab girls to lure them into three-ways and four-ways."

"Three-ways? Means what?"

"You know, multiple wives."

"Not in America?"

"Not on your life," said Althea. "You better have my cell number. Give me your phone."

"I don't have a cell phone."

"Then tell Chris you need one. You do. And call me when you get it. I'm your go-to for dating customs in the U.S. Some guy tries to come on to you, call me first. At least until you get your sea legs, girlfriend."

"She means she's up on American social norms," said Christine.

"What about you?" Sevi asked. "What about Christine herself?"

"Tell her about Ed, Chris," Althea said.

"Yes, what about that stud?" asked Winona. "I see him watching you around the office."

Christine shook her head. Her dark eyes narrowed. "It's still about Sonny for me. That won't go away. I've tried some things, but the feelings are all wrong. I'm still in love with my husband."

"You said someone shot him," said Sevi. "On the plane coming here you told me about that. And you can't forget him."

"It's not just about forgetting. It's dealing with the feelings. I was never one who could hop into the sack with someone when I loved someone else. In fact, Sonny and I were virgins when we first got together. We were both inexperienced in that department."

"So when he died you were still inexperienced?" Sevi asked, all innocence.

Christine rolled her eyes. "That, dear girl, is my own secret. Never let it be said I discussed my sex life with three fools at lunch."

"Sisters in Law," said Althea. "Not fools."

"Speaking of which," said Winona, "Sevi, I think it would be a good idea for you to join us every week. At least until you get your bearings on America."

"I could do that?" asked Sevi. "I would like that. Very much."

"Sure you can," said the other two women. "Please feel free."

"I was going to invite you again next week," said Christine. "Now consider it done."

"I accept," Sevi said. "This is a good introduction for me."

"Then it's done, girlfriend," said Althea. "Just remember, what you hear here, leave it here."

"Okay," said Sevi, "I will leave it here."

WHICH DIDN'T HAPPEN. An hour later she was meeting Hussein on Wacker Drive. There, she told him everything over their new custom of coffee and pastries.

What she had heard there at lunch, she definitely didn't leave there.

Nor would she.

"Go slow," Hussein admonished. "I need to understand everything that was said. Begin with the talk about settlement negotiations with Blackguard. Tell me word-for-word."

She did.

"Now about this Althea woman. You got the idea she was working for Blackguard? How could that be?"

The talk ranged over all the lunch topics for an hour or more. It was left at the point where Sevi would be trying to find out all she could about Althea and Blackguard.

ISIS wanted to know everything about Blackguard.

But most of all, it wanted to know about the Sisters in Law. Every detail would be relayed to Syria and pulled apart and examined. Some of it would be useful, even actionable. Other parts would be nothing.

Either way, ISIS wanted it all. By a huge stroke of luck Sevi had been placed right in the middle of it.

It couldn't have been better planned.

18

On a bright May morning, Sevi withdrew her remaining
funds from the bank and prepared to go shopping. Her
list comprised the ingredients for making the bomb she
would plant outside a grade school.

It had been two months since she had been couriered by Christine from Turkey to the States. She was working the 4-12 shift at Randall Dynamics, a downtown Chicago software engineering startup where she was coding embedded systems to calibrate industrial thermostats and couplers. It was boring work but it paid almost fifty dollars an hour, so Sevi was satisfied with her lot. More important, the late-afternoon/night-time shift pretty much gave her her days free and she was using that time to move ahead with her plan to attack America. For her, nothing had changed.

From two a.m.--bedtime--and after, as she lay in her bed and tried to sleep, her mind was restless and sought to avoid the pain of her loss. The wedding day drone attack had left her a shell of herself--withdrawn, depressed, and socially inept.

At work her co-workers had learned to keep their distance after receiving blank stares and guarded replies when their friendly approaches had been turned aside. Her only social activity was the weekly lunch she attended with the Sisters in Law where, much to her surprise, she felt comfortable and welcome.

The Sisters In Law were kind to her and always gave her opportunities to verbalize her thoughts on the topics under discussion, whether love lives or work lives or children or exciting events or clothing or intellectual or creative interests--Sevi was allowed to have her say. Which was causing her to grow into a woman she had never imagined she could become. She was, when all was said and done, becoming wise in the ways of the world, thanks to her lunch group. Moreover, she rather liked the woman--herself--she was coming to know. The bottom line was that the lunch bunch was bringing out the best in Sevi. There were even moments of self-doubt: moments when she questioned her motives in coming to America. At those moments the notion of murdering American school children was rejected by her heart of hearts. But, thank Allah, those moments were rare.

At the end of her second month, she was still living with Christine. The lawyer had told her guest that there was no hurry for her to find her own place. She wanted the transplanted Middle Easterner to get to know her way around the city first, to get firmly ensconced in her profession and geographically centered, before she entered into a lease on an apartment or condo. After all, Chicago, like any city, had its safe areas and its high-crime areas, and had areas that were affordable on Sevi's salary and those that were out of reach on her salary. No, Christine told her guest, you're not overstaying your welcome.

And there was another development in the household, something neither woman would have predicted. Jamie, it seemed, had become fascinated with Sevi and her grasp of software engineering best practices, including writing smart algorithms and avoiding lapses in his code where hacks might be made. Systems programming was her forte and, while Jamie was writing server-side code for web projects now, the same best-practices theory and standards applied equally in both areas of the software engineering endeavor.

In short, Jamie thought the sun rose and set on Sevi. He sought her out day times before she left for work and after he arrived home from school. He showed her the projects he was developing. He showed her his FACCE facial recognition software. He explained that it was now being developed for commercial use by a startup. And he showed her his ideas for evolutions of FACCE as he remained the R&D arm of the team. "Research and development is my middle name," he told Sevi over mid-afternoon tuna sandwiches he had prepared for them both. "My company doesn't add one new feature without my okay first."

"Are you selling this FACCE software?" Sevi asked.

"We have it installed in three police departments in Cook County. So far the feedback is terrific. It seems like we have a tool that helps law enforcement in bringing criminals to justice. How much better can that be?"

She had smiled and nodded.

Yes, how much better could it be than to bring criminals to justice?

Then Christine approached Sevi and asked whether she would tutor Jamie in her academic areas of interest.

Sevi smiled. "Too late. We're already tutoring each other!"

Christine nodded and accepted the fact--again--that she had a prodigy in her son--and in Sevi too, for that matter. So the two software engineers fed off each other and their conversations became increasingly animated as they discussed this and that and upcoming developments in their world. Jamie read Wired; Sevi was writing an article for Wired, one that had been tentatively accepted for publication. Her work supervisor insisted she submit the article. So Sevi had agreed and now spent much of her off time researching and writing for publication. It was good therapy which challenged her and kept her mind from tragic musings.

All except for that time when she worked on her shopping list for her bomb. There was that part of her that wouldn't blink. She was going ahead with her plan to strike America no matter what else might be going on in her life.

So in early May, she withdrew a large sum of money from Fifth

Third Bank in downtown Chicago and set out on a shopping task. She had ridden the Blue Line downtown early that morning, arising after five hours of sleep to begin preparations for what she believed would be the most deadly attack against an American grade school in history. The prospect at once both increased her resolve and revolted her. Nevertheless, she plunged ahead.

Her time with ISIS had been a huge learning experience. The ingredients for her bomb were available in America and for the most part required the use of only a small degree of deceit. Her shopping list included explosive-grade ammonium nitrate fertilizer, diesel fuel, nitro-methane and the commercially manufactured explosives, Tovex and Primadet. A federal building in Oklahoma City had been totally destroyed by such a bomb. And yet the ingredients for making such a horrendous explosive remained freely available.

But first on the list came storage. She needed some way to store the chemicals she would procure. Which required she re-think the ISIS concept, because ISIS' bombshell consisted of a two-ton truck. A cube truck, usually white with small lettering indicating the truck was part of some small business from out-of-state. Sevi considered this and decided that she would downscale. She knew a large truck would draw attention, given the tenor of Homeland Security procedures; the truth was, the authorities ascribed high-profile scores to such vehicles. It was no secret they could easily be used to accommodate massive quantities of explosives, and so the cops regularly pulled them over on pretense stops and searched them. It was the American climate and Sevi knew this.

She reviewed *Van and Driver*. She searched for deals on *Craigslist*.

In the end, she decided on a two ton Ford van for sale in Kirksville, Missouri. When she arrived she found a backwater town off the beaten path where few questions would be asked. Even when a clearly Middle Eastern woman showed up wanting to buy a van that was obviously far too large for her needs.

"How can I help you?" the farmer asked. His eighty acre farm was five miles northeast of Kirksville. It was a quiet, wooded area with maybe sixty acres that could be plowed without fear of tractor over-turns on steeply rolling hills.

"I'm here about the ad on *Craigslist*," Sevi said with her best smile.

The man eyed her closely. Foreign, his mind registered. Leaning on a cane and dressed like someone who clearly didn't live in the country. But his need to sell overcame any preliminary reservations he might have had.

"Well," he said, "it's got good rubber and only a hundred and fifty thousand miles. All put there by me."

"What do you use it for?"

"Tires, mostly. I moonlight fixing flats on the highway up from St. Louis. So I carry the most common sizes of rubber plus my jacks and stuff. It's got lots of rubber scrapes in the cargo area, I ain't gonna lie to you. But most of that will come off with elbow grease. I might even do it for you if you're not in some big damn hurry."

"I am," said Sevi. "My husband is a carpenter and needs it on his job site this week. We'll need to close the deal fast. Like today."

The farmer pushed the feed store hat back on his head.

"I see," he said. "Got cash?"

"Cash, yes. Got a title?"

"Yep. I'm asking fifteen-five."

"I'll give you thirteen cash now, this minute. But the title must be blank."

"I don't care if the title's blank. That's up to you. Fourteen will carry the day."

"Done. Fourteen thousand it is. I'll start counting while you watch."

He took her inside and she plopped down on the couch and began counting hundreds out of her shoulder bag onto the coffee table. Actually the bills were wrapped, hundreds, ten to a wrap. She fished out fourteen and aligned them vertically, side-by-side.

"You should count each pack," she told him.

"I plan to," he said, and lowered himself onto his knees on the other side of the coffee table. She watched as he counted. He was painfully slow but thorough. He placed the bills in a single stack as they each added up to one thousand dollars. Ten minutes later there was one stack and fourteen thousand dollars had been presented. In cash. The title appeared from nowhere and he turned it over and handed it to her.

"No need to have it notarized," he said. "Already on there."

"You've already had it notarized?"

"Look it over. I've already signed it and notary already did her stamp. You're good to go. That thing's like cash until someone fills in the new owner's name. But that's between you and God. I'm out of the picture on that one. Hell, I don't care if you put the devil's name on there. No skin off my nose."

"That's fair. Well," she said, standing up, "I won't take up any more of your time."

He gave her a curious look at that point.

"Why dinchoo even start her up?"

"Because I trust you. And because I know where you live. Which means my brothers and husband know where you live. But why do you ask? Is there something mechanical you haven't told me about?"

"No-no-no--I was just asking. Hell no, that van runs like a top. I'd trust my life to it."

Sevi rounded the table and folded the title carefully along its creased fold.

"You have," she said, and held out her hand. "Keys. And one favor."

"Sure."

"Drop my rental car at the airport. They're expecting you."

"I can do that. Won't even charge you for the service."

"Well, that's mighty white of you," she said, lapsing into language she'd heard in TV movies.

The farmer laughed.

"White, I guess. Everyone in this county is white."

"Well, enjoy that."

"We do. We do."

"Now, point me toward my new vehicle. I've got a long drive looking back at me."

"Where you headed to?"

"Louisiana. Gulf Coast."

"You'll have no problems with tires, either. New rubber and rims all around. I always do that at one-fifty."

"Sounds exciting."

She held out her hand. He took it and they shook, though the expression was lost on both of them as they neither cared about one another nor wished to ever again see one another. But Sevi had learned that everyone in America shakes hands on any, even the most modest, occasion, and she executed the action as expected.

She then climbed in, inserted the key, and cranked the engine.

Perfect. All the dash lit up, needles swerved into place, and the engine was all but soundless. Relieved of fourteen thousand of her dollars, she was satisfied with her purchase.

Should she have told him she planned on making the van into a bombshell?

She grimaced and shook her head at him as she floated by backing up.

At some point down the road he might read the article about the attack on the grade school. And he might realize the van described in the attack was the same one as the one he had sold. But that's probably as far as his mind would proceed with the information.

He just wouldn't want to know more.

IN ST. LOUIS she met up with Hussein and gave him the keys to the van. She flew back to Chicago while he continued to Little Rock, Arkansas. He told her he had a line on six fifty-pound bags of explosive-grade ammonium nitrate fertilizer. This was a chemical that was all but impossible to procure, especially since the tragedy in Oklahoma City.

He headed south and west out of St. Louis on Interstate 55 until he reached Memphis, where he took the bypass and caught Interstate 40 west to Little Rock. He then drove north of Sherwood and took a county road west, as instructed. It was raining and early evening when he came to a gate across the turnoff he had been directed to follow. So he dialed the number given to him by the supplier and was told to wait there at the gate.

Thirty minutes later, an old, rusted-out Chevy Scottsdale pickup pulled up to the gate on the opposite side and turned off. Two men came out. One of them was holding a pump-action shotgun and the other was carrying a garment. Garment man inserted a key in the lock holding the chain in place and swung the gate. Shotgun man pointed the weapon at Hussein and motioned with his left hand to drive through the gate and then stop. Hussein complied.

The gate was then swung closed. But it wasn't locked.

Shotgun man came to the driver's window of the van. He indicated the glass should be lowered, which Hussein did. He felt drops of rain blow across his face and squinted into the hazy evening light-- what was left of it.

"You alone in there?" Shotgun man asked.

"I am alone," said Hussein.

"Hey. Where you from?" asked Shotgun man.

"Chicago. Like I told you."

"That's bullshit!" the man cried. "You sure'n hell ain't American. What you think, Freddie? We just blow this sumbitch's head off and feed him to the river? Or what?"

Freddie pulled open the passenger's door. He slid into the seat and leaned over to look at Hussein.

"You got twenty grand like you said?" asked Freddie. Hussein smelled the man's rancid breath as he leaned too close. Something like onions and heavy grease. He drew away, which made Freddie raise a finger and shake his head. "Huh-uh. Don't you pull away from me, not if you want to leave here alive!"

Hussein placed both hands on the steering wheel. He meant to show them he was unarmed and posed no threat.

Freddie took note and nodded. "Now, we're going to just drop this feed sack over your head and then I'm gonna drive. Get your ass out!"

Hussein exited. He was roughly pushed up against the side of the van. Instantly a burlap bag was dropped over his head and shoulders.

It was coarse on his face and smelled like some kind of grain or seed he didn't recognize. He realized that his knees were weak and felt his hands shaking. He forced himself to calm down. He drew a deep breath and said nothing.

"Now," said a voice, "I'ma goan ta lead you around and put you in the other side. Got it? Gimme your hand, boy."

Hussein extended his hand and allowed himself to be walked around the van. He stepped up and slid inside.

The engine turned over and instantly they were lurching and swaying along a bumpy dirt road. Judging from the rough ride, Hussein knew the road was deeply rutted and slippery in places, where it dipped and the rain had created mud baths they skittered through. He made a mental note to run the van through a car wash and take great care to wash the undercarriage. He knew the FBI would at some point be collecting dirt samples off the tiny pieces of van left over after the heat and fire and he didn't want them to locate dirt samples that could place the van where he'd been. Already he knew the gas pump and convenience store cameras had been making a record of his journey, try as he did to turn his face from the cameras as he pumped gas and made his purchases. Of course there was the matter of the van's license plates showing up on video, but that couldn't be helped. Besides which the van was unregistered except to the Kirksville seller. By the time the bomb was set off all VIN numbers would be removed, including the hidden ones. He would make sure of that and had acquired the resources and schematics to make it happen.

The lurching ride along the washed-out dirt road took a good ten minutes. But at long last they slowed and the brakes were applied to bring their trip to an end.

"Now, I-Ran boy, open your door and step down. I'll come 'round and get you."

Hussein did as he was told. He wasn't surprised to hear a vehicle pull alongside. Shotgun man then jumped out and strode up to Hussein and jammed what he thought must be the muzzle of the shotgun against his temple.

"Where's the Benjamins, boy?" asked Shotgun man.

"Put the damn gun down," said Freddie. "We don't need that here, Roy. I-Ran boy only wants to pay us and pick up his fertilizer and be on his way. Right, I-Ran?"

"That's right," said Hussein. "I will make no problems here today."

The burlap bag was jerked roughly from his head. Hussein blinked in the rain and saw that the light was gone and it was dark, and saw that he was in a heavily wooded area with only one road in and out. To his left was a small shack with tire rims leaning on either side of the front door. Why tire rims? Why, Arkansas? he wondered. Why any of this? Because. Because there were American school children to murder in payback for so many Arab deaths. Allah required no less of him.

Roy pushed at Hussein with the shotgun stock and ordered him to circle back behind the shack. With Freddie leading the way, they walked around the frame shack, where Hussein now found himself looking into the lighted maw of an open garage. Placed neatly against the rear wall stood six bags of fertilizer. Fifty pounds each, said to contain his explosive grade fertilizer. His pulse quickened.

"So where's the Benjamins?" asked Roy.

"Under the seat of the van. Driver's seat."

Roy nodded and grunted in disbelief. It was clear he believed nothing the Arab said and he made no effort to hide his dislike of the man. Hussein had the feeling they would just as soon shoot him as allow him to leave with the fertilizer. He began to consider his options--which were limited.

Within minutes, Roy returned with the nylon drawstring bag dangling from his right index finger. "Our Bens in here, boy?"

"Sure. Please count them. I wouldn't try to cheat you."

"Cheat us?" Roy chortled. "Ya hear that, Freddie? He wants we should trust him!"

At which point Freddie pushed Hussein from behind and ordered him inside the garage. He guided him to a lighted work bench and held out his hand for the nylon bag, which Roy produced while never taking his eyes off Hussein. "Count better be perfect, I-Ran boy, or you ain't leavin' here alive."

"It is all there," said Hussein. "Please count."

Which they did. Both of them, counting in unison, through two hundred bills, one hundred dollars at a time. When they were finished they turned to Hussein.

"Now comes the hard part, for you," said Roy. "We're goin' down by the river."

He was roughly handled and forced to walk ahead of the two men--now his captors--out of the garage, where they skirted behind and began following a path. The sound of running water was faint at first but then grew in volume as they trudged through the night, the rain, and the mud.

Two hundred yards later they were at the edge of what Hussein could hear was rapidly flowing river water.

"Now on your knees, I-Ran boy," said Roy. "On your knees and close your eyes, boy. You ain't even goan' to feel this."

"Feel what?" questioned Hussein. "What are we doing here?"

He asked the question but he knew the answer. In the dark his captors didn't immediately see his first move to the side and he spun around and kicked with his right boot at Roy's closest kneecap. As the kneecap dislocated, Hussein rose upright and seized the barrel of the shotgun. Almost immediately he flipped the gun around and pointed it at his antagonists. Without hesitation he fired off two twelve-gauge blasts into the dark outlines of the men from Arkansas. Both men were blasted backward and lay still. No moans, no groans, no sound.

Hussein came fully to his feet and again flipped the shotgun around so he was now holding it by the barrel. He pulled his shirttail free and wiped down the trigger and barrel and stock. He went up to Roy's body and placed his foot in the dead man's abdomen. With his free hand he tore loose a square of the man's bloody shirt. He used the square to then grasp the barrel of the shotgun and fling the gun far out over the river, where it plunged into the water and disappeared. He had no concept of current flow or how far the gun would tumble along in the swift waters, nor did he care. Point being, it wouldn't be traced to him.

Hussein riffled through Roy's trouser pockets and located the van keys. He jerked them free and turned away with a scowl. "Asshole," he muttered.

As he hiked back to the garage, he had one pressing concern. There were tire tracks from his vehicle that would be traced by the authorities. Coming in and going out.

Ten minutes later, he had the fifty-pound bags lifted into the back end of the van and was closing the vehicle doors. He then retrieved the nylon bag of money from the workbench where the rednecks had left it. He was elated; so far, so good.

Three hours later he pulled into an all-night Tire Masters and bought new rubber all around. There would be no tracing and tracking of tire tread after the van was blown to bits. No connection to the tire tracks in Arkansas would be found.

Hussein paid for the new tires with cash. As he went about his business he wore a slouch cap pulled low across his eyes. He took careful note of the security cameras coming and going and made sure to avert his eyes.

Hours later he stopped in Ferguson, Missouri, where he helped himself to the license plates from a Nissan sedan parked on Washington Street. He placed the plates beneath the passenger's seat.

Now he had new rubber, new plates, and he knew where the VINS were etched into the van's steel.

It wouldn't be traced, which meant he wouldn't be traced, either.

At least not by the van or its components.

A second step was completed; an important second step following acquisition of the van. The ammonium nitrate in an explosive grade was all but impossible to acquire. Yet...he had done it.

And all it had cost was fourteen grand for the van and three tanks of gas and twenty-two hours.

Chicago was just up ahead.

The storage facility was just outside Palatine, a northwest suburb of Chicago. When he arrived he tapped his code into the storage facility's sliding gate and parked the van inside his unit.

He then roared into the night on his Harley.

Tossing his head back and raising a gloved fist, he shouted.

"Allahu Akbar!"

19

S he wasn't all that happy with Ed Mitchell's work on Sevi's case. She pulled out a yellow legal pad and wrote Edward Mitchell's name and slowly nodded. Then beneath that she wrote:

PROBLEM

Ex-Army JAG - Loyalties definitely still are with military
Dragging feet on Sevi's case - difficult to attack military establishment???

FACTS

Immature: young - 29
Unmarried - not afraid of losing job and starting over elsewhere
Beneath all that she wrote

GOOD POINTS

Undergrad major = criminal justice

Law school heavy in criminal law

~~Good-looking dude~~

Loyal Bears fan

She tore the sheet of paper from the pad and wadded it up. On second thought, she then flattened it and ran it through her shredder.

Then she tapped Ed's office line. She asked him to come into her office.

Ed knocked once and entered. He was carrying a legal pad of his own and he nodded at Christine as he took a seat in one of her visitors' chairs.

"Hey," he said, and gave her a cheerful smile. "What's cooking?"

She drew away from her desk, leaned back, and clasped her hands behind her head.

"You're a week late with the Sevi al-Assad interrogatories. Is there a problem?"

The smile faded from his face. She watched this with heightened interest, mentally kicking herself for having dated him a few times. That fact made the present need for her to be his boss--his unhappy boss--that much more difficult. Never, she swore to herself, mix business and pleasure. Hadn't she heard that somewhere? Damn!

Still, every time she saw him she fell into a half-swoon. He was amazingly handsome by anyone's standards and he was attentive, polite, and always ready to jump in and help. Worst of all, she had introduced him to Jamie and her son adored him. They did sports together, movies, Saturday afternoon projects around the house. She had to admit; she had let it go too far with someone who was actually an employee. She sighed; she had only herself to blame.

But the fact remained: he was a damn hard worker, extremely productive and proud of his work product. Careful to the nth degree. Except with Sevi's case. This was his first time off the rails. What the hell was going on? She wondered. She plunged ahead.

"Sevi's case requires us to sue the government, the DOD, and Blackguard. Is that a problem for you?"

He sat bolt upright, as if coming to attention in his chair. A small frown creased that soft spot between his eyes.

"Is it a problem? Well, truth be told, it isn't easy, Sevi's case."

"Why's that? Clearly the defendants murdered a houseful of innocent people. You disagree?"

He clasped his hands around a knee and pulled.

"I don't know if I would say I disagree. But we've both been there--
the military. Sometimes missions go awry and innocents suffer. That's
just the nature of war."

"Does that mean the government goes scot-free just because it's
war?"

"No, I guess not. There should be responsibility."

"You mean to say there should be consequences?"

He slowly nodded. "That too, I suppose. Yes."

"So why are we having this work slowdown? Things have been
going great around here, but I've messaged you three times this week
asking about the interrogatories and all I get back from you are vague
responses. You tell me tomorrow, tomorrow, and tomorrow. Yet,
tomorrow comes and still no work product. You tell me you'll get back
to me and you don't. Frankly, Ed, it's all making me uncomfortable."

He drew back, defensive. "Hey, Christine, it's only a week past the
deadline. I can catch it up."

There it was, the defensiveness. Too much togetherness away
from work had emboldened him. She took it as a challenge and the
hair along the back of her neck buzzed ever so slightly. It wasn't a
fight, not yet, but it was definitely a tug-of-war.

"Playing catch-up and meeting deadlines are two different
animals. To tell the truth, I am uncomfortable with you this minute.
In fact, I'm unhappy."

"Sorry, jeez. I'll have the paperwork to you first thing in the morning. Does that work?"

"Sure, it works, but I don't want this to happen again, Ed. Look at
it from my perspective. I've taken on a lawsuit and now I owe a client
a duty to perform in a workmanlike, professional manner. Toward
that end, I pay you to pitch in and help. But you have a kind of
agenda, I would call it. That would be your antipathy toward suing
the government over a military mission that went to hell. So who's at

risk here? Me, that's who. And you put me there because of your feelings. Sorry, but I can't have that. If it's true that you just don't want to be assigned the case, speak up, man. I'll get someone else on it."

"It's not that. Let me do some soul searching. Can I get back to you on that?"

"Sure. Take an hour. Search your soul. Then get back in here, either ready to jump all in or tell me where to shove it. Bottom line: I need your truth about the case. That's all I'm asking. Are we good?"

"Yes."

"Have I made myself clear?"

"Definitely you have made yourself clear. Very clear."

"Good. Then back out of here and go do your thing. I'll expect to see you again in fifty-eight minutes. Goodbye, Ed."

"Thanks, Christine. I'm on it."

"Here's hoping."

With that he turned and hurried for the door. As he went, there was an awkward buckle in the air between them. They had clearly been headed toward a romantic encounter before that morning. Was that off now?

The door was shut softly behind him--no slamming, no outbursts, no displays of any kind. For that, Christine was thankful. She hated to have to ream a good worker like Ed, but her first allegiance was to the client. Always the client. And not just because of the professional liability exposure, either. She actually felt a moral obligation to do whatever she could for anyone whose case she had accepted into her practice. Whether it was the military she was suing or the timber industry or whatever--they all would be kicked and punched by her until they finally threw in the white flag. She owed her clients no less than that and, by God, she was going to stand and deliver, Ed or no Ed.

She stood and stretched. Her muscled shoulders rippled beneath the suit coat. She outstretched her arms and flexed her hands. Then she moved to the wet sink and poured herself a cup of coffee and picked up a donut. It felt hard so she put it back. Why couldn't her receptionist keep up and provide fresh pastries? she found herself wondering. It was her week, so was that so hard?

Which was when she realized. She was restless, irritable, and discontent.

And it all came down to Ed.

Or was it just Ed?

Lately she had become increasingly morose. She did her own soul searching--which took fifteen seconds. Then: damn it, she was lonely. Sonny was gone over a year and she was lonely. Sure, she missed him and loved him dearly yet, but that didn't undo her loneliness.

Life had to go on.

She owed it to her kids to be happy.

And she owed it to herself.

If not Ed--he was a hunk but he was her employee--then who?

She laughed. She had never in her life thought of men as hunks.

So maybe that was her problem: she kept trying to pin faces and feelings onto hunks of flesh. Maybe she should stop that.

But she knew she never would. More than anything, she needed the big, stiff R:

Relationship.

20

"What are we trying to accomplish today?" said Winona. The sisters in law were meeting in Christine's conference room. Lunch was a quickie, catered from Quik-Sand sandwich shop downstairs in Christine's building. Tuna, Turkey, and Roast Beef sandwiches were distributed, plus diet-everything to drink.

"We're trying to protect my ass," said Althea as she bit into her roast beef.

"Exactly that," said Christine. "We need to make sure that once Blackguard figures out you're one of us they don't murder you."

"That would be nice," said Althea. "Uh-huh."

"So how do we protect her?" Sevi asked. She had the veggie burger and was spreading mayo across the "burger."

"By making them fear us," said Christine. "And there's only one way to do that."

"Go ahead," said Althea, "I'm listening."

"We need to hand you a bigger club than they've got," Winona said. "You need to have more power."

"I'm thinking you're thinking documents," Althea said to her two friends.

"Bingo!" said Christine. "Here's how I see it going down. First, their systems administrators are going to notice the document transfers. I don't know how or when, but they probably will."

"Agree," said Althea.

"They always do," said Winona. She peeled up the bread on her tuna sandwich and examined it. "Not enough onions. Damn!"

"Next, they're coming after you because they'll trace it back to you. First rule is, you do not show fear. If you show fear they'll take advantage and head down that road."

"Meaning?"

"Meaning they'll try torture. They'll see if they can cause you enough pain that you tell them where their records are."

"That would happen," said Althea. "I'm a sucker for pain. Not!"

"Okay, so here's what we do," said Christine. "We take—"

Winona interrupted. "We take the records out of your control so you don't know where they are. You couldn't tell them even if they're pulling out your toenails."

"Shit, girlfriend, enough on that!" cried Althea.

"Agree," said Christine. "Let's take her idea, though. I like it, Win. We have Jamie hide the records so Althea can't give them up. That's beautiful."

"Of course then we're in charge of the records and they'll know that if anything happens to our friend, we go public."

"There it is, ladies," Christine announced. "There's our strategy."

"I can live with it," Althea said. "Except for the torture part. How do we avoid that road?"

"By not showing fear," Christine told her. "When they threaten torture just throw it right back in their face. Laugh at them. Threaten them right back, as in, you torture me, I expose you. Exposure is huge with these assholes, I can promise you that."

"Seems simple enough. Okay, I can live with that," Althea decided. "Let's get this done."

"I'll talk to Jamie. We'll move the records out of Haiti but you won't know where."

"Then I can't tell."

"Then you can't tell."

"Who ordered this stuff?" Winona said. "My turkey is dry."

"You ordered it," said Sevi. "It's your office."

"I did," said Winona. "I did order it. Short memory."

21

I t was a systems administrator by the name of Don Nelson who discovered her theft. Althea was at her cubicle inside the Watergate in Washington when Nelson leaned inside her cube. "See you a minute?" he said. It wasn't a question. He crooked a finger at her and walked off, expecting her to follow.

Always the systems administrators, Althea thought as she fell in behind Don Nelson.

SA's were the bad boys who tracked and traced everything that happened on a company network such as Blackguard's. They knew everyone's password. Check.

They knew all data sent and received by all users. Check.

They knew modifications users made to all data and systems themselves. Check.

They knew all attempts to jack their data. Check.

But did they know that Althea had scored a SA's credentials and had been downloading tons of documents and transferring them to the real world? That was something she was about to find out.

She swallowed hard and watched the bouncing globe of Don Nelson's bald head as he led her through Blackguard's labyrinthine halls. Everything in her wanted to resist, turn and run, but she knew

she'd never escape. Not by running. So she had to use her head. Then
it occurred to her: the only thing these people understood was a
threat. She would threaten them, manipulate them--and hope she
lived to tell about it.

After a final left turn and oblique march of another thirty yards
the SA threw open the door to a dark conference room. Althea passed
him by and went in and switched on the lights. The neons blinked
and threw their icy light around the small room. Althea sized it all up.
Table, four chairs, ubiquitous conference phone in table center, tray
with pitcher (empty) and four upside-down water glasses. Best of all,
no one else there. She took a far chair, sat, and clasped her hands
before her. See? I have nothing to hide, her body language trum-
peted. She was many things, but she was not afraid. She had the
goods on them and the goods were in a safe place where Blackguard
could not reach them. They could threaten her, but she could
threaten them right back.

Nelson took the chair closest to her and turned in his chair so he
was facing her. He was maybe eighteen inches from the side of her
face when he spoke first.

"Well, Althea, you know, and you know I know, what you've been
up to."

"SA's know everything. That's my beginning premise," she said.
"But you brought it up, so tell me what you know."

"We know you've taken data. And we want it back. If you refuse
then bad things will happen to you and your family. This isn't a game
we're playing."

"Oh, that's where you're wrong. It's a game of keep away and I won
two weeks ago when I began downloading terabytes of data and
storing it off-site. Where it is--that's the game, because you'll never
find out and you'll never make me tell you."

"You can't be made to tell us? Are you serious? Are you sure?"

"Serious and sure."

"We have our methods, dear woman. Never forget that Blackguard
is populated with some of the heaviest hitters in the world. Men and
women who create new modes of torture as a contest among them-

selves. I can assure you that when your eyes are about to be cored of their pupils you will speak up. Or when snakes are introduced into your body, you will want to cooperate. Don't flinch, dear woman. There, there."

She had recoiled at the suggestions. Recoiled and scowled in disgust--against her will, of course. Just like that--snap!--she had been cowed. And he knew it. Then she caught herself. She had practiced this answer many times before:

"See, even if you make me talk, I don't know where the data is. Someone else does and you don't know who. But if you even so much as frown at me, then it's over. My person will upload your data to WikiLeaks and the world will come after you."

"Then let's talk about who else has seen the data you've stolen from us."

"So far, no one has seen it."

"And how do we know that? Do you have proof?"

She shrugged. "Guess you'll just have to believe me."

"Already we don't believe you. No, you'll have to do better than that."

At that moment Nelson removed his eyeglasses and tugged a white handkerchief from the breast pocket of his beige shirt. He wore no tie--systems administrators wouldn't be caught dead wearing ties. He held the eyeglasses up to the neons and peered through first one lens then the other. As he passed each lens by, his eyes jumped to twice their size, magnified in the frail light.

Althea watched this display with disgust. Try as they may, SA's always reverted back to the geeks they were. He'd had her there with the cored eyes and the snakes--but then he'd lost the rhythm and meter of his presentation when he stopped to spot clean his eyewear. What a doofus, she thought, and relaxed in her chair. Now he wouldn't get squat out of her.

But then he surprised her. Surprised her in a way she'd never forget.

He cleared his throat several times. "Miss Berenson--do you mind if I use your real name? We have one of your children."

Althea froze. Then she slowly turned in her chair so that her face wasn't twelve inches from his.

"Mister, you'd better be kidding. If you've touched one of my children I will take down this entire place. Everything goes on WikiLeaks immediately."

"Do that and your child disappears forever."

"Do that and I will hunt you down and personally kill you, your wife, your children, your parents, your siblings and your friends. Then for fun I'll take out the DuMont brothers themselves. And their wives and their children--you get my drift?"

"I hear what you're saying. Should I be frightened?"

Her back stiffened. "Know this, mister. If anything happens to me, your documents are automatically delivered to WikiLeaks. If anything happens to anyone or anything I love, your documents are automatically delivered to WikiLeaks. Now, if I were you, I'd assign someone to me and to my family and to my dog to make sure nothing bad happens to any of us. Are you frightened yet?"

He smiled.

"So we're at an impasse," he said. What do you suggest?"

The power play was hers.

"I don't suggest, I demand that my child be returned to my home immediately. Once that is done I will return the documents in my possession. Except the Sevi al-Assad documents."

"I don't know what those are. Sevi who?"

"Your missile killed her family in Syria. The lawyer who employs me is suing you. Those documents I keep."

He frowned. "No, no exceptions, dear woman. You keep nothing."

"Then we don't have a deal. Time to hide your loved ones because my sisters and I are coming after you."

"Your sisters have what to do with all this?"

"My Sisters in Law. Believe me, you don't want that pack coming after you."

"Please, no threats. That doesn't work here."

"Then I'll tell you what. You keep my kid and I'll upload Blackguard's entire universe to WikiLeaks. Everything. From Vietnam forward, every black deed, ever homicide, every evil ever done by the DuMont brothers becomes public knowledge around the world. We're done here, Mr. Nelson."

She stood to leave.

"Hold it. What makes you think you can just leave? What if I have security waiting outside that door?"

She leaned down and placed both hands on the table. She leaned toward him.

"WikiLeaks."

"That's it?"

"That's all I need. Now I'm leaving. You better damn well hope you can bring Malie home by six o'clock tonight because at six-oh-one I'm clicking UPLOAD on the WikiLeaks page. Now, we're done here."

She turned and abruptly strode from the room.

Nelson rubbed both hands back over his bald head. He punched the green button on the conference phone.

"What?" he spoke into the phone.

A metallic voice came back.

"Return the kid."

"You're sure about that?"

"Are you seriously challenging me?"

"No, sir."

"Six o'clock, Nelson. Have her home."

"She isn't actually out of the country."

"How stupid do you think we are?"

"She's on her way."

22

"When I flew to London I drank too much," Winona confided to the sisters.

They were gathered like birds on a wire at Moe's Grill, a slum name for an upscale eatery on North Wacker Drive. As they waited at the bar for a table, Winona made her announcement to the group. "I drank too much and I cried myself to sleep."

"Girl," said Althea, directly to Winona's left, "That scumbag ain't worth that. Uh-uh."

"Have you found a lawyer?" asked Christine.

At Althea's left, Sevi studied the menu. Without lifting her eyes, she asked, "Scumbag? Is that a real American word?"

"You'll get the hang of that word once you're in the American singles scene," said Althea, patting Sevi on the arm.

"Which we don't recommend you get involved in until you've lived in the States at least a year," said Christine. "Too toxic for newbies like you."

Then Althea's face darkened. "They caught me yesterday."

All faces turned to her.

She nodded.

"Yep. Systems admin found out I've been stealing documents."

"Why didn't you call me?" said Christine. "You knew I needed that kind of development without delay!"

"Sorry, sister. I know you do. But I knew we were meeting today. It's all been taken care of. I'm terminated from Blackguard. They even found the bugs."

"What are they going to do?" asked Winona. "Cops called?"

"You kidding? No way the criminals are calling the cops. I just dropped one word on them and it all shriveled up and blew away."

"What was that?" said Christine.

"WikiLeaks."

"Yes."

"Yes."

"It did the trick. And...I wasn't kidding. I still might do it."

Christine's eyes grew wide. "Uh-uh. We don't need that kind of news traffic now. The feds would be all over us if you did that. No, you're going to sit tight and hang onto what you have. I'll tell you when it all changes, if it ever does. But for now, no WikiLeaks. For God's sake, please."

"All right, all right. They just shouldn't have threatened me. I hate bullies. Speaking of," said Althea as she changed the subject, "Winona, how's that trim your man Gorman is playing house with? Is he still hitting that?"

"'Course he is. The little head's doing all his thinking anymore."

"So your husband is dipping his wick in his secretary. That's a load on, girl," said Althea. She snorted scornfully.

"Yep. My turn in the barrel."

"How can we help?" asked Christine. She took a long drink of her tonic water. No alcohol for her at lunch---that was forever a no-no.

Winona toyed with her cocktail napkin, slowly wiping away the drink condensation beneath her glass when she moved it away. "Hard. To. Say. Point me toward a good divorce lawyer, I guess. What about you, Chris? Can you take my case?"

"That's an option. Someone needs to give Gormie a good drubbing. It's definitely time."

"Think about it."

"Let me talk to Ed. I would be more comfortable with Ed Mitchell actually doing the case."

"Ed would be great. Maybe he would even take me to his breast and pat me on the back. I could do that with Ed."

Christine laughed.

"Or do you have first dibs on him?" asked Winona. "I see how you two stalk each other around the office. Always just happening to bump into each other at the copier, or in the kitchen, or going or coming from the restrooms, or talking to paralegals--it happens constantly, ladies. There's a real game going on here."

"All your imagination," said Christine. "Ed's my employee."

"But he comes to our house all the time," chimed in Sevi. "He helps Christine around the house, plays catch with Jamie, and studies me like I'm from another planet or something."

"Comes to your house?" said Althea. "Exposed to the kids? Now we're talking serious, honey."

"It's not like that," Christine protested. "He comes around to play with Jamie. More like a big brother to him since Sonny's gone. I appreciate everything he does."

"Really?" said Winona in a needling tease of voice, "What all might it be that he does?"

"Rubs my back, kisses my toes--you know, the typical big brother stuff," Christine laughed. "Get outta my face, you two."

"I haven't seen him rub your feet," Sevi said, her look perplexed. "But I have seen him take your hand and kiss you."

"Oh God," said Christine, "it's definitely time we find you your own place."

"I could do that," said Sevi. "I need my own place. You've been wonderful but I make enough now to pay my own way."

"Plus you've gotta know your way around town by now," Winona said.

"Plus you probably want to throw your leg over some dude by now," said Althea, "am I right? Do you need your privacy so certain physical violations and inspections can proceed?"

Sevi slapped the mahogany bar. "I'm not like that! Stop, please, even if you are teasing. Only Hussein is my--"

"God, sorry," said Althea. She pulled her head into her shoulders turtle-like, and shrugged at the other two women. "I honestly didn't realize. Please forgive me, Sevi."

"You're forgiven," said Sevi. "I know you're trying to be good to me. It's just not easy for me to move on from my love."

"Got that," said Christine, raising her glass of tonic water. "Here's to lost loves."

"Lost loves."

"Lost loves."

"Lost loves."

They touched glasses and drank deeply. Each had her own private look on her face. And each face was somewhat pained, to varying degrees, for they all had suffered losses that still niggled at them.

"Better to have loved and lost--"

"Than never to have loved at all."

And at that moment the hostess came to lead them away to their table. They fell in behind her, twisted and turned around tables to the rear of Moe's Grill, and were shown to a dark corner with a candlelit table. Two candles, in fact, a foot apart in the center of the table. The cutlery was silver inlaid with pearl and the napkins were linen. The women made themselves comfortable, unfurled napkins, and began going over the menus.

"I understand the FACCE software for falsehood recognition. And it's amazing work, Jamie," said Sevi.

They were sitting in Jamie's office in the spare bedroom on the third floor of Christine's house. It was windowed on two walls and sprawled beneath dormers and a raised ceiling. The ceiling beams were oak and the framing stanchions were left uncovered but faced with oak too. He had done the room in blood red and written favorite words vertically in a wide orange font. "Singularity," said one word on the front wall. Four feet west was another, "Non-locality." Above his two-wall desk ran the phrase "quantum makeover," upon left wall and right wall. Jamie loved words and, obviously, was deep into quantum mechanics.

"Thank you, Sevi. FACCE is now patented, like I might have told you. It's being tested now nationwide. That's new. But we're a year away from our first sale. So now I'm working on this," he said, and hit RETURN on his keyboard, which brought to life a slide show of the same person doing various things such as standing at a gas pump; handing a credit card to a clerk; squeezing mustard onto a hot dog in a convenience store; looking into a camera lens in a rest stop restroom, and on and on.

"What are we looking at?"

"It's a montage. A montage of the same person traveling from Illinois to Missouri and his face and features being recorded on CCTV as he makes the trip."

"And what is unusual about this? Couldn't that easily be done by hand?"

"It could. But let's say the police are looking for someone who kidnapped a child and must be found without delay. Using my system, all closed circuit TV video is fed onto my server in Chicago."

"Then what?"

"Then my software analyzes a mug shot of the suspect or even an old yearbook photo. Using my facial recognition software algorithms, my new creation then searches all video feeds, locates the same person as he is traveling from point to point, and returns a slide show of his movement. Along the bottom of the screen is the location, time and date of each piece of video. This way the authorities can determine a direction and route of travel and all-points-bulletins can be narrowed to a known route and direction of travel."

"Allahu Akbar!"

"Yes, God is great."

"This is amazing. Have you shown it to anyone?"

"No, and I'm at a point where I could use your help. With the video resolution. I'm trying to jack it up--computer enhance the resolution--but it's slowing the product way, way down. It's becoming much too slow for those emergency cases. Well, too slow for any usefulness, truth be told."

"I've done video enhancement. Can you copy the source code onto a thumb drive and let me take it to my room and check it out on my computer? This will take some time."

"Sure, then you can just feed it back into my code repository. We'll make a branch in the code and I'll put your name on it. I'll email you a user ID and password. We good?"

"Good. We are great, Jamie."

"Okay."

He unplugged the thumb drive and passed it back over his shoulder to where Sevi was standing behind him.

"Can you get back to me in twenty-four?"

"More like half that, I should think," she said.

"That would be cool. Okay. Onward and upward."

Sevi, the thumb drive in hand, walked down one flight of stairs to the second floor and entered her bedroom. She closed the door behind her and quietly slid the latch, locking it from within.

She sat at her desk and entered the password on her MacBook. The screen resolved and she checked her email. Two messages from Hussein, one attachment:

"We need to meet. I have good news." Message 1.

"I have found us a place. Cash rent accepted. Pack and we can move you." Message 2.

Attached to the email was a PDF. She opened it and studied it corner to corner. It appeared she was viewing the inner walls blueprint for Windsor School District's Elementary School Number 9.

They had selected School 9 for several reasons. First, there was a hill just across the street from the front of the elementary school. The hill would redirect the blast of the bomb back toward the school. Hussein had discovered this effect and tactic by studying the United States' bombing plans for World War Two's nuclear attack on Hiroshima. That city had been selected at least in part because of the surrounding mountains. They would keep the blast force focused rather than blowing out and harmlessly dissipating. Same with the grade school and its hill. Second, the grade school was selected for its high population. It was in an upper middle class neighborhood where two lesser grade schools a mile apart had been consolidated into one "super school" as they were called by the Chicago School District. CSD also had moved another 250 students from a third school that wanted in; it was a parochial school that had closed its doors due to seriously declining enrollment after a key parish priest had been indicted. It had been a sad occasion and a shocking one, but the authorities thought the kids would be better served by integrating them into a public school.

At the time of Sevi's receipt of the blueprint, the school's enroll-ment was 2500 students. Hussein predicted an 85% mortality rate if the bomb in the van exploded in the school parking lot; a 70% mortality rate if parked along the street. An ancillary plan called for blocking both ends of the street on the morning of the attack with rented vehicles. That would make ingress and egress difficult, if not impossible, for first responders, including EMT vehicles. The plan, he assured Sevi that same night as they met for dinner, was hard-ening day by day.

"Hardening?" she asked.

"More difficult to prevent."

After meeting that night with Hussein, Sevi returned to her room and again locked her door.

She inserted Jamie's thumb drive in the Mac's USB port. For the next ninety minutes she traced through his code. It looked profes-sional, she decided. She would give him an A. Then she found the routine for the video enhancement and began sketching ways to improve the execution of the code to make it run faster. By eleven o'clock that night she saved all her work and shut down her machine. She then unplugged Jamie's thumb drive and took it upstairs to him.

He was awake, of course, hunched over his machine.

"Can I come in?"

"Sure."

"Here's the code enhancement."

"Shit, that was fast!" he exclaimed.

"I would have had it sooner. But I had a dinner date."

"Anyone cool?"

"No, not cool. Just an old friend from home."

"From Syria? That sounds interesting."

"From Turkey."

"Wow."

"Anyway, please try the code and tell me what you think."

"I'll have some metrics for you by sunup. Maybe we can have breakfast and talk?"

"Sure," said Sevi with a smile. She stretched her arms overhead. "So sleepy. Off to bed for me. Good night."

"Good night. And thanks."

"Oh, before I forget. I came up with a name for your new software."

"Tell me."

"What about calling it TRAC?"

"Means what?"

"TRACE RECOGNIZE AND CAPTURE."

"TRAC. I love it, dude."

She raised her hand for a high-five and they slapped together.

"TRAC it is."

"Good night, Jamie."

"Night."

Eager to move his project along, Jamie lodged the thumb drive in his laptop's USB port. He located the port with his finder and double-clicked the code file. His development software opened the file Sevi had saved and he went straight to the routine for video enhancement. He tested it, measured it, sampled it with a real video feed, and was happy to learn the speed had been increased to a useful state. Now that was something, he thought. He was delighted.

Then something else caught his eye. There was an attached document, a PDF.

24

S he parked in a visitor's slot in the north lot. The grade school was a multilevel complex, sprawled along two-thirds of a city block. Its sidewalk was tree-lined and NO PARKING signs and a red curb kept the traffic flowing smoothly in and out of the lot throughout. Hundreds of cars pulled up and loaded and unloaded. It added a flavor of small chaos to the large chaos of the yellow buses that sat nose-to-tail in the early morning, restricting access to the sidewalk that paralleled the huge parking lot.

Across the street was a row of houses built on the downward slope of a jutting promontory of a rather large hill. For the Midwest the ground swell was remarkable, probably five hundred feet in elevation.

Christine exited the Escalade and fixed her sunglasses on her face, as it was a bright, sunny June day and hot. She was alone; she had purposely told her driver to wait behind at her building's coffee shop while she visited the school rendered in the blueprints given to her by Jamie.

"Why would she have these, mom?" he asked the morning after Sevi had returned the thumb drive.

Christine plugged the drive into her laptop and viewed several screens, noting though the legend at the bottom edge of all drawings: Windsor School District Elementary School Number 9.

"Did she say anything when she gave you the drive?"

"No, she just said she thought she'd improved the routine I was working on."

"Has she ever mentioned anything to you about schools or grade schools or students or anything like that?"

"No. I mean we talk about lots of things. But nothing about a school."

Christine's first impulse was to casually ask Sevi about the blueprints. Why, she wanted to ask her, would you have the blueprints to a grade school?

But she reconsidered. She decided she first would visit the school and nose around for herself.

After climbing out of her car and slipping on her sunglasses, she began the walk up to the school entrance. She was immediately surrounded by fifty or more school children walking past. She watched as they chattered, played tag, breaking off in clutches of three or four and talking as they stole glimpses at members of the opposite sex--smiles, laughter, all the sub-mature expressions and eruptions common to the grade school era. Christine threaded her way through them, coming up to the door and encountering a security desk. Two fortyish gentlemen--armed with pistols on their utility belts--blocked her admittance.

"Purpose of your visit, ma'am?" asked the nearest guard.

"I'm here to see--the principal."

"Do you have an appointment?"

"No. Uh--I'm a lawyer and I have a legal matter to discuss with the administration."

"Do you have identification?"

"As a lawyer? Sure, I have my bar card."

"May I see that?"

Christine opened her shoulder bag and retrieved the card that proved she was a member of the Illinois State Bar Association. She held it up for review.

The guard read it, took it from her hand, flipped it over and examined her signature, then raised a finger. "Excuse me one minute."

He turned to the mike mounted on his shoulder and pressed a button. He spoke rapidly and quickly into the mike. Within seconds a response crackled back. Evidently they were going to see her even without an appointment.

"Please proceed to the end of this hall and then take a left. All the way to the end, glass doors. Thanks for your cooperation."

"Thank you."

The waters parted and Christine began her walk.

At the glass doors she paused and checked her agenda with herself. She planned some kind of inquiry about some manufactured issue. Maybe an injury report. That would do.

The receptionist told her the wait for the Assistant Principal, Evelyn Ridnour, would be fifteen minutes. Would Christine like a bottle of water?

Christine accepted the water and found a waiting room seat next to a lamp. She withdrew her tablet from her shoulder bag and began logging into her office network. Within seconds she had the PDF of the blueprints up on the screen. She began her review. Minutes later she had grown restless. Something wasn't adding up here. She went to the receptionist's window and got directions for the restroom--an ostensible need.

Back in the hall, she continued further into the building. Along the hallway she passed a chemistry lab--chemistry in grade school?-- and at the far end found herself trying the locked door to the gymnasium. Through its glass panes she viewed a collection of girls about thirteen playing volleyball on four different courts. It was a huge gymnasium and Christine was impressed. She watched the games for several minutes, going over in her mind what she might have expected to find in coming here.

What was it?

The blueprints included the interior walls of the school. Why on earth would Sevi have blueprints of the exterior and interior walls of a grade school?

As she watched the girls batting the volleyball back and forth, an idea began to coalesce in her mind. How could she have been so blind?

What do we have here? Children. Acres of children. Just like the children Sevi lost in the Hellfire attack.

Christine turned and began a hurried walk back to the Assistant Principal's office. When she arrived at the door, she walked right on by, continuing to the end of the hall and beyond the security station, until she was back outside in the hot June sunshine.

As she placed the sunglasses back on her face, she realized her hands were shaking.

Sevi--could it be? Could she be planning to attack this school?

Restraining herself from breaking into a run, Christine race-walked to her Escalade.

She pulled the seat belt across and fastened it. Her chest felt tight and a sour taste had come up in her mouth. She pulled out her cell.

"Win? Chris. We need to meet. Durant's restaurant. Be there in thirty."

DURANT'S WAS a beloved Chicago steak and chop shop where many of the legal community's older members often took their midday break. It was dark inside and the maître' d' told Christine that her party had already arrived. She was shown to a side table and found Winona, sitting facing the kitchen. Christine came up behind and patted her friend on the back. "Hey. Thanks for coming."

"You sounded upset. What's happening with you today?"

Christine explained to Winona about Jamie's coming across the blueprints on the thumb drive. She recounted her visit to the grade school and the moment she'd had her insight.

"Is it possible, Win? I mean you know Sevi almost as well as I do. What's your take?"

Ever the suspicious police officer--retired or not--Win's forehead furrowed. "It bears looking into, certainly. I mean we're not going to come right out and accuse her or confront her--that gets us nowhere."

"Right, we don't tip our hand because she then goes off on her own and does whatever she has in mind anyway. We've got to stay in close contact with her. So here's what I'd like to do. I know you've got a full caseload you're working up--"

"Not the least of which is Sevi's case itself--"

"So I'm thinking. Maybe you should take up her surveillance. Get on her. Thoughts?"

"Exactly what I was thinking. Do we have access to her computer?"

"She keeps her laptop with her at all times. Even when she showers. No, I'm exaggerating there. I don't know what she does when she showers."

"Hey, that's not so far out there. We should definitely think about that. What about Jamie, can he access her laptop?"

"Well, she does use our WIFI at home."

"Can he hack that?"

"Jamie? Are you kidding? Just say the word with that kid."

"Okay. Let me talk to Jamie. Let me take it from here. You need to stand aside on this and let me deal with Jamie. I don't want any suspicious glances or words between you two that Sevi might pick up on."

"I agree. You approach Jamie."

"Where is he now?"

Christine checked her watch. "Still in school. Another hour. Why, you heading there?"

Winona was already standing. "I'm on my way. Madison High?"

"Yes. Junior class."

"I'm on it."

Winona hurried from the restaurant.

Christine's waiter appeared with two menus and a puzzled look. "She had to go," Christine explained. "But I want a drink."

"A dry martini," she told him.

"And I never drink before five."

Never.

25

It was like someone ordered all thirty-one Baskin-Robbins flavors, there were so many of them.

Lawyers, that is.

Some came from the Department of Justice. These were the wise owls (three-piece suits, black eyeglass frames) who would protect the United States government from the likes of the woman whose family was murdered by a missile.

Some came from Blackguard (early-to-late fifties, round bellies, sagging jowls) who would protect the DuMont brothers' two hundred billion dollars from the greedy hands of the Syrian woman whose wedding day was incinerated by a Hellfire missile specially delivered by the DuMonts. (The brothers had privately joked: "Never let it be said we didn't bring a little something to the wedding party to light up the festivities.")

To top it off, the manufacturers of the Hellfire missiles and the sub-contractors also off-loaded a passel of black suits from crammed Cadillac Escalades lined up along Dearborn and blocking through traffic. By the time Judge Alphonse LaJordia took the bench, every seat in the courtroom was claimed. And every seat claimed was populated by the smooth, fatty butt of some lawyer who looked and thought like all the other lawyers present.

"You would have thought one lawyer per defendant would have sufficed," said the red-faced jurist as he took the bench in his flowing black robe. "Maybe next time I'll enter an order. Or maybe the Northern District should have a local rule that, on photo-op day in any lawsuit each defendant may be represented by but one lawyer. Gentlemen--and ladies--I presume that after the TV crews dissipate and the newspapers smell foul elsewhere, that the teams will be winnowed down to one lawyer per name on the complaint? Am I right, here?"

Failures at improvisation, the entire retinue was momentarily struck dumb. No one had even a monosyllable in reply. Instead, they studied each other and a frantic digging through briefcases ensued while everyone waited for the alpha dog to show.

The quiet was shattered when a husky female voice replied, "Federal Rules of Civil Procedure make no attempt to limit the number of attorneys a litigant may field. It may be presumptuous of me, but please allow me to maintain that a local rule that seeks to narrow and confine the FRCP would die on the vine if tested in the Court of Appeals. That said, I would think no, Your Honor, our teams probably will not see our seconds and thirds left in the dugout when the plate beckons."

Christine, alone at counsel table--not even Sevi was along for this organizational meeting--turned to see the speaker. She had, Christine thought, used a whole bunch of words to say damn little. Who could it be?

Maybe half or just less than half of the defense lawyers were female. Christine was at a loss to discern which of them in the entire crowd had piped up. So, she waited.

Judge LaJordia pursed his lips and blew a steady stream of oxygen as he eyed the speaker. "And you are? For the record, madam?"

"Sorry, Your Honor. I'm Martha J. Mattingly and I represent the Department of Justice. First chair."

"Well, Ms. Mattingly of the first chair, despite your protestations methinks we'll just go ahead anyway and issue the first order of the court. All counsel except first chair counsel for each defendant shall leave the courtroom at once. There's so damn much hot air blowing through my courtroom I'm opening the windows. Not literally. Leave now, please."

A sudden clamor erupted at the judge's order. Everyone leave except first chairs? What the hell was the judge thinking? Had he suddenly collapsed in on himself, a supernova whose light was blinking off? After all, Judge LaJordia was the Chief Judge of the Northern District of Illinois. He was well known--not only throughout the Seventh Circuit but through the other circuits as well, all the way out to Hawaii--as the thinking judge's judge. He was a nonpareil jurist, his nearest challenger in the brains department probably being Big Blue over at IBM. Could he even issue such a decree? Just chase everyone out? Shoo them away like flies?

The less testicular-enhanced among the bar slammed shut brief- cases and shoulder bags and closed down laptops and began leaving en masse. Within minutes the courtroom was eighty percent cleared-- cured, rather, as one newspaper wag would have it. Then, what was left of the first wave proceeded to inventory its remaining numbers. Eleven; that was it. Eleven attorneys to defend against the lone woman at the plaintiff's table. Her presence momentarily stumped them again: she hadn't yet been heard on the judge's previous order.

"May it please the court, my name is Christine Susmann and I represent Sevi al-Assad, the plaintiff in this case. If your honor hadn't *sua sponte* cleared the courtroom of the briefcase-bearing second and third strings, I would have made the same motion to do so myself. So, for the record, I join with the court in its efforts to whittle our numbers down to a manageable size. Short of that, we faced an hour of self-introductions any time we came into court for even the most mundane business."

Judge LaJordia immediately raised a hand, shutting her off.

"Miss Susmann, I can assure you--and everyone remaining--that mundane business is never transacted in my court. All business here is important."

"Sorry, Your Honor, I didn't mean to suggest--"

"I know you didn't. But in case anyone else might get the wrong idea, I felt forced to characterize further what it is we do here." He looked directly into the TV camera when he said this. He even spoke slowly enough the newspaper writers could get it all down word for word. Then he smiled broadly at Christine. No harm, no foul, said his smile. She returned the smile and took her seat.

"Now, ladies and gentlemen, let's get down to some of that important business I just referenced moments ago. First up, standing orders. Number one, today is June fifteen. Trial in four months. Madam clerk, that means our trial date will be--"

"October nineteenth, a Monday," the clerk shot back.

"Exactly the date I wanted," said His Honor, "the nineteenth of October. The World Series is over by then and the NBA is just getting its first paycheck of the new season and leasing its first Mercedes and moving mom out of South Chicago. Perfect time for a trial. Second, the length of the trial will be fifteen court days. Those days are given eight to the plaintiff, who has the burden of proof, and seven to the defendants, who can divvy up the court time among them. Take what's left, you defendants, and fight it out. But know this: the court will entertain no motions regarding who gets how many court hours among the defendants. You men and women will decide that among yourselves sanely and quietly without my help. In this regard I would recommend you elect a litigation committee from among your numbers--let me suggest a threesome--and that you defer all such decisions to that committee. Believe me, your clients will love you for it once they realize they're not being billed every time there's a discussion but only when there is a solution. And so on."

His eyes dropped to the papers spread before him. It grew quiet, the atmosphere still.

The DOJ then thought it incumbent on it to replace the unused airtime with words. "Your Honor," Ms. Martha J. Mattingly began in her smooth, but husky, tone, "please let the record reflect that the United States Department of Justice objects to the court's limiting trial days to just fifteen. The DOJ's case alone could take twice that."

"Yes, in theory I suppose it could, but we don't have twice that. We hardly even have the fifteen days I've already given you. One, your objection is noted. Two, I respectfully suggest the United States pony-up several million to this injured woman, to whom, if the complaint I am now reading may be taken at face value, you have terribly injured. Give her ten million and save us all much to-do, keep a lid on the case, covenants-not-to-reveal-terms-of-settlement and yada yada yada. What say you, madam?"

"We've done nothing wrong, Judge," said Mattingly. "The injuries were suffered during war time."

"Yes, but it wasn't the United States' war that was going on; it was the Syrian civil war. What, does the United States just get to latch onto whatever war is going on in the world and lob missiles into the fray? Is that seriously your defense? Counsel," smiling benignly at Christine, "I wouldn't accept less than ten million, just off the record, based on what I've just been told by the DOJ. It appears their defense is that the U.S. has legal authority under international law to send in the marines anytime a shot is fired anyplace on God's green earth." He poured himself a tall glass of water and took two gulps, shaking his head as he swallowed. "Lord help us all."

"There is more, much more, Judge," said Mattingly. "We will brief the court on the law as we go."

"Yes, you do that. And maybe, just maybe, the next time your locution is introduced into my courtroom in an attempt to sway me, you won't lead with your weakest point, please. Agreed?"

Dead silence. He had just cut the lead attorney for the DOJ off at the knees. Christine knew better than to speak. When your enemy is hanging himself, try not to replace the stool. So she sat, arms folded on counsel table, fingers interlaced, staring at the dimple on Judge LaJordia's dark chin. Her eyes wanted to meet his eyes, but she knew better. She knew better because she knew he would recognize in her eyes the young girl doing somersaults across the courtroom floor. Yes, she had been soothed and energized in an instant.

It was coming true again: they could only talk one at a time. No

matter the head count, there is only one to face at a time. That's what
she loved about courtrooms: not everyone all got to speak at once.

She was imbued with a new sense of completeness about the
case. There was their side, her side, and the judge's side. All too often
their side also included the judge among its numbers. Not so here.

For a moment she loved all federal judges equally. Appointed for
life and not subject to re-election, they were thus given the freedom
to actually do justice with regard only to a case's merits, never
needing to consider the political influence of the litigants.

Judge LaJordia drew a deep breath that could be heard over the
court sound system. All ears listened up.

"Discovery will be complete by August 31. That gives everyone ten
weeks, and I am going to enter a special rule just for this case. When
each party's attorney returns to his or her office, you will prepare and
file within seventy-two hours the names, addresses, and expected
testimony of all witnesses. Now, before you begin with your
objections--"

There was already a clamor among the defense counsel. Even
Christine found herself confronted with an unbelievably near and
short deadline. She would have to work around the clock for the next
three days to comply.

"Before you begin with your objections," the judge repeated, "let
me say that I have reviewed the case, reviewed all parties' answers,
and all I have seen so far is boilerplate. Granted the federal rules
require only notice pleading, but from here on out I want all plead-
ings attached to a verified statement of facts in support. In this way, I
can quickly get to know who your key witnesses are and begin to
settle on a trial plan in my own mind. The time for interrogatory
answers is shortened to ten days and--"

"Your Honor, if I may," said a short stocky attorney with a hairline
that began just an inch above his eyebrows. The hair was clipped
short and the man resembled more a pugilist than a well-heeled
lawyer from a silk-stocking firm. But Christine knew better than to be
fooled by first impressions, for she knew this man. He was Boris
Adizkov and he represented Blackguard in the first chair. Secretly

Christine had prayed it would be anyone but Boris but she knew she had been dreaming if she had thought he would pass up this case. No way was that going to happen. He was a scrappy in-fighter before a jury and master manipulator of judges and clerks. His settlements and court victories were recorded around the world. It was said he lived on his own private jet as he moved around constantly keeping Blackguard's feet from the fire. He continued in his loud, jack-hammer voice.

"If I may say, while I appreciate the court's desire to foreshorten the Federal Rules of Civil Procedure and bring this matter to trial, there are some matters that simply are too complex for your deadlines. For instance, all parties will be seeking Blackguard documents. Judge, Blackguard's data repositories are strung around the world. It generally takes us two weeks to pull together all documents in response to a simple document request. In a case such as this, that same effort will require months."

"Counsel," said Judge LaJordia, who was nodding appreciatively, "I understand your problems with a multinational corporation as your client. So I would suggest you call your people as you're being chauffeured back to your office and get the ball rolling as early as possible. We will stay with my case timing."

"That's easy for you to say, Judge," said Martha J. Mattingly in her husky voice, "but the truth is, the Department of Justice represents not only the DOJ but also the military forces of the U.S. To require documents from us in two weeks is almost laughable. That will take months."

"Then you can expect sanctions, counsel," said the judge. "If you fail to comply with my timing you can expect that I will consider certain facts alleged by the plaintiff to be true as a matter of law. Second, I will award money sanctions--legal fees and fines, if you violate my rules. Are we all hearing this?"

Christine couldn't help but allow a small smile. This was going to actually be fun. At this point she had nothing but high praise for the trial judge. He wasn't going to be pushed around and he was going to take this case to trial in four months. There would be none of the usual contentious continuances and foot-dragging by defense counsel as they begged and wheedled the court for more time for every little thing in an effort to delay, delay, delay. Delay was anathema to plaintiff's counsel and it was a beloved tactic to defense counsel. Judge LaJordia had made it clear that he would entertain none of it.

For another hour the orders kept coming and the attorneys kept making their notes. The judge told them that all details would be supplied that same day in a written format so no one could later claim they hadn't understood this or that.

At the close of the proceeding, after the judge had left the bench, Christine could overhear the first-chairs making plans for a committee selection meeting right after lunch. It sounded to her like they were going to take things seriously. She also overheard that several of them would be filing for a change of judge but she didn't let that worry her. The judge who was selected and accused of some sort of bias in a motion to change judges was always the same judge who would hear the motion. In the history of courts in America, she could think of no occasion where a judge had admitted bias and accordingly removed him or herself from a case. It just wasn't going to happen.

But they could bill for such a wasteful motion, and that was the point.

They could bill it out at $1,000 an hour so the motion made damn good sense.

If you were the biller.

Not so much for the billee.

26

The 4-12 shift at Randall Dynamics had one no-show on a Friday evening. Her name was Sevi al-Assad and she was long gone from Chicago when it came time to clock-in for the shift.

At four p.m., Hussein driving a rental SUV, the two terrorists had reached Eau Claire, Wisconsin, where they planned to cross off some items on their shopping list. Dauntag Excavations and Explosives sold Tovex and Primadet to licensed contractors. Hussein had obtained a federal license for $5,000 and had that along, plus a letter of introduction from the president of the company where he was employed in Chicago. All phony, of course, but all designed to obtain the explosive and detonator.

The Primadet was a non-electric delay detonator commonly used as the primary initiator for mining, quarrying and construction blasts. Tovex was needed to detonate the ammonium nitrate, which would level the entire school to rubble.

They were met at the MTI plant by Ed Novik, a plant manager who supervised sales of small quantities of Tovex, used mostly by small private companies for one-time shots, as he explained to Hussein and Sevi.

"You're using this for clearing dead trees?" Novik asked Hussein.

"Yes, we're clearing an old wetland that's been drained. It runs north-south along the Mississippi River maybe twenty-five miles above Hannibal."

"Down in all those drainage districts. Got you. Well, Tovex is malleable, meaning you can cut it to length. Totally safe to manipulate in the field. In most cases like yours, crosscut saws and chainsaws are too hazardous to remove dead wood. So just do a wrap or two of this stuff around the base of the trunk. Following me?"

Hussein nodded. "I think so. We've used it before." He was telling the truth. A Tovex plant was licensed in Islamabad, Pakistan. The jihadists bought the stuff by the ton over there, Hussein among them.

"Now your blasting caps will be ignited using hand-held boxes of some kind. Got that?"

"Cell phones."

"Oh, that works but it's pretty much unnecessary. What's wrong with the box?"

"Just don't want to spend the extra bucks. Budgetary, Ed."

"Got you. Now your det cord is the Primadet. Correct?"

He knew the answer, because the invoice listed it.

Again Hussein nodded. "Forty feet is all we'll be needing."

"Why so little?"

"Actually we've only got four trees that are blocking ingress to our area. Once we get those monsters cleared out we can reach everything else with saws."

"Got you. Now the blast will completely utilize the Tovex. There is no discernible residue. Of course the crime labs can easily ID it with microscopes. But that won't be a worry for you. Will it?"

Hussein realized Ed Novik was eyeing him with some degree of suspicion. He was actually amazed that they had come this far with no one asking more questions. Two Middle Easterners buying explosives in America? Are you kidding me? He thought.

"It's private property where we're working. No crime labs within a hundred miles," Hussein laughed.

"Well, not my worry, anyhoo, as my daughter says. None of my business. Your invoice is right here, I've made copies of your license and ID and letter of introduction from your owner. So it's all good. Can I get someone to load the stuff for you?"

"No, the boxes are small and we're in a hurry to get back to Illinois."

"The stuff is safe to transport, very stable. You can drop it from high altitudes or even shoot it with a rifle and it won't detonate. So you can feel safe on the road. Even if you hit a semi this stuff won't ignite. Not that we'd want that, of course."

"Of course not. Well, my friend will drive safely," said Hussein, indicating Sevi.

Sevi gave Ed Novik her best smile. He returned the acknowledgment with a shy smile.

"We're all good here, then, folks?"

They backed their rented Toyota Tundra up to the loading dock and a short young man loaded the explosive and det cord into the bed. Hussein covered the load with a tarp and bungeed it down on all four corners. They shook hands with Ed a last time, and he gave them a military snap salute as they drove out of the yard.

"Stupid asshole," sneered Hussein as they cut into the flow of highway traffic. "Who would believe that Americans would sell Muslims high explosives? Don't these people read the newspapers? Such a joke!"

Sevi was smiling broadly. "The same people who taught them to take off in 747s without teaching them how to land. Americans are so stupid."

Hussein reached across and touched her on the leg.

"Stay with me tonight?"

"Yes. We'll be back after midnight. I won't need to awaken Christine and her bunch."

"Good."

"But separate rooms. That is all I will do. Then I will cook your breakfast after prayers."

He smiled and turned to his window.

"What more could a man want?" he mused.

"So where does that leave us?" she asked.

"Just about finished. Nitro-methane and fuel oil and we're done. Ready for payback."

"Have you selected a date?" she asked him.

"I have. I'm thinking October 20."

Her heart jumped. "My wedding day. Or would have been, one year ago."

"I picked it out just for you."

"My trial starts that day too. No, it starts one day before." Thank you for honoring that special date for me."

"What a great success for you to have!"

"The irony. This is good. I didn't expect this."

"See, Allah provides. You are getting your revenge as it should be."

"Yes," she said. "Allahu Akbar. God is great!"

27

C hristine began depositions on July 7th, the first regular work day after fireworks day.

She set up the depositions in Conference Room A in her own suite of offices. It was a large room centered with a magnificent conference table as big as four table tennis courts pushed end-to-end and surrounded by twenty-six chairs done in pink leather. Christine wasn't one to engage in Pink-dom, but she wanted an effect in the room that would momentarily throw off visitors when they first came inside. The pink leather seemed to do just that.

"I want us to dissect these people like the bug under the microscope," she told Ed Mitchell. Ed, who'd done a complete about-face on his feelings over suing the U.S. military, was now anxious to leap into the fray and begin hitting the visitors hard with tough deposition inquiries.

"Today we have Colonel Joachim Martinez, in charge of the drone room in Reno. I've done his workup and mapped out questions you'll want to pursue."

"Can we get to him?" she wanted to know.

"Is he vulnerable? Yes. See my suggested questions. They're interlineated with the basis for each question, including my background comments."

"Sounds good."

They were sitting in Christine's private office, having their second morning coffee as they planned their approach for the day.

"And next we have Lieutenant Randolph Cunningwood, who actually pressed the button that launched the missile."

"Yes. The man behind the actual slaughter."

"What do we know about him? See your notes?"

Ed smiled. "Yes, please, see my notes. Winona and I have done an extensive workup on the guy."

"Roger that."

She took a sip of coffee and glanced to her right, out the windows, at Lake Michigan. The sky over the water was hazy with the remnant of a light fog that had crept ashore overnight. The sun was busily burning it off, seagulls were floating on thermals, and sailboats were presenting their wind-catching triangles of white and yellow and red against the near horizon. Each attorney was thoughtful for several minutes. Quiet times, times without speaking, were comfortable enough between them. They had been out together and had spent weekend days together where very little actually needed saying, as comfortable as they were with each other. Plus, with lawyers, it seemed like everything got said during the week anyway, and weekends allowed time away from words. That ability to be still together had accompanied them into the office. As she watched the sails skitter along the water, Christine realized she was quite comfortable with Ed. She found herself wishing, in the next thought, that he wasn't an employee. She missed having times out with him. A thought occurred next. She turned back to him.

"Ed, I am happy with your work here, overall, you know that, don't you?"

"Except for my lapse over the suing the government thing, I think I've done a fairly good job for you."

"Totally agree. And your salary is commensurate with what the top firms across the nation are paying, correct?"

"Correct."

"Well...what would you think if I sold you an equity share in the practice?"

"I could become a shareholder?"

"Yes."

"Would that mean you would go out with me again since I would no longer be just an employee?"

She realized her cheeks had flushed. Momentarily she had forgotten why she'd hired Ed in the first place. Perspicuity and all that as a given, the guy was also a mind reader.

"Maybe we could do that. If you were on an equal footing with me, then there wouldn't be the employer-employee thing."

He smiled wanly. "You're afraid I might get in a tiff and sue you for sexual harassment?"

"Something like that," she said with a laugh that wasn't all laugh. There was some small modicum of truth in what he was saying.

"No need to worry. I've never sued a date. At least not yet."

She laughed again. She had to admit, she had missed the guy and his outrageous sense of humor. What the hell, she thought. Let's do it.

"I'd like to invite you for dinner at my house Friday night. Seven-ish. I'll have the equity paperwork with me and we'll celebrate with gourmet food and expensive wine. The gourmet food will be prepared by me. Something like spaghetti with meatballs."

"Would you please put black olives in the sauce? I love it with the olives."

"My, we're getting presumptuous already, aren't we?"

He laughed. "Yes, I'm feeling the wind beneath my wings."

"Good on you. It's your turn, I'd say. Hey, it's time to hit the conference room and bury these mothers. You good to go?"

"Ready, Sarge. Lead the way."

"Up and at them, then. On me."

They gathered pads and files and headed down the hall to Conference Room A, the well-lighted, glassed-in room directly across from the receptionists' counter. They went inside, closed the vertical blinds, and greeted the court reporter. Several others were already there and seated; Christine and Ed began shaking hands.

"You are?" said Christine to a Hispanic man in his mid-forties. He was fit and capable and his thin black hair was combed straight back from the widow's peak low on his forehead. His teeth sparkled as he smiled and held out his hand and said his name.

"Colonel Joachim Martinez," he said, ignoring the attorney who had come to her feet when Christine entered the room.

"Martha J. Mattingly," said the female attorney in her familiar husky voice. "Representing DOJ and the military branches you've sued. These three gentlemen to my right, and the lady at my far right, are all attorneys in my office. They'll be sitting in and may occasionally need to go on the record too. You won't have a problem with more than one of us going on record today with the same witness, will you?"

Christine shook the woman's hand. "Just as long as you don't all try to talk at once, I'm cool with it. I'd only ask that you ID yourselves for the court reporter before each speaks up. It'll help her out."

"Will do," said Mattingly, with a look and a nod at her retinue. They all expressed understanding of the ground rule and would ID themselves when speaking on the record.

"The second deponent--is that him in the reception room?" asked Ed of Mattingly.

"It is. That's the lieutenant. You wanted the colonel first, am I right?"

"Right," said Christine. She then addressed the second group across the table, and recognized Boris Adizkov, Blackguard's first chair. His hair was clipped close to the skull and his shoulders bulged beneath his pinstripes, giving him the look of a boxer, with his flat nose and strong chin.

"Did you ever box?" Christine asked him out of the blue.

The man smiled and leaned across the table, extending his right hand. They shook, Christine and Adizkov and Ed.

"Not a boxer. I was a wrestler in college. NCAA second place nationally my junior year. Then I tore a rotator cuff and my career was over. Does that qualify?"

"Does in my book," said Christine.

"How about you, any sports?"

"If you call shooting terrorists a sport, yes. I did my athlete years in the Middle East with the army. Demanding stuff."

"So the depositions today of military people will present no mystery to you."

"Actually," she said, ignoring him, "Ed here is ex-military too. But he still drills on weekends."

Ed was arranging his files and folders and looked up. "Captain in the reserves."

"So, two ex-army folks. Well, thanks for your service, both of you."

At those moments, Christine always wanted to say, "You're welcome," but held her tongue instead. No need to start off on the wrong foot. That would come of its own accord anyway, soon enough.

"So is Colonel Martinez ready to be deposed?" Christine asked Mattingly.

Mattingly nodded and placed a hand on the colonel's shoulder. The colonel ever so slightly shrugged away. Military doesn't like its uniform touched, Christine remembered, and smiled to herself. Mattingly's attempt at familiarity and rejection by Martinez was duly noted. Maybe we have someone who will give us the truth here today, thought Christine. That would be huge.

Everyone took a seat, arranging themselves around the table as Christine requested. The court reporter fed a new spool of paper into her machine and nodded her readiness to Christine. Christine asked the reporter to swear in the colonel, which she did.

"Would you state your name?" Christine began.

"Joachim Jonathan Martinez."

"What is your occupation?"

"Colonel, United States Air Force."

"Tell us about your military career thus far, beginning with your promotion to colonel."

"You don't want the earlier ranks?"

"Nossir. From Major on."

"I was promoted to the rank I now hold twenty-two months ago. At that time I was serving at Creech."

"Explain Creech, for the record."

"Creech Air Force Base is a United States Air Force command and control facility used to engage in daily Overseas Contingency Operations of remotely piloted aircraft systems which fly missions across the globe. In addition to an airport, the military installation has the Unmanned Aerial Vehicle Battlelab, associated aerial warfare ground equipment, and unmanned aerial vehicles of the type used in Afghanistan and Iraq."

"And Syria?"

"There have been times when a drone crossed into Syria, yes."

"Such as Deir ez-Zor, in Eastern Syria?" She was referring to the town where Sevi's family was murdered.

"That would be classified."

"Colonel, what preparations have you made for today's deposition?"

"Reviewed the logs from the day in question, met with my attorney--"

"Ms. Mattingly?"

"Martha Mattingly, correct. Reviewed my own calendar from the date in question."

"Hold it. You keep your own calendar?"

"I do. Unofficial, of course."

"Did you bring it with you today? There was a *subpoena duces tecum* seeking documents of that sort."

"I did. My lawyer has it."

"Counsel," said Mattingly, reaching and passing out a stack of one-sheet calendar entries. "The day of, day before, and day after entries of Colonel Martinez are included on the sheet I'm passing to you."

"Madam court reporter," said Christine, "please take one of the pages, mark it Plaintiff's Exhibit A, and attach it to the deposition booklet."

The court reporter nodded. She would comply.

"Now, Colonel, directing your attention to what's been marked as Exhibit A. Tell us what that is, please."

"It's a copy of my calendar for three days. The day before the drone attack, the day of, and the day after."

"Why three days?"

"Just trying to comply, I guess," he said, with a look at his attorney. She didn't acknowledge his look.

"Please read the calendar entry for October twentieth of last year. No, first tell us what you recall about October twentieth of last year."

"Nothing specific. We launch drones every day, under my command. Twenty October last year would have been unremarkable. So I would have to refer to my calendar for what actually happened that day."

"Because you have no independent recollection?"

"Exactly."

"Then please read your calendar entry."

"Twenty October, 2014. Attacks in Islamabad and Syria. Casualties. Deir ez-Zor."

"Do those calendar entries jog your memory?"

"The one in Syria does. Rarely were we hitting Syria back in mid-2014. Now we are, of course, since the President decided to pursue ISIS. But back then it would have been rare. Unheard of by me, in fact."

"You're saying you can think of no prior occasion where a drone was launched against a target in Syria?"

"None that I can recall. I didn't search my calendar specifically for that."

"So it might have happened, you just don't have an independent recollection."

"Correct."

"What's it like, firing Hellfire missiles at human beings from an armchair in Reno?"

The colonel pulled away from the table. His look said, "This one has sharp teeth!"

"War time is never fun. Whether I'm on the battlefield or in Reno, the feelings are the same."

"Describe those feelings."

"Sorrow that people have to die. But when they're clearly terrorists, as this al-Assad gentleman we hit, no sorrow. Only relief that we killed another bad guy."

"What about when you kill a houseful of innocents, as you did here?"

"Objection!" cried Mattingly. "No foundation. He hasn't said whether he knew who was in the house or not."

"Did you know who was there?"

"No idea."

"Isn't that something you would want to know?"

"Not necessarily."

"Seriously? You just fire missiles into residences without having the full skinny on who's inside?"

"Pretty much, yes. When we have a high-value target, the issue of collateral damage becomes less weighted."

"Less weighted?"

"It lessens in importance. Sometimes in war, innocents suffer and die. It's always been that way."

"Is that official government policy? That innocents have to die?"

"I don't know about government policy. I only know about doing my job."

"Which is to kill bad guys, as you put it."

"Yes, ma'am. Killing bad guys is my job."

"You understand that your order to fire the Hellfire was directly responsible for the deaths of about forty innocent civilians?"

"I understand now that you're suing for something like that. You're claiming we killed many civilians. But we didn't."

"How do you know you didn't?"

"Our visuals indicated the house was empty."

"What?" Christine cried. "What visuals?"

"I would have to check that. I think there might have been a second predator in the area."

"Okay, hold on. We'll take a five minute break here."

Christine motioned for Ed to follow her into the hallway, where they quickly ducked back into her office and closed the door.

"A second Predator? Did you know this?"

"Hell no," said Ed. "No mention of it in any of the paperwork we've received. We've combed it with a fine tooth, too. No second drone."

"What the hell?"

"I know. How convenient we now have a second drone that saw no one enter the house."

"Are they just making this up?"

Ed shrugged. "Knowing Blackguard, I would guess they might be. But the military, that's a lot of people you'd need to get to lie. I don't think they could pull that off."

"Neither do I. Besides, there're too many patriots serving who wouldn't lie for anybody."

"Agreed. There must be something to it, then."

"So we need to find out what proof they have of a second drone."

"Seems like it. Astounding, Chris. I'm frankly shocked."

"Then that makes two of us."

"All right, let's rejoin."

They made the trip back down the hall to Conference Room A, where they went back on the record.

"Colonel," Christine began, "we're back on the record. You were saying there was a second drone in the area, correct?"

"Correct."

"Were you in command of that second drone?"

"Negative."

"Who was?"

"Unknown."

"What do you mean, unknown? Are there other drone bases that would have controlled it?"

"Yes, ma'am."

"Well, what are their names?"

"Ma'am, I don't know their names."

"Explain that answer, please."

"The United States presently has over fifty drone bases."

"Fifty!"

"Yes, ma'am. There's a facility outside Las Vegas where the troops work in climate-controlled trailers. More and more of these are springing up around the world."

"Where else that you know of?"

"Some camp in Africa that was once used by the French Foreign Legion. There's a third in Afghanistan. I'm guessing that's where the second one was controlled, but it's only a guess. There's another in the United Arab Emirates. Location top-secret, almost no one talks about it. We're not allowed to."

"And it's the Air Force that runs all these?"

"No, ma'am. Some are run by the military. The CIA runs many. It's the new way the United States is projecting power abroad."

"All right, let's back up a minute. If I wanted to find out who controlled this second drone so that I could get its video, who would I ask?"

"Objection! Foundation."

"Let me re-phrase. Do you know who I would ask?"

"No, ma'am."

"But you're sure this second drone had surveilled the Deir ez-Zor residence for twenty-four hours prior to your drone launching its Hellfire?"

"Yes, ma'am."

"How did you know that?"

"My headset told me."

"Your headset?"

"Some of the time we have no idea who's feeding us info through the headsets. We just know they're on the Net, so we believe them."

"So an unknown voice told you the house was empty?"

"No, ma'am. It told me no one had been seen coming or going for twenty-four hours."

"So you assumed that meant no people inside?"

"Wouldn't you? I mean twenty-four hours with no one seen?"

"Why would a second drone be watching this particular house if no one knew al-Assad would be going there?"

"I believe it was high-level, not necessarily focused on this particular house but the area in general."

"That's convenient."

"I can only tell you what I know."

"Would it surprise you to know that Syrian wedding festivities can last a week? And no one may come or go during that time?

"I don't know about that."

"When you ordered the missile strike were you relying on the headset information?"

"That no one had been seen? Yes, I was. We would never fire a missile into a house without knowing who was there."

"I don't doubt you mean that. But why is that so? Is there a rule book or something?"

"Just the rules of engagement. We always try to spare civilian lives."

"Can I get a copy of the Rules Of Engagement?"

"The ROE? Yes, ma'am."

"What about civilians? What are those rules?"

"A civilian under the laws of war is a person who is not a member of the military and is not taking a direct part of hostilities in a situation of armed conflict."

"How are you to treat civilians?"

"Don't engage them."

"What else?"

"That's my understanding--don't engage. The trouble is, from the air, where we live, it's often hard to tell who's doing what down on the ground. Are those figures running along a wall one street over from American troops engaged in direct hostilities? That's where the rubber meets the road."

"Now, coming back to the specific day. Twenty October. Describe what your day was like."

"Typical. Got up, shit, shower and shave--pardon my French. Drive out to the base, report in, get the day's briefing, assume my post, do my job. At the end of my shift we would debrief and go home. Some would stop off for a drink. Not me, I don't drink."

"Do you have a memory of twenty October?"

"No, ma'am. Not specifically."

"When did you first become aware that you had ordered the deaths of dozens of civilians that day?"

"Objection! Form of question!"

"Please answer."

"I never did become aware. Not until we got sued."

"So you don't get reports on casualties inflicted or who you took out--none of that?"

"No, ma'am. Much of that information is classified. I'm too low in the food chain to know those things."

"Seriously? You might not even know whose death you ordered?"

"That's correct. Oftentimes we have no names. It's rare that we have a name."

"But if anyone would have a name, it would be you?"

"Correct. The troops flying the planes wouldn't know."

"Because it's non-essential information to them?"

"Correct."

Christine paused and poured a glass of water from the pitcher separating her from the colonel. She tilted her head, asking him if he would like a drink. He nodded and she filled a second glass and passed it over.

"Thank you."

"Back on the record. Colonel, when you gave permission to fire the missile on twenty October, did you stop and think there might be civilian casualties inflicted?"

"No, I didn't."

"Why not?"

"Well, because drone two reported no movement in twenty-four hours. They reviewed its video data and focused on the house. I don't know how I can make that any clearer."

"What if drone two was wrong?"

"Well...that's war, I guess."

"Who were you attacking that day?"

"Arum al-Assad."

"Who was he?"

"An ISIS operative. A high-level bureaucrat in the oil ministry."

"Why was he a target?"

"Unknown."

"The reason for killing him was unknown to you?"

"The reason that I had was that he represented a high value target. Why he would be a high value target, I couldn't possibly know."

"Not necessary."

"My job is to review targets, to make sure they're who we think they are. Not by name, but whether it's the guy we've been tracking. I help keep them sorted. A 'did he go into building one or building two' sort of thing."

"You surely must do more than that."

"That's on the detail end. On the strategic end, I evaluate what our civilian cohorts say."

"What is a civilian cohort?"

The colonel took a drink of water. He pulled out an Air Force blue handkerchief and wiped his mouth.

"A civilian cohort is what we call a civilian contractor."

"Who was the civilian contractor on this drone strike?"

"Blackguard."

"What was Blackguard's role in this drone strike?"

"They were the requestor. They wanted the strike."

"So a military strike was made because an American civilian company requested it."

"In a nutshell, yes."

"Is Blackguard under the authority of the military?"

"Nope."

"Takes orders from the military?"

"Nope. Other way around."

"Blackguard gives the military orders?"

"Blackguard requests ops. On twenty October they wanted al-Assad taken out. In my headset I received Blackguard's request and combined that with drone two's surveillance and made the decision to order the strike. That simple."

"Was there anyone above you in this chain of command?"

"Nope. Buck stops with me. Harry S. Truman."

"Indeed. Colonel, I think we're done here, unless your counsel has questions."

"No questions," said Martha J. Mattingly. "Read and sign."

"Thank you, colonel."

"Yes, ma'am. Thank you."

28

I t was early afternoon by the end of Colonel Martinez's deposition. They had taken a lunch break and were now ready to proceed with the deposition of the actual pilot.

Assembled again in Conference Room A, Christine asked the court reporter to swear the deponent, which she quickly did.

"State your name for the record, please."

"Randall C. Cunningwood."

"What is your occupation?"

"I fly drones."

"Who do you work for?"

"The United States Air Force."

"Rank?"

"Lieutenant. First Lieutenant."

"How long have you been in the military?"

"Little over two years."

"Did you attend college and where?"

"University of Illinois, Champaign-Urbana."

"Major?"

"Aeronautical engineering."

"Are you a licensed pilot?"

"I'm commercial licensed multi-engine. Also certified to fly the Predator."

"That would be the Predator drone?"

"Yes, ma'am."

"Tell me about the Predator."

"Not much to tell there. I fly the MQ-9 Reaper. It's a UAV--unmanned aerial vehicle. You call them drones, we call them remote piloted vehicles or RPVs."

"General usage?"

"Well, the MQ-9 Reaper is the first hunter-killer designed for long endurance, high altitude surveillance."

"Mechanics?"

"950 horses. The original Predator had only 115. So my aircraft carries fifteen times more ordnance than your original Predator."

"Who has it?"

"Air Force? Well, the New York Air Guard dumped all its F-16s and migrated to the MQ-9. First full fighter squadron to do that. Then we use it out of Creech. Also used by NATO, CIA, NASA, Border Patrol, and Navy. Probably more I don't know about."

"What does your job entail as the pilot of the Reaper?"

"Takeoff and landings. Transition to target. Acquire target, operate weapons, surveillance--stuff like that. Plus classified stuff. Please don't ask me about that."

"Tell me about the classified stuff."

"Objection! Classified!" cried Martha J. Mattingly. "Don't answer, Lieutenant!"

"Fine," said Christine, rubbing her face. "We'll take it up with the judge." She turned back to the pilot: "Does the classified information have anything to do with twenty October twenty-fourteen?"

"Negative, ma'am."

"Fair enough, then. We'll leave that alone for now."

"Thank you, ma'am."

"Now, directing your attention to twenty October twenty-fourteen. Do you remember that day?"

"No, ma'am. That would just be another workday for me."

"Do you remember flying into Syria that day?"

"That would be classified, ma'am. Sorry."

"Did you fire a missile in Syria that day?"

"Classified."

"Did you fire the missile at Deir ez-Zor on twenty October?"

"Classified," said attorney Mattingly of the Department of Justice. "He is under orders not to answer questions about flights into or over Syria."

"Then we'll have to talk to the judge. This deposition is continued until I can get a ruling. And counsel, you better have a damn good reason, you and your clients, for not answering my questions. I'll be after sanctions."

"Good on you," said Mattingly. "You rock, girl."

"Off the record. Go f--screw yourself, Miss Mattingly."

Christine and Ed rose up out of their chairs and indicated the others should leave. The herd mentality kicked in and no less than a dozen lawyers, all carrying bulging briefcases and CPA cases, made their way for the door.

"See you in court," Christine called after them. "I'll tell Judge LaJordia that the Air Force has decided to classify my case so you don't have to talk about it."

"Go for it," said Mattingly in a parting shot over her shoulder. "But I'm betting on the United States Air Force, ma'am."

"Sons of bitches," Christine whispered to Ed. He gently reached and brushed a lock of hair back over her ear when they were alone.

"Sorry. I've wanted to do that all day."

"Don't be sorry."

"Well, I am."

"Well, you don't need to be. I'm starved. What do you say we run downstairs to Starbucks for a protein box?"

"Lead on, boss. I'm starved too."

"Not boss; partner. Lead on, partner."

"I like the sound of that much better, actually," he said.

"Me too. An idea whose time has come."

"Just be warned. I'm now officially pursuing you."

"What, you're going to stalk me now?"

"Yes, I am. You need to be stalked."

"Maybe so, Ed Mitchell. Maybe I do, by you."

29

He was fifteen when he fell in love. Her name was Diana Apersain and she was a senior, while he was a junior.

So why would a senior girl be interested in a junior boy who hobbled around on forearm crutches and geeked everyone out? For one thing, they were in math club together. For another, they had partnered that summer at Science Camp. They had developed a software project: Diana had provided database work while Jamie had done the actual coding. It was Diana's goal to become a database designer after she got her Ph.D. in computer science at the University of Chicago. It was Jamie's goal to get a Ph.D. in computer science and teach and develop code. As Diana told Jamie one night in early July, "We're a match made in heaven."

"Isn't that from a song or something?" he asked.

"I don't know. My mom says I need a match made in heaven. That's all I know."

"How about a match based on data points instead? Like, I'm fifteen, you're sixteen, so we're both teens. Your IQ is above one-forty and my IQ is above one-forty. We're both in MENSA. We both love computers. I have a dog, you have a dog. We both love Science Camp and science fiction books. You love Hugh Howey's book *Wool*, I love his book *Sand*. I think data points make more sense than heavenly matches. Don't you?"

"Plus you're handsome," she said.

"You mean even with these?" he asked, raising a crutch skyward.

"Don't even go there. Lots of people have challenges. You're a CP kid. Me, I'm anorexic, in case you haven't noticed."

"You're skin and bones."

"Let's get out of the hallway. Time for lunch, speaking of."

"Will you eat?"

She did a fake faint up against their adjoining lockers, where they had actually met.

"I think I can force something down. Maybe celery and carrot sticks."

"Let's try some meat and potatoes on you, girl. Todays' menu is beef pot pie and fries."

"Ugh. I don't do animals."

"I do. You should too. It's protein."

"I want veggies, not protein. I want my body to eat its own protein."

"TMI. Let's go."

Together they made their way down the hall, Jamie running interference on his crutches and swinging his legs, Diana bringing up the rear. It was crowded, sometimes the path was jammed closed, and Jamie made honking noises with his mouth.

"Queerbait!" yelped a senior.

"Doofus!" cried a junior.

"Watch it dude," said a freshman, who then swore under his breath at Jamie and his swinging legs.

"It's the genius twins," said Margo Hagelman, the head cheerleader and a senior. She was wearing a short gray pleated skirt, green tee, and her letter jacket, even though summer school classrooms were warm.

"Just can't get over yourself, can you?" Jamie said to Margo as he swung past her. "Letter jacket in July? Really?"

"Screw yourself, Jamie," said the head cheerleader. "If you were half as smart--"

Diana, who pushed past the cheerleader and laughed back over her shoulder as she went, interrupted her words. "Go cheer about that!"

They made it to the lunchroom and headed for the serving line. Jamie dislodged two trays from the spring-loaded tray service and pushed one to the side for Diana. She pulled napkins and flatware and placed them on the trays. Then the serving began. Jamie asked for two beef potpies and double fries. Diana wanted only veggies. Jamie shook his head and scolded her with his eyes. "Need protein, Di," he said, shaking his head. "At least take a grilled cheese."

"Half of a grilled cheese."

"Okay, then."

She helped herself to the half-sandwich and they selected fruit juice for their glasses.

Jamie had learned to hold his tray with his left hand and work that crutch with his forearm, keeping all his weight on his right side. He slowly but gracefully led them to a table with two seats together. The rest were filled with freshmen, who no upperclassman would ever be caught fraternizing with, but Jamie and Diana didn't seem to notice. She slid in first and he slid in beside her. He balanced his crutches at the end of the table and rolled up his shirtsleeves.

"My God, you're diving in up to your elbows?" she chided him.

"All the way. Maybe to my shoulders. Growing boy's gotta eat, Di."

"What do you think of us learning to program in C++?"

"Nothing to it. We're already doing C#, which is object oriented all the way. C++ shouldn't be much of a challenge."

"Agreed. Let's take it this fall."

"Let's."

They chewed quietly, staring ahead, but he was aware of her left leg pressed against his right leg. She was warm and firm: he hadn't lost the feeling in his legs, just the use of. The feelings were just fine.

They had kissed and held hands at the movies. He had wanted to do more but she had told him no way, not in a public place like a movie.

So they met up to study in her bedroom. With the door closed.

One thing led to another that long June afternoon.

Now he had a girlfriend.

A real one.

30

Office time was scarce, so Ed and Winona agreed to workout together at lunch. That way they could get in their workouts and discuss her divorce problems too.

The Chicago Women's Athletic Club was a misnomer. It accepted memberships from men and women both.

Ed and Winona trotted at a good clip around the springy indoor track as they talked.

"So he's got a girlfriend. That has to hurt," said Ed as they ran.

"Gorman's always fancied himself a ladies man. But he's never done this before. At least not that I knew about."

"Who is she?"

"His secretary. Talk about cliché, huh?"

"Whatever you call it, I'm sure it must hurt." There he was again, trying to get her to talk about her feelings. This time she walked through the open door.

"I cry myself to sleep every night when he's out. When he's not out we sleep in separate rooms. We don't talk anymore."

"So his romance is open. I mean, he's not trying to hide it from you?"

"Exactly. He's so much as told me he doesn't give a damn how I feel about it, he's in love and he's not going to give her up."

"So you cry yourself to sleep and feel pretty powerless. Am I getting that right?"

"Exactly. I feel powerless. I feel like I'm lost inside a hurricane that's about to blow me away. I can't sleep, can't eat, my head hurts and throbs, I can't concentrate at work--it's a miracle Chris hasn't fired me."

"She won't fire you. Christine knows what it is to lose someone. She'll stand behind you all the way."

"So what do you recommend?"

"I recommend you file suit against him and bring him up hard against the financial hole he's dug for himself."

"How do I do that?"

"We ask for alimony. At least temporary spousal support. How long have you been married, fifteen years?"

"Yes, but I make more than he does."

"What's he do?"

"Big pharma sales. He calls on docs."

"I thought those people did quite well."

"At one time he did. Now the field is crowded and competition is fierce. I'll be lucky if I'm not ordered to pay him alimony."

"What about your condo? Rent or buy?"

"Paid for. We doubled-down on the mortgage payments. Paid off a thirty in fifteen."

"So there's an asset you can go after. What about retirement funds?"

"I've got my city retirement. But that won't kick in until I'm fifty-five."

"That's twenty years."

"More or less."

"What other assets are there?"

"Well, I have a lawsuit pending against the man who shot me when I was a cop."

"Tell me about that."

"We broke down his door and stormed his house on a warrant. He'd set a spring gun inside the front door. I was first through so it fired one round that entered my abdomen and severed my urethra. Now I pee into a bag I wear."

"Seriously? You're wearing that now?"

"Yep. My shirt covers it."

"And so you're suing this guy. Who is he?"

"He's the son of a state senator. The senator owned the house where this happened. He's a co-defendant. We're trying to get the house awarded to me in damages."

"Well, that isn't property that the divorce court is going to split with Gorman."

"Not?"

They rounded the track for the fourth time and Ed was starting to breathe harder. Winona, however, not only was keeping up she was having to shorten her gait so as not to leave him behind. She consciously was forcing herself not to outrun him.

"No, personal injury awards usually belong a hundred percent to the party who was injured. How much are we talking about?"

"Well, the house is one of those monstrosities on the Gold Coast. Probably six or seven."

"Six or seven what? Million?"

"Uh-huh."

"So you're going to be a rich divorcee one of these days."

"I keep getting UTI's. The bag and tubes cause it."

"Urinary tract infections are terrible."

"Tell me about it. Constant pain, discomfort, and embarrassment. I deserve five or six million for having to live like this."

"I'd say you do. Okay, here's what I'd suggest."

He then went on to describe how they should approach the divorce litigation. By the time they were done with their back-and-forth, they had run four miles on the indoor track. He was breathing hard; she was breathing through her nose.

And Winona felt happy. For the first time in months. She no

longer had to sit back and be the victim. She was about to go after the man who had betrayed her, and that was feeling just fine.

As they separated at the entrance to the men's and women's locker rooms, she took his hand and squeezed it. She was saying thanks to him.

31

On July 20th the plaintiffs and defendants appeared before Judge LaJordia on Christine's motion. The motion was entitled, *MOTION TO COMPEL TESTIMONY* and it had been written by Christine. Sevi accompanied Christine to court and took her place with Christine at their counsel table.

"Your Honor," Christine began; she got to speak first since it was her motion. "The defendant DOJ has refused to allow the pilot of the drone to testify about the day of the drone attack. Even the drone attack itself is classified, according to the DOJ. We're here today seeking your order compelling the DOJ to give us the testimony we deserve and that we need to properly present our case at trial."

Judge LaJordia's eyes moved over to Martha J. Mattingly, who was wedged among a dozen other lawyers around the defense table, six in the first row, seven in the second. She rattled the papers before her and gathered her thoughts. Then, "It's not the Department of Justice that has claimed classification of the events of that day. It's the Air Force itself. To compel the Air Force to openly discuss how it oper-ates--selects targets, surveils them, weighs their value--would be a huge help to the enemy. The terrorists of the world would rejoice to be handed that information."

"Counsel," said the judge, "what about giving the information in a closed hearing with a jury sworn to secrecy? Would that solve the problem?"

"It would for us," said Christine. "Assuming we first got our deposition testimony, even if it's in a closed deposition with everyone sworn to secrecy."

"No-no-no," cried Mattingly. "Civilian secrecy vows are meaningless. We've seen this repeatedly. They never work, the cat always jumps out of the bag and American lives are lost over it."

"Oh, so now we're making American casualties more likely because we're after the truth about what happened that day? Is that what counsel is asking the court to conclude?"

"I'm wondering the same thing, counsel," said the judge. "How is the American military disadvantaged by telling exactly what happened on the day of the attack? In fact, let's take it a step further. What if I granted the plaintiff's motion except for policy decisions made that day? Would you still try to tell me American lives would be endangered? I'm afraid I don't get that."

"Judge, all I know is that the information is classified, so I can't speak to your question. Truth be told, I don't even have access to the information and I'm their lawyer. Classified is classified and I am not in that inner circle."

"So you don't even know what it is your client is refusing to say? Is that it?"

"Correct, Judge."

Christine spoke again, rising to her feet to be heard. "Your Honor, I subpoenaed the deponent-pilot, Randall C. Cunningwood, to attend today. I saw him outside in the hallway when I came in. I would request at this time that I be allowed to put him on the witness stand and ask him my deposition questions--out of the range of the press. The court could clear the courtroom and include in the evidentiary portion of today's hearing only the lawyers for the DOJ and myself. Everyone else scoots outside. Then Your Honor could hear the testimony and decide if it should remain classified or not."

Mattingly then took to her feet. "Judge, under the Classified Information Procedures Act, the government may ask the court to protect against the disclosure of classified information disclosed by the United States to any defendant in any criminal case."

Christine responded right back. "Emphasis on criminal case, Your Honor, which is quite different. In criminal cases, where the government claims national security is at risk, the court can level the playing field by saying, 'okay this remains classified, but along with that I'm going to dismiss the indictment against the defendant.' That's not our case here, unless the court says, 'Okay, it's going to remain classified, but we are going to find, as a matter of law, that the facts alleged in the complaint are taken as true.' That would include that the defendant did wrongfully and negligently attack my client and her family. We get an automatic win on the issue and the government gets to stay silent. It's a win-win."

Mattingly erupted as though poked by a fork. "Wouldn't she love that?! She wins on the issue of liability just because the nation's national security has been put at risk by her lawsuit? Absurd!"

Judge LaJordia shook his head. "No, I think the nation's national security has been put at risk by the Air Force striking and killing forty-some civilians in Syria. I don't think you can blame the plaintiff's attorney for that, Ms. Mattingly."

"Well Judge, I was only speaking metaphorically."

"No, you were speaking quite literally. I disagree. At this point the court is inclined to preserve the question of national security and allow the Air Force to keep quiet on its classified information. Still, the plaintiff shouldn't find herself penalized for this. Miss al-Assad lost her entire family due to the Air Force's actions. The court finds, as a matter of law, that the Air Force was liable in the deaths of all forty-some named decedents. The only issue remaining then is the issue of monetary compensation to Miss al-Assad. Trial will proceed on that issue only. So ordered. We're adjourned."

He rapped his gavel and left the bench.

Christine sat at counsel table, stunned. Beside her sat Sevi, who wore a puzzled look that had replaced her normally calm countenance. "Chris, what happened?"

Christine dropped her *Illinois Civil Practice* manual into her shoulder briefcase.

"You won. We won."

"We won? How much did we get?"

"We have to have a trial on the issue of damages. That's in October."

By now the reporters in the courtroom were clamoring for a statement from Christine or Sevi or both.

Christine turned and pushed open the gate separating the spectators from the litigants and counsel.

"Let me just say," Christine began, raising her hands to speak, "we are gratified with Judge LaJordia's ruling here today. His ruling has put the United States military on notice as to further drone attacks: You may or may not be attacking combatants legally, that's for another day. But if you murder innocent civilians in the attack, you will be found liable and you will be forced to pay damages. After all, this is America, whether it's acting inside the borders of the fifty states or clear around the world in Syria. American law doesn't change, the military doesn't get open season on innocents. Needless to say, we're elated. Now we have to wait until October to find out how much Sevi al-Assad is to be awarded."

"What about others like her?" said the reporter from the *Tribune*. "Won't this open the floodgates to other litigation against the military and government?"

Christine smiled. "I certainly hope so. The United States wasn't created to go roaming around the world killing civilians at will without consequences. So, yes, I hope others do follow us into court and bring their cases."

"Miss al-Assad," said the reporter from the Daily Sun. "What about the money? How much are you asking for?"

Sevi took the question head-on. "Enough to give each of my relatives an honorable burial and a respectable headstone."

"That's all?"
"I'll leave that up to the jury," said Sevi.
"Are you after anything else?"
Sevi shook her head and turned away.
"No. Nothing else."

32

He came to her house that Friday night after work. Jamie was at the movies with his girlfriend and Janny was at a classmate's sleepover in Palatine. So the house belonged to Christine.

She answered the front door on the first chime of the doorbell. To say she was excited to see him didn't adequately express the excitement she felt.

He came inside and extended his hand. He was carrying a single rose, a small tube of water on its distal end, the bloom full and fragrant.

"Let this express how I feel. Better than words, no?"

She accepted the gift.

"It speaks volumes. Here, come into the kitchen with me. I'm cooking pasta."

He then quickly came to her and encircled her with his arms before she could turn away. He reached with his hand and tilted her face to him. He brushed his lips against her forehead.

"I am so happy to see you," he said. "It makes my whole week."

She laid her face against his shirt. A discernible male fragrance mixed with a dot of aftershave found her senses and she closed her eyes. He kissed her hair and tightened his arms around her.

"Let's eat first," she whispered. "We have hours ahead of us."

"No," he replied. "Let's not miss this opportunity to be together. Take me to your bedroom."

She turned off the stove as she felt herself yielding to his desire. She turned her face up once again and pushed her mouth against his. His lips parted and he tasted her mouth. His hips pressed forward and she could feel him move against her, wanting, desiring, even demanding.

"It will be our first time," he whispered. "I want it to be unhurried, a time for us to hold on and become better acquainted."

She pushed away and took him by the hand. She led him to the stairs and went ahead of him, her hand behind and pulling him after her. But he didn't need her assistance. He was only too anxious to stay close and be with her. She knew it was time.

Christine's bedroom was at the far end of the hall. Double doors guarded her private sanctuary when she needed to be alone, away from the kids and their friends, away from clients, calls, and demands upon her. Inside the doors, Ed found himself looking at an L-shaped configuration. Her room was divided two-thirds along the vertical of the L and one-third along the horizontal. Except he didn't have time to take it all in. The smaller room contained a chaise lounge--evidently for reading or plain old staring out the floor to ceiling windows--small table, and a floor lamp turned to low. The larger room contained a massive bed, two nightstands, huge flat screen, and a full wall of closet doors. A darkened bathroom lay to Ed's left; the smaller room lay straight ahead and to the right.

She immediately turned to him and pulled his arms around her. She moved up against him and urgently pressed her pelvis against his. She was wearing a white silk shirt, a slipover, and she raised her arms, indicating he should remove it, which he did. Now he reached behind and unhooked the black bra. Her breasts spilled forward and found his eager hands. He touched her and dropped his head to her. His lips moved against her and she arched her back with a small gasp. She had felt none of these feelings since Sonny's death. Even the one night with Hussein in Ankara had meant absolutely nothing about feelings. That had been about business. But now, here, tonight, she was all in. Ed suddenly came upright and lifted her from her feet.

He moved her to the bed and placed her on her back. She lifted her legs while he slipped away the khaki slacks she'd been wearing. Then he dropped to his knees and approached her with his mouth. He pulled the filmy panties aside and--

"Wait," she said. "Come up here to me."

He climbed up onto the bed.

"Now, kick off your shoes and pants."

He obeyed.

"Now the underwear."

He was wearing Jockey mini-briefs and he removed these with a single sliding move of one hand. He tossed them to the floor.

Now she reached across and took him in her hand. She caressed him and encircled the head with her good hand. She massaged him until he was ready. He used protection.

"Now," she spoke, and spread herself open to him.

He entered her and she shuddered. His lips found her ear and he said softly, "I have wanted you since that first day. You are the definition of desire and female-ness. I have dreamed of this moment."

She closed her eyes and felt him begin moving against her. He was slow and giving like the Ed she had imagined he would be. Which relaxed her even more. He was the man he had presented to her. He was tender and gentle and considerate. And he was experienced.

He paused and reached beneath her hips, lifting her to him, and in the same moment he rose up to his knees and gazed down at her.

"You know I love you," he said.

"I know," she said. "And I--"

He plunged deep inside.

"I--I--"

Even inside her, he was experienced enough to find her clitoris with a gentle probing finger. He knew enough not to touch it directly, moving along its tiny shaft, bringing her along with him, and then releasing and plunging himself even deeper inside her body.

WHEN IT WAS OVER, they lay languorously side-by-side. She absently toyed with him and traced his hairline with her fingertips. He pressed his lower half against her and absorbed her heat. Then he came up on an elbow and touched his lips to hers.

"You were saying?" he asked. "Your feelings?"

"You are my love, my happiness tonight. Isn't that enough?"

"It is. You are."

She refocused her gaze, looking beyond him to the ceiling over her bed.

"There's a part of me that still wants to cling to Sonny. But that part is growing smaller as this new part becomes larger. Please, just be patient with me. It's all good."

"There's no hurry. I can express myself freely with you. This is a safe place to be and that's all that matters."

She again moved her focus to his face as he lingered above her.

"Come to me again," she said. "I'm not done with you."

"Then we are thinking alike."

"And that is good," she said with a sudden gasp as he moved against her.

Good, she thought, and she floated back to that place where she saw only his eyes and thought--even for an instant--she saw his soul.

And it was good.

And it was safe.

33

Hussein was driving, Sevi was pressed up against the passenger door, staring at the Chicago streets as they whizzed by. They were headed to a mosque where they had an appointment to speak with the Imam.

"You told me I would lose," said Sevi. "But I didn't lose. I won."

"But it's not over. You still haven't been paid for the deaths of your loved ones."

"But they are going to pay me. Christine said so."

Hussein slapped the steering wheel of his newest acquisition, a blue Volvo titled in the name of one of his many identities.

"Going to pay you! Do you believe that, stupid woman?"

"I am not stupid. I'm quite intelligent."

"Maybe you have the books, it might be so. But in the ways of the world you are dumb, dumb, dumb!"

"I'm learning America isn't what I first thought," said Sevi. "The judge was fair to me."

"One time someone is fair and that turns your head? Are you kidding me here?"

"He decided the Air Force was at fault. That's all I'm saying. In

Syria a woman could never win her case against the military or the government. It's different here."

"So--what? Are you saying you want to call off the bomb attack?"

She swung her head around and stared at the side of his head.

"Did I say that? Where do you get that from?"

"Good; there are people who wouldn't like it if you called it off."

"You're threatening me now? I'm the one who lost her entire family and you're threatening me?"

"Hey," he said in a strident voice, "don't forget, I lost my wife to these animals too."

"Maybe you should talk to Christine. My lawyer might sue them for you, too."

"That would violate everything I believe in."

"What do you believe in, Hussein? Murdering children?"

Again he struck the steering wheel, this time hurting his fist. "No, no, no! I believe in avenging my wife's death and the deaths of your family. That is all I believe in."

"Well...I'm not sure. My mind is changing. There, I said it."

He swung around to stare at her full on. "You have been warned, Sevi al-Assad. There are people who won't let you just walk away from our plan."

"And why is that?"

"Because. For one thing, you know too much."

"I plan to tell no one. I plan to just live my life and be left alone."

He rubbed his hand back over his black hair. "That's not going to happen. The people I work with will not leave you alone. The plan is set. Now leave it be."

She turned her face away from him. "It's not what I want. I want no more of killing. It's done."

"I'll say when it's done! Since when do women tell men what is and what isn't?"

"Since we came to America! That's since when. You don't own me over here like you do over there. I am free here!"

"We will say when you're free. If you continue with this, I shall have to report you, Sevi. You have been warned now a second time. Don't make me tell."

"Tell, tell, tell! You can all just go to hell!"

"All right. I'm stopping this car. You will not go to the mosque with me."

She picked up her backpack and slung it over her shoulder. "Fine. Pull over right here. I'll catch a cab back to work."

He pulled over and slowed at the curb. "Jump!"

She threw open her door and leapt from the still-moving car. She rolled onto her right side and twisted over onto her abdomen. The pain of the old injuries shot up and down her spine. Momentarily she was numb from the knees down.

She pulled up onto her knees, but the frozen knee wouldn't bend, forcing her to stand fully upright before she was ready.

At that exact moment, a black woman pushing a grocery cart stopped beside her.

"Here, darling, take my hand," said the woman. "I seen it all. He pushed you out!"

"No, he didn't push me. I jumped. Good riddance, I say."

"That's good. Now hold onto my cart and catch your breath. Atta girl."

Sevi stood at the cart, both hands along the horizontal push bar, breathing deeply and wondering how she was going to walk away without her cane.

"I can't walk without my cane," she told the woman. "It's in his car."

"Let me get you a cab," the woman said, and she stepped down off the curb into the parking lane. She began hailing cabs. The fifth one approached in the middle lane but then swung to the slow lane when the driver saw the hail. He pulled up and stopped. He was wearing a Sikh turban and smiled across the seat at Sevi.

"Do you need help, Miss?" the cabbie called.

"Yes."

He punched on his hazard lights and opened the driver's door and got out. In a second he crossed to Sevi and took her forearm. "Let me help you. Easy now."

With the black woman on the backpack arm and the cabbie on the other, the threesome made it up to the passenger door, which was opened, and Sevi sat down with a thump. Taking both hands she pulled the frozen leg inside and guided it beneath the dashboard. The cabbie slammed the door. The black woman waited beside the car.

"You be careful, girl," said the woman. "Stay away from that bastard threw you out."

"He didn't throw me. I jumped."

"I seen it. Pushed you right out. You want, I can go to court and tell what I seen."

"No, no need. I'm fine now. I just need to go--home."

"What's the address, ma'am?" said the cabbie.

Without thinking, Sevi gave him Christine's--and her--address.

She was going home.

Actually, she was home. And for the first time in months, she felt at home.

At home with people who were actually good. Tears came into her eyes and she began sobbing as the cabbie pulled away from the curb. He plucked two tissues from a box on the console.

"I know," said the man in the turban, "America rocks."

"It rocks," she said. "I like it here."

"You and me both, little sister. You and me both."

34

Sevi borrowed the cabbie's phone on the ride home. She was immediately connected to Christine and, through her tears, asked Christine to meet her at home. Christine said she would be right there.

Christine found Sevi in the family room, sprawled across the couch with her feet up and a handful of ice cubes wrapped in a towel and secured around her frozen knee. Her right forearm was abraded and oozing where she had come out of the Volvo and landed on her right side, breaking her fall with the forearm. Tears washed through her eyes as she cried softly and moaned. Her abdomen hurt, she said, and she had vomited twice since arriving home.

"What happened?" Christine asked. Her voice was steady with a hint of anger at whoever had caused Sevi's injuries. "Who did this?"

"Hussein. He made me jump out of his car."

Christine stopped. Her mind reeled back, back to Ankara and the night in the hotel.

"You're not talking about the Hussein I met--"

"Yes, he found me. It's horrible what we did. We bought fertilizer and explosives and detonation cord and--"

"Whoa, whoa, whoa. You did this? Or Hussein?"

"We both did."

"Why? That's a big damn bang you're putting together. What the hell?"

Tears began streaming down the young woman's face.

"I was angry. It made me crazy to lose all my family. I hated America. I wanted to sue America. And I wanted to explode a bomb and kill Americans. Oh, oh, oh!"

"Where is the bomb now? Please, stop crying and talk to me!'

"The bomb is in the white van. Hussein has it somewhere. I don't know where it is today."

"When is he going to detonate the bomb?"

"The - the anniversary of what would have been my wedding day."

"You're sure of that?"

"Yes."

"So tell me exactly why he made you jump out of the car today."

"Just because I told him."

"Told him what?"

"I told him I didn't want to do the bomb. American people are good to me. The American people aren't like the American military."

"So what happened with Hussein? What did he say and what did you say?"

"He told me someone would hurt me if I didn't go ahead and explode it."

"Who would hurt you?"

"Other people. Muslims."

"So you told him no more bomb and he threatened you with bodily harm?"

"Yes."

"Have you told anyone else about this?"

"No."

"Where is the bomb going to go? Does this have anything to do with the grade school blueprints we found?"

Sevi's mouth worked but no sound came out. Then, "How--how--"

"When you gave Jamie the thumb drive you must have accidentally copied the blueprints onto the drive. Jamie gave them to me and

I went to the grade school. Is that where the bomb goes, the grade school?"

"Yes."

"When? Tell me exactly when, the date and time."

"It is going to be one year after my family died."

"October."

"Yes. That day. At the grade school."

"Why that day?"

"That was to be my wedding day one year ago. It was because of the irony."

"Hussein and you decided it would be ironic to explode the bomb on what would have been your first wedding anniversary?"

"Yes."

"And whose idea was that? His?"

"Both. I thought it was good too."

"Now. Tell me Hussein's address. Where does he live, where does he go? Does he work? What kind of vehicle does he drive? License numbers?"

"Christine, slow down, please. I can give you all that."

"Go ahead. I'm waiting."

"He lives on the South Side. We kept the bomb van in a fenced lot there. In a garage by itself."

"Can you take me there?"

"Y-y-yes."

"Then let's go. We must go now."

"All right. But I need my other cane. He has my good one."

"Where is it? I'll get it for you."

"In my closet. Just inside, below the switch."

"Wait here."

Christine took the stairs two at a time and returned with the cane.

"Let's go. Let me help you up. Easy, easy."

"Thank you."

"Now, grip my arm and use the cane on the bad knee. Don't worry, I can support you."

"Your arm is as good as a cane."

"Let's go. Now walk with me."

Together they went down into the garage and Christine clicked the doors of the Escalade with her keychain. They climbed inside and Christine backed the vehicle out of the garage as the door finished rising.

It was hot outside; the A/C roared to life.

"Now direct me."

"Go up to the corner and go right."

Twenty-five minutes of driving in heavy Chicago traffic as the city fled work for the weekend.

"Now slow down, slow down. This is it. Go down along this fence to the corner and go right. The entrance is right there."

Christine did as instructed.

"You know the gate code?"

"Yes, 67723ZZ."

"All right, here we go."

Clicking the keypad the gate came open; they passed on through.

"Up two rows and then go left, down three rows."

Christine followed the route and took a final left.

"Number 447-A."

She stopped at the indicated storage garage.

"Now what?"

"Now we need a key to open the lock."

"Do you have the key?"

"Yes, I have one and he has one."

"Give me the key, please."

Sevi handed over her keychain and pointed out the padlock key. Christine jumped out and opened the lock and in one motion raised the door.

They looked inside.

Empty.

"This is where the van is kept? You're positive?"

"Absolutely positive. I put it here myself."

"All right. Now think back, how did you leave it with Hussein?"

"Leave it? How did I leave it? He told me they would hurt me if I tried to back out."

"So he thinks you're still in on it with him?"

"Yes."

"Even after he threw you out?"

"It's not unusual for a Muslim man to make his wife walk. Or worse. He knows I'll still be there for him."

"Wait, wife? Did you marry this guy?"

"No. That's just my example."

"Okay. Good."

"So he thinks you're still with him. I want you to call him on your cell. Call him and tell him you're sorry. Make him think you still want to help with the bomb. Can you do that?"

"Yes. I've been lying for almost a year now. I'm getting good at it."

"All right. Call him, now."

Sevi pulled out her cell and punched Hussein's name. It began beeping to get through.

"Put it on speaker, please."

She did as she was told.

"Hussein? It's Sevi. I'm sorry, Hussein!"

"You should be. That was stupid and unforgivable."

"Did you tell anyone about me? Are they coming after me?"

"Not yet. I'm meeting with my group tonight."

"Your cell?"

Silence. Then, "We don't call it that. The stupid newspapers call it that. We're all just friends of Allah."

"Please don't hate me."

"I don't hate you. Sometimes I just don't understand you. The evil Americans deserve to die. Do we still agree?"

"Yes, we agree."

"They are infidels and idolaters. They worship money and flesh. They hate Allah. They hate the Quran. They hate you and they hate me. They killed your family. They killed my wife. They deserve to die! Many of them must die!"

"When are we going to do it?"

Silence again. "Are you alone?"

"Yes. You know that."

"We must meet. Come to my house tonight. Ten o'clock, after my meeting. We will discuss it. I need to see your face and judge you."

"All right. But I'm hurt. It hurt when you made me jump."

"No excuses. Come anyway."

"I will."

The phone went dead as he clicked off.

"Well?" Christine said. "What about meeting him?"

Sevi shrugged. "Of course I will. It is too late for me to back out. We will fool him. He will kill me in the end, but he must be stopped."

"Exactly my thoughts. But he won't kill you. I won't let that happen."

"Really?"

"All right, let's go home and make our plans for tonight. You won't be there alone."

"What do you mean?"

"I'm going with you."

"But then he will know."

"Not to worry. He'll never see me."

"What is your plan?"

"Let's go talk."

Christine was already backing away from the garage. Then she put it in DRIVE and sped away to the gate and back to the highway.

"He has the van," Sevi moaned as they pulled into the traffic.

"Yes, he does."

"Allah, Allah, Allah."

35

The United States Attorney for the Northern District of Illinois wasn't surprised when the charging documents showed up on her desk. All she had to do was give the okay, and warrants would issue. After all, classified documents had gone missing.

The United States' Attorney's name was Racquel MacAdams and she was a rising star on the Democratic front around Cook County and the collar counties. She attended all party events--official and unofficial--appeared at fairs and beauty contests, helped serve roast pig at the summer Democratic festival in Grant Park, and waged war against the mob and the non-mob alike. She personally had shaken the hands of all attendees at the most recent Chicago Bar Association convention in the SRO-only hotel auditorium along the Loop. She was a fixture and a mainstay among federal officials in the city, and she was a no-nonsense prosecutor.

So who was this Christine Susmann, she wondered as she flipped through the charging documents. She studied the attached one-sheet. Susmann was an attorney on the East Side, a notable among the supporters of the Shedd Aquarium, a decorated war hero, and a mother of two. Her husband had been murdered less than two years ago and yes, she evidently had hired one Althea Berenson to infiltrate Blackguard, Inc. and steal documents. At least that was the crime charged. Coupled with a second count of conspiracy to commit theft and a third count of conspiracy to illegally obtain government documents, the woman was firmly tagged in the crosshairs of Racquel and her hit men. They were savage prosecutors, poised to tear into the lawyer, and all they needed was Racquel's signature on the memo giving the felony team the go-ahead.

MacAdams sighed and leaned back in her chair, absently scratching her chin with the Montblanc pen her father had gifted to her upon her appointment to her current position.

"So tell me, Gerry, why are we so determined to go after her when Judge LaJordia's already ruled in her favor? Isn't the damage already done? How does my prosecuting her undo that damage?"

Gerry Alexander Smits pulled at his red necktie and smiled at his boss. Smits was the chief felony prosecutor on the government agency side. He prosecuted crimes committed against the United States, as opposed to those crimes committed against private individuals and private corporations. Others prosecuted the latter within the U.S. Attorney's Office.

"Blackguard wants its documents returned. I want the documents returned. They're classified, many of them, and their theft greatly jeopardizes the CIA and military."

"What are the documents taken by Miss Berenson?"

"Battle plans. Airstrikes. Black ops. Crap that we don't want floating to the surface of the Blackguard cesspool."

MacAdams nodded. "I fully understand. Well, what about just asking for their return? Can't we strike a deal before we actually prosecute? Give it a try first?"

Smits snorted. He was still choking on his boss's naiveté at times. She never failed to amaze him when she would think out loud.

"Not at all. We must arrest them and hold them while we execute search warrants so the evidence isn't destroyed or, worse, moved. It's computer files, easily moved hither and yon. I don't trust either of these women and neither does our employer, Uncle Sam."

"Sure. That makes sense. Well...all right. Here."

She signed the prosecution memo and Smits gathered the yellow sheet and interleaved it into the file. He stood to go.

"I'll get the marshals right on this," he told his boss.

"Yes, you do that. And Gerry, for the love of God, let's keep the lid on this. We don't want Blackguard looking like the dumbest sons of bitches on earth for hiring the enemy to work for them, do we." It was rhetorical and not a question.

Gerry nodded. He would see to it that the press was blindsided.

"Gerry. Hold up. I want dailies on this. Understand me?"

"Yes, ma'am. Dailies it shall be."

"And move fast. She has millions. She'll probably be out of jail ten minutes after you put her in."

"We'll get four overnights out of her first."

"Yeah, you do that."

"Monday is Labor Day. We'll take her into custody Friday afternoon late. I just checked the court's website and all judges and magistrates are out of town. We can hold her until Tuesday before she sees a judge. That gives us plenty of time to toss her home and office."

"This one has fangs. Don't overstep, you hear me?"

36

He lived in a one-story walkup above a mechanic's garage. The place smelled of gasoline and automobile exhaust at all hours of the night and day. But it was cheap and anonymous in the center of South Chicago and no one would think to look for him there. Among many dark skins he fit right in, so it suited him perfectly.

Hussein answered the door wearing a silk robe and flip-flops.

"Come in. The air conditioning is out, so be ready."

Sevi walked by him and he closed the door behind her. She was wearing her backpack slung over one shoulder and took a seat at the kitchen table and removed her laptop from the backpack.

"I have the blueprints up on my screen. Is this what we will talk about?"

"Not yet. He took the seat opposite her. She could see he was nude beneath the robe and he made no effort to cover himself. She averted her eyes and tried to stay focused on his face and her computer screen as they spoke.

"Let me just say again, I am sorry about today."

He placed both hands down and leaned on his forearms. "That

must never happen again. That was a meltdown. Did you lose your nerve?"

"I am just exhausted. I am working long hours and feeling lonely. You and I no longer meet and satisfy each other. I don't understand why not and I lost my way."

"Because our sex is unclean. We are unmarried. We should marry and be together."

She sighed. "I have told you that is not possible until it has been a year. He is still in my heart."

"Even though I have been in your bed."

"Even though, yes."

She touched the pen in her shirt pocket. It had to be clipped properly and pointed directly at Hussein for Christine to receive the audio and picture of the conversation.

"Why did you do that?" he asked.

"Do what?"

"Don't play dumb. What is that pen in your pocket?"

"Just my pen."

"Here, let me see it."

He didn't wait; he reached and jerked the pen from her pocket. Its design was such that the lens was made to repeat the manufacturer's icon. In all respects it appeared to be an ordinary pen. He pulled it apart and hit it against the tabletop, trying to eviscerate any wiring or electronics it might be holding. But nothing came out.

She reached and jerked her pen away.

"What is wrong with you, Hussein? Now you don't trust the woman whose family was murdered by the Americans? Is that it?"

"I don't trust anyone. It's not just you."

"I went to look at the van today. Where is it?"

"It's been moved."

"Is there another storage garage?"

"Yes. It's many miles from here. After our fight, I moved it."

"And what of your meeting tonight? What was decided?"

"It was decided you would be given a second chance. My friends consider you a high-profile public relations individual. Your engagement with the bomb will make Americans know we will no longer tolerate murder. You are a valuable asset and must go with us to the end."

"You have come to your senses, you and your friends."

"That wasn't all. You will be staying here with me from tonight on."

"That's impossible. All my stuff is at Christine's."

"You can get new stuff."

"But what do I tell her? She's my lawyer!"

"Tell her you have met a man. Tell her you've moved in with him. She'll understand that."

Christine had driven and had dropped Sevi a block from Hussein's. Now she waited in her Escalade around the corner from his place. She was following the conversation on her smart phone's screen when Hussein told Sevi she would stay with him from then on. She knew that was going to make matters more difficult, but not impossible. There would still be opportunities for the two women to meet at Christine's office in the normal process of making the case ready for trial.

"But I will still go to her office about my case?"

"Negative. You will meet with her by phone. You have moved to New York. That is what you will tell her. That will explain why you no longer come to her office. I will monitor your conversations."

"This is because you no longer trust me, Hussein."

"It has nothing to do with trust. It has only to do with the integrity of the plan. Every precaution must be taken to guarantee its success. I don't trust you or not trust you. This is the same way my friends judge me. They neither trust me nor not trust me. It is all part of our cell."

"Your cell. There is that word."

"Cell, cell, cell. Yes, we are a cell. But you will never use that word. And you will never reveal our existence to anyone. If you do, you die. It is that simple. My friends want you to know you are at the end of your rope with them. One more slip and you will join your family in paradise."

"Understood. I will be careful."

"Yes. Now, we will make you a bed on the couch."

"All right. I understand now."

"Yes, you understand."

Around the corner, Christine watched as the scene changed and Sevi moved across the room to the couch. The video feed then presented views of blankets and a pillow being arranged on a beige couch.

She turned the key on the Escalade. It was no longer safe for her to be in the vicinity of Sevi's new life.

She would just have to leave.

She turned to the man in the passenger's seat.

"Seen enough?"

"Yes, Christine. I've got the picture."

"You know she's being held against her will, then?"

"Yes. Clearly."

"At this point, we know there are others. We don't know who they are. We no longer are sure of Sevi and Hussein's roles. Will they plant the bomb, or will the others? The rules of the game have clearly changed since earlier tonight."

"Yes, we can only pray he leads us to his friends."

"Then go back to your car. You've got a long night ahead of you."

"Yes, we'll take it from here."

"And you'll update me on all movements of this man."

"Yes. We will be his new skin."

"Fine, thank you, Rolf."

The man named Rolf opened the passenger door. No light flared inside the car. He began walking back up the sidewalk and toward the corner of the block where Hussein lived. He then crossed the street and disappeared from Christine's view.

So the surveillance was in place.

Now to pray it was enough.

37

F riday night, the marshals came for Althea at her condo. She lived in a gated community. The gatekeeper--when the black Crown Vic pulled up at his window--asked no questions once the badges were flashed. "Gentlemen," he said, and immediately raised the gate.

Althea thought it strange when her doorbell chimed without a call first from the guard. No one was expected. It could only be a neighbor, she thought, even though she knew none of them because she had only lived there since returning from Washington, D.C.

She used the peephole. A black face and a white face peered back at her. Then a badge was displayed. The security chain in place, she cracked the door and looked out.

"Yes?"

"U.S. Marshals, ma'am. You're Althea Berenson?"

"Yes."

"The same Ms. Berenson who recently lived in Washington?"

"Yes, why?"

"May we come in?"

She slid aside the security chain and stepped away from the door. The officers came inside.

"Please, come in and have a seat," she offered.

"No ma'am," the black officer said. "We have a warrant for your arrest. We're here to take you to jail."

Althea was a strong woman and had been around the block. She knew that whatever it was about, it was all about leverage from then on.

"May I call my lawyer first?" she asked.

"No, ma'am. After you're booked you'll be allowed to make calls to your attorney or family member. Please turn around and cross your wrists behind you."

She did as she was told and the handcuffs were firmly put in place.

"Now, ma'am, I'm going to place right here on your dining table a copy of the search warrant we're going to execute tonight. It will be here for you when you make bail and return home."

"Search warrant? What are you searching for?"

"Contraband," said the white, smaller officer.

"Contraband means what?"

"Evidence of a crime."

"What crime am I accused of?"

"We have a criminal complaint charging you with multiple counts of theft and multiple criminal conspiracies. You will receive the complaint after you're processed into the jail and we then talk to you."

"I won't be talking to you. So you can save your criminal complaint and your efforts to fool me into making a statement. Ain't gonna happen, Gents."

"All right, then. We are going to take you downstairs to our car. We'll be passing a group of marshals on their way up. They'll be searching these premises. Is there a storage room apart from the condo that you use?"

"You mean here on the grounds somewhere?"

"Yes, ma'am."

"Well, there's a storage room off my porch. At the far end."

"Do you keep computer parts in there? Hard drives? Old computers? Floppies?"

"No. It's got some interior paint I saved, some ant powder, maybe an old roller or two. Stuff like that. But no computer parts."

"Your computer is here?"

"Yes, it is. Right there on the coffee table."

"Is that the only computer you own?"

"Yes, it is."

"Is that the only computer you use?"

"Yes, it is."

"Do you use cloud storage with your computer?"

"I do. Dropbox."

"Will you give us that password?"

"I would if I knew it. It's been so long since I had to enter it, I don't remember it."

"Any other external drives, thumb drives, CDs or other magnetic data repositories?" asked the white marshal.

"No--no. Why, what you looking for?"

"We're looking for the documents you stole from Blackguard, Inc. while you worked for them in D.C. Mind telling us what you did with those?"

"No comment."

"No comment because you don't want to tell us?"

"No comment."

"All right, then. We're done here. Let's go now, Ms. Berenson."

They took her into the hallway, down to the elevator, and downstairs to the waiting Crown Vic.

"Don't tell me," she said at the car. "I get in back, you two up front. I've seen this movie before."

"Correct," said the black officer. "Easy now, don't hit your head."

"Wait! I didn't bring my purse!"

"You won't be needing your purse, Ms. Berenson."

"But it has my blood pressure pills!"

"The prison nurse will cover all that once you're booked in. You wouldn't be allowed to take drugs with you into your cell anyway. Not drugs from the outside."

"If I have a heart attack or stroke, I'm suing. Can I get your cards?"

The white officer, in the passenger seat, held up a business card.

"Here you go. Oops, you're handcuffed. Maybe you'll just have to wait and read the police reports to get our ID's. Is that all right?"

"Now you're being facetious. That's sarcasm, officer."

"Yes, it is. I'd suggest you sit back now and enjoy the ride. We're an hour away from the jail, so you can relax."

"All right, I'll relax. Or try to."

"Yes, try to. All any of us can do is try, Ms. Berenson."

After booking she was allowed to make no calls. She objected and demanded to speak with her attorney. She was ignored.

LONNIE RIFFER, PH.D.--"DOCTOR RIFF"--HELD a Ph.D. in computer forensics from a university in Zurich, Switzerland, where he was born and grew up. He had been hired by the U.S. Marshal's service for his expertise in extracting usable evidence from computer systems. This included computer hard drives, storage modalities, systems analysis, on- and off-site storage including cloud computing, as well as the analysis of how data had been put to whatever use by its interloper. He was a six-footer, lithe and blonde, and wore a scruffy blonde beard and eyeglasses with blue lenses that would have made Elvis jealous.

Doctor Riff went into Althea's townhouse with a team of five marshals and marshal's office employees and directed the seizure of all electronic storage media. He then spent all night tracking data acquisition and distribution under the seventeen user accounts maintained by the defendant. Yes, seventeen, he told his associates, the most he'd ever seen one individual maintain. "She was a walking User ID," he laughed. "I still don't know if I have them all. But I will, definitely."

Doctor Riff debriefed with U.S Attorney Racquel MacAdams on Saturday morning at her office on Dearborn.

"So here's the preliminary shakeout," said Doctor Riff. "I located seven Dropbox accounts and inventoried them all. You'll be receiving my report of those items after Labor Day."

"Tuesday?"

"Thursday at the latest."

"What, essentially, are we talking about?"

"Lots of Blackguard material such as employee handbooks, system analysis recipes, fire drill plans, even a menu from May's cafeteria offerings."

"God-Almighty!"

"Yes. But most important, I came across a private key, the kind commonly used between two computers to access and store data."

"Did it unlock anything?"

"It did. A certain European moving and storage company has an off-site data dump. As near as I can tell, it's a room full of servers, maybe thirty, all told. Their system had been hacked. They had no clue. And the data from one server had been redistributed to a sister machine and was made accessible there. Then the empty server was accessed remotely, of course, over the next two weeks by a machine with Althea Berenson's credentials."

"Accessed for what purpose?"

"She used their data server to store Blackguard documents there."

"Describe, please."

"You name it, she has it stored there. Action items, photographs, schematics, conversations--written and verbal--communications between officers and agents of Blackguard--including the owners themselves."

"The DuMonts."

"Yes. But the dates are what blew my mind. This stuff she stole and squirreled away goes back to 1973 and the Vietnam War."

"Blackguard started operating during Vietnam."

"Exactly. After the fall of Dien Bien Phu the call went out for CIA intervention. The CIA didn't have the horsepower, so it called on America's largest security company. At that time Blackguard was totally domestic and it wasn't known as Blackguard. DuMont Investigations and Security was its name way back when. Anyway, the two brothers reformed the company, named it Blackguard, and went international. They basically put into effect all CIA schemes and plans during the remainder of the war. All of that stuff--Vietnam to this year in Syria--all of it has been accessed and stored off-site on this server in Europe."

"Must be a huge server."

"Oh, but she's much smarter than that! The documents have been segmented. Ten percent are on the server we discovered, another ten percent are on a second server we found, this one at a startup pharmaceutical in Hong Kong, and it goes on and on. Slowly but surely we're tracking them down. But it will be months, probably, until I know I have them all located."

"Is there a master list of the data? Foolish question?"

"Great question. You have raised one of the key problems with all this. We don't know what's been taken or not. So no, there's no master list. Which means we'll probably never know how completely the government's classified data has been compromised."

"So she's hit us hard."

"Harder than hard. Even if you were talking wartime explosives, this one's a hydrogen bomb."

"Who else knows about this?" asked MacAdams, her mind already veering off to damage control.

"So far it's closed door. Just two staff members who're helping me. One's a cryptographer; one's a security expert. They're both geeks; they don't know anyone to tell."

"And they have clearances?"

"Yes, both top secret clearances. Just like yours truly."

"You."

He smiled happily. "That's right."

"All right. Look, this goes no further. My first inclination is to take this personally to the Attorney General. No, it's not an inclination, that's what I'll be doing. In fact, I'll see if I can track him down this weekend."

"Yes, good."

"You keep a lid on everything. Don't go back on those servers or do anything else. Got it?"

"You're shutting me down?"

"Just until I can talk to the AG. He might want the FBI in on this."

"Roger that."

"Lordy, here we come!"

SHE LOCATED the AG at half past noon by phone. He was out on the waters of Chesapeake Bay in the family spinnaker and would be back around three. So she waited. She went downstairs to the corner and retrieved Buffalo Coffee with a sesame bagel. She bought a Trib. She went back up to her office and called her daughter. She chided her for wearing too much makeup to the "Welcome Back to School Holiday Dance" at her high school last night. She sprayed her computer screen with cleaning solvent and carefully wiped it away with a diaper she kept on hand for that purpose.

Finally her phone rang on the private line.

"Racquel? Anders Livingston here. What national security matter did you call about?"

"I did say it was matter of national security, sir, because I believe it just might be."

"All right, cut to the chase. We're getting ready for burgers and wine coolers here."

"You know Blackguard."

"Of course I know Blackguard. And what--what, woman?"

"Their data has been mined and scattered around the globe."

"They did this?"

"No, an employee did this. A woman we've just arrested. We got her computer, tracked down logins and trails over the last few months, and found Blackguard's data on a server in Europe. We found more of it on a server in Hong Kong."

"Whose servers?"

"People--companies--that know nothing about the data they're storing. These were soft firewalls. High school level stuff, I'm told. Anyway, Blackguard's entire history as demonstrated by company documents has been compromised."

"You don't mean classified stuff?"

"I do. I mean all of it."

"Holy shit, woman. All right, slow down. Where are you, MacAdams?"

"At my office. Downtown Chicago."

"I'm calling in the FBI's Emergency Response team. Our national security is on high risk status as of now--three-twenty-four p.m."

"Copy that, sir."

"You wait there, MacAdams, the FBI is on its way. And get your computer people on site. Are these U.S. Marshals?"

"Yes, sir."

"Good. Call them into your office. No talking to anyone about this. As for me, I'm calling the President at Camp David. He's going to have a miserable holiday."

"Sorry for that. Please give him my--"

"Sit tight, MacAdams. That's an order!"

"Yes, sir."

38

FBI agent Bernard L. Janssen had flown in from Washington to take the suspect into custody himself. Why would the DOJ send a high-ranking FBI agent to Chicago to effect a mundane arrest in a government theft case? Because, as the President had passed along, this was anything but a mundane arrest. From what they had been able to gather, the suspect, Christine Susmann, was the mastermind behind the Althea Berenson theft of Blackguard documents. She had to be arrested without delay and, most important of all, she was to be held incommunicado. It was key that she not be allowed to speak to anyone, especially any lawyer she might wish to call. She was to hit a dead end.

So Janssen was uncomfortable when Christine invited him into her home that Saturday night. Uncomfortable because he knew they were about to play hardball with the woman, hold her without bail and without communication with the outside world.

It just had to be done that way. At least until they could get a tape measure around the tonnage of documents that had been made off with. They still didn't know how inclusive the theft was. Which was the most critical item on their checklist of all the items hastily put there by the President, the AG, the Director of the FBI, and the D.C. AIC Bernard L. Janssen.

He accepted her proffer of chilled water and thanked her for the courtesy.

"Why we're here, Ms. Susmann, you already can guess."

Christine sat cross-legged on the white sofa across from Janssen and two of his subordinates.

"Actually I can't guess. I'm thinking it has something to do with the al-Assad case, maybe."

"What's that?" Janssen asked.

"The girl--young woman--whose family was murdered? You've heard about that case and her success in getting a plaintiff's verdict on the liability issue?"

"Actually, I haven't heard," said Janssen, gulping down a mouthful of the chilled water. He wiped his mouth with the back of his shirt cuff.

Christine was perplexed. She had finally decided to turn over the surveillance of Hussein and Sevi to the Chicago PD and already the Illinois Bureau of Investigation had swooped in and was working the case day and night. Christine was satisfied with that call; the matter threatened to involve the deaths of hundreds of innocents and Christine had wasted no time calling in the cops when Sevi's life was taken over by Hussein. Yet, that wasn't what the FBI visit pertained to. So, she decided to decry all knowledge and information about any other matter the FBI might like to know about even though, deep down, she knew certain documents had been lifted from the Blackguard servers; she just didn't know the full extent of it.

"Well, my client is being held against her will by a Syrian terrorist. He is threatening to set off a bomb in a populated area. The IBI has taken over that case. So my guess is, you're not here about that."

"Actually, no. This is the first I've heard about that. But that's not why I'm here."

"Then, how can I help?"

"Actually, Ms. Susmann, I'm here to arrest you."

39

J amie knew his mom was a moving target. She played hard and she fought hard. Likewise, those she opposed hit back hard.

When the FBI took her away, he didn't freak out; in fact, it came as no surprise.

To him, her arrest was just another result of her being on the front lines fighting the good fight and standing up for what she believed. Besides, she had told him long ago, when first adopting him, that her job would keep her in jeopardy some of the time and that he shouldn't be surprised at the odd things she would sometimes ask him to do or the aberrations that would sometimes come their way.

So when she was arrested he kept all this in mind and waited for his mother's mother--his grandmother--to show up at the house to keep an eye on him and his sister. Her name was Rosalind Albright and she was a retired baby doctor from Orbit who always responded to Christine's requests for help in a flash. This time was no different and, because of the arrangement, Jamie and his sister felt fully supported when mom was led away. Just another day, they said, knowing full well she would soon extricate herself and be back home.

To stay busy, Jamie turned back to his software. While he wasn't worried about his mother, he was worried about Sevi's sudden disappearance from the house. She was his good friend and he wouldn't rest until he knew she was okay. He doubted she had the same ability to care for herself as his mom had. The IBI was tracking her, he had been told, and that should have been enough. However, Christine was updating Jamie on the IBI's efforts and it was turning out that the IBI wasn't enough. They kept losing Sevi.

The problem the IBI ran into was that the Muslims they were concerned about were slippery. Consequently, the cops were thrown off the trail, or they simply lost the scent altogether, repeatedly. When they lost their quarry, all they could do was cross fingers and pray that this wasn't the time the bomb was being taken to a school and set to explode.

"Cross our fingers and pray," IBI Director Hans Schaffuler told the governor of Illinois.

"That's not good enough, Schaff," said the governor. "I expect a hundred percent proficiency from here on out. Or I'm looking for a new director. Especially if this thing goes off and kills a bunch of kids. Heads will roll and yours will be first. Mine will be right behind. And we don't want that, Schaff. So get the hell on the ball!"

Despite such encouragement from his boss, the director and his IBI continued to find themselves sabotaged in their tracking efforts. It would happen in traffic when the twosome would jump from one vehicle going north to an approaching vehicle heading south. Or jumping from a vehicle, abandoning it in traffic, and running in and through a building downtown. An old trick, but an effective one. As the IBI was tracking in fits and fails, Jamie Susmann was putting the finishing cosmetic touches on his new TRAC software. "TRACE RECOGNIZE AND CAPTURE," Sevi had named it. Jamie thought back to that night and he felt lonely for Sevi. She was just so damn smart, he told his mother. Why did she have to leave them? And she didn't even tell me goodbye! What's up with that?

So...Jamie did the next best thing.

He talked to his FACCE users and begged video feeds. Just city-wide, but it was a start. And when they said yes, he almost exploded with joy. At last he had a chance at finding Sevi and learning what had happened to her. Christine had confided in her son that Sevi had been forced to leave them by a determined, evil man. Is this her husband? Jamie wanted to know. No, not her husband. An evil, terrorist sort. Jamie resolutely decided then and there that he would find her and do what he could to help extricate her from the situation. They were scientists and engineers: every problem was simply a solution waiting to be chosen.

TRAC went live the same Friday that Althea Berenson was arrested.

Jamie's determination to help his Muslim friend had redoubled. For sixteen hours he toiled at his monitor and keyboard, implementing the video feeds provided to him.

Then, at midnight Friday, he went live.

Slowly, but with increasing speed, the system began comparing the headshot Jamie had snapped of Sevi for his cell phone contacts list. TRAC compared the picture to all connected service station feeds, convenience store feeds, security cameras on every street corner in the city, video feeds coming from intersection monitoring equipment, and hundreds of thousands of other cameras pointed and turned on around the city for a thousand other purposes.

Slowly, the system located her. First, a shot of her walking into a 7-Eleven. Next was a shot at a Marshall's in the western suburbs. Then a picture of her filling a white van with gas at an Exxon station.

And on it went.

By noon the next day--Saturday--he had his first film of Sevi moving around the city.

Now to establish a starting location and a destination. If they turned out to be one and the same, then he would have what he needed. He would have learned where she was living. Who knows, he thought, there might even be a video camera smack in the middle of the block where she lived. If only he could be so lucky.

He followed her forty-eight hours straight on Saturday and Sunday. He analyzed his videos. He had two locations where she appeared both days: an Exxon and a diner in South Chicago. The software kept spinning along, analyzing video feeds, and looking for the Sevi al-Assad model that it knew through its machine learning algorithms. As the software grew smarter, Jamie's friend began turning up more places.

Then he did an interesting thing. He went back through the videos to the beginning of the feed and re-ran the TRAC system, smarter now the second time through. New images/locations began surfacing. Now there was a department store, exterior and interior hits when she had shopped and purchased summer weight slacks and a cotton shirt. There was a video series of her walking along Wacker drive as she went into 100 West, where she worked. Those feeds followed her inside, even up to views of her in her cubicle at work, her head bent low to her computer.

Jamie was fascinated with what he had invented. And he was fascinated with the feeds. He knew that his system had huge potential for law enforcement and industrial security, but he was no fool, either. He knew his software had the potential to be a disruptive influence where it came to sorting out human rights and the right of people to be let alone and not be tracked in their daily lives by video feeds of their activities. Was there a legal right to be let alone? Jamie discussed this with Christine. Her advice to him: Continue on with the engineering but leave the legalities of his invention and its work product to the lawyers and courts. She told him he couldn't be expected to work both rings of the circus, her words. So he settled into what he did best: software engineering. And he freed his mind from concern over misapplication of his invention.

WHILE JAMIE WAS TWEAKING his software and watching as its IQ grew and grew thanks to its machine learning code, Christine wasn't sitting idly by in the Cook County Jail just hoping for a lucky break.

The interrogation failed, of course, so they allowed her to call her attorney. The first person she called was Ed Mitchell. He had dropped what he was doing and immediately appeared at the jail, where they met and talked. Their conversation was general, without reference to case specifics, as they were communicating through Plexiglas over a phone system they knew to be hacked. The FBI was listening in and probably recording every word that was said. It was a federal crime to violate the attorney-client confidentiality rules. However, the FBI didn't give a damn. They played fast and loose with rules every day. It was part of who they were and how they rolled. Agents Janssen and Akim received transcripts of the conversation and they agreed there was nothing startling there.

ED MITCHELL: Do you need anything?"

CHRISTINE SUSMANN: A crab salad, lots of greens.

ED MITCHELL: Bleu cheese?

CHRISTINE SUSMANN: Yep. And a tall iced tea. It's sweltering in here. The AC is on the fritz.

ED MITCHELL: I've called around for a judge. Everyone's out of town until Tuesday.

CHRISTINE SUSMANN: I can do Tuesday in my sleep. They've got a bunch of John Grisham novels here. I can catch up.

ED MITCHELL: I've checked in on the kids. Your mom has everything under control on the home front.

CHRISTINE SUSMANN: Is Jamie taking his Cogentin?

ED MITCHELL: He is. I checked that with him myself.

CHRISTINE SUSMANN: And what about Little Bit? How's she holding up?

ED MITCHELL: Janny is great. She's doing her colors and listening to her iPad music. She asks about you, but having Nana and your mom there is keeping her busy. They're taking up the slack, if that's possible.

CHRISTINE SUSMANN: All right. We'll talk about this when we can have some privacy. That's all I have for now.

ED MITCHELL: Agreed. I'll check in again tomorrow.

ON SUNDAY, Jamie confirmed Hussein was holding Sevi where Christine had accompanied her.

It was a walkup above a mechanic's garage on the South Side. He knew this because almost directly across the street was a Speedway and that service station's video feed from pump seven had captured her face as she was coming down the exterior stairs. Following behind was a dark male who Jamie didn't know, but he cropped out the man's face and sent it to Ed Mitchell to show Christine.

Sunday noon found Ed back at the jail, again talking to Christine through the Plexiglas. The first thing he did was bring up the picture on his smart phone and plaster it against the Plexiglas screen-side to Christine.

Her eyes grew wide.

"I know him. He's the man holding her."

"Well guess what? Jamie has them located."

"Pure genius. His TRAC did this?"

"His TRAC did this. I have a feeling Jamie is going to need to pay another visit to his patent lawyer."

"Astonishing. Tell him how proud I am."

"Do we tell anyone?"

They were comfortable enough talking about it. Those listening in neither saw the picture of Hussein nor knew for sure to whom she was referring. They had their ideas, but there was no hard and fast evidence. So the conversation about Sevi could continue without being about Sevi.

"We don't tell anyone yet. Let me think about this. But tell Jamie to stay focused here. It might even be a good idea to bring in additional surveillance."

"Do this myself? Or authorities?"

She pointed at Ed without verbally responding.

"All right," he said, "if you don't feel comfortable answering me, then don't. But I have other appointments, so I'm out of here."

"Enjoy our day off."

"Whose day off? I've been at the office since sunup. Just because you're on holiday doesn't mean I am."

He smiled and placed his hand against the glass. She immediately raised her hand and placed it on her side of the glass. They would have been holding hands if it weren't for the inch of Plexiglas between them.

He smiled. She smiled.

He nodded: instruction received.

Then he left.

ED'S next stop was at Christine's house to visit with Jamie.

"Good work, Jamie" he told the teenager. "Evidently you've found her."

"So what do we do now that we know where she is?"

"XFBI has put a van in place. From here on, a constant video feed will be made directly to you."

"Excellent. Will the van attempt to follow them?"

"I don't think so. Too risky. We need it to go unnoticed and if it follows them, it might be spotted."

"Will we tell the IBI what we've learned about where she's being held?"

"Your mom and I are working on that one. I'll get back to you."

"Cool."

40

The DuMont brothers were horrified. Their entire dark world was stored somewhere on servers beyond their reach. Whether classified government documents to which they were privy and had in their possession, or internally classified documents, the hack was unimaginable. They had paid over five hundred million dollars in IT funding to guarantee their online systems were burglar-proof and their firewalls unbreakable and their networks unhackable. Now it seemed the payouts had all been for naught. A single woman, someone without a world of computer expertise between the ears, had managed to not only penetrate their servers but also to make off with millions of pages of documents. The brothers were stunned.

And not just a little frightened.

Frightened because the world would learn of Blackguard's vile deeds if those documents went public.

"How did we get here?" said Edlund DuMont to his brother, Wilfred, as they met over the Labor Day weekend and circled wagons. They were in the study of Wilfred's Dallas home, overlooking Lake Dallas on the lakeside of Westlake Park. A hearty dinner of rock lobster and steamed rice with shrimp had just been enjoyed, and now they were relaxing and speaking to each other through clouds emitted by Cuba's finest tobacco.

"We got here because oil is our god," Wilfred replied. "Mother taught us better."

"But father gave us the keys to the kingdom."

"Here's to wildcatters."

They each raised a brandy snifter and nodded to one another.

"Arum al-Assad had to die because he was planning to sell our oil to the Chinese."

"That was a no-brainer."

Wilfred said, "I called in the drone because he had to go. The problem was the collateral damage. Who would have guessed the house was full of Muslims waiting for a wedding ceremony?"

"No one is faulting you, Wilfred. I would have done the same thing."

"Yes, you would have."

"But lo and behold, a Muslim woman gets blown out of the house and lives. Then she comes to the United States and sues us. Along with the government. Now that's perplexing. It hasn't happened before."

"And her lawyer plants this Berenson woman inside our Washington offices."

"And she proceeds to rob us."

"They say she has put our documents on servers around the world. There's so many they don't even know where to start."

"How did she learn that?"

"Unknown. What are we thinking?"

"Our internal security service has just provided me with its workup. It appears Ms. Al-Assad's lawyer has a son who is a certified computer genius."

"Are we thinking it was him?"

"Unknown, for sure, they tell me. He's only fifteen."

Wilfred blew a plume of blue Cuban smoke at the ceiling. He tapped the fingers of his free hand against his knee. "Do you know what I'm thinking?"

"I think I do."

"Tit for tat."

"Quid pro quo."

"His value to his mother equals our documents' value to us."

"We can make a trade."

"If we have a chip."

"So grab him."

"Done."

"But don't hurt him. I'm sure he's a good kid."

Wilfred tapped his cigar against the enormous crystal ashtray beside his chair. "I doubt that. And frankly I don't give a damn whether he ever sees his mother again. I just want our property back."

With a wave of his hand Edlund replied, "Then do what you must. Throw him in the goddam lake for all I care."

"I'm thinking there's even more to be done with him."

"Such as?"

"Well, it's clear, isn't it? She has a judgment against us on the liability issues for killing the family. We trade the kid for a document evidencing a satisfaction of that judgment. We pay zip. We get our documents back. We dump the kid in deep water and wash our hands. He won't be around to tell the cops who took him."

"I say we go the extra step as well. Father would have."

"What would that be?"

"We take out the al-Assad woman. There's no other family after her. No one to collect on any judgment. No one to push the case forward. Poof, it evaporates and we're back to square one."

"How do we find her?"

"We've already found her."

"How did that happen?" asked Wilfred.

Edlund smiled. His smile was the smile of a man in his eighties: long in the tooth and yellowed with coffee and cigar stains. "We hacked the son's computer, a simple task. Evidently he has hammered together a piece of software that takes video feeds and analyzes them. So our people tell me. Using his little software, he's located the al-Assad woman. She is staying in a walkup over a garage in South Chicago."

"Then by all means. Do what's indicated."

"Her demise is indicated."

"Don't tell me. Just do it."

"Consider it done."

41

J amie found the same black Chevy sedan passing in front of his house four times Sunday morning and afternoon. He knew this because his own video system monitored the street that ran along their security wall. The same vehicle going past more than twice in any given day made the system flag Jamie and he took a look. Now the Chevy Impala had gone past four times.

Four times, dark windows, slowing as it passed by--all the signs of a car that should be watched.

On its fifth pass, Jamie's cameras caught the license plate number when the brake lights flared at the corner and the sun had just set. Now he had something to work with, so he fed the license plate number into TRAC and waited.

While the system began searching new video, Jamie's thoughts turned to the car and the possibilities. He reasoned it was probably nothing, just someone visiting one of the other families in their housing development. But he also had a reservation about that kind of Pollyanna thinking: what if someone was after him? Or after Janny? Shouldn't he be prepared to provide protection now that his mother was incarcerated?

Ever so quietly he stole from his room and crept in the early dark toward his mother's double doors. Once inside her bedroom he closed the doors quietly behind him.

He knew the gun safe was built into the floor of her closet and he went there.

He also knew the combination.

Doubtful that his mother had any real secrets from him, he spun the dial on the safe. Left-right-left-left-right, he could actually hear the tumblers falling into place.

Then he stopped and twisted the handle and the safe door swung upward, assisted by pneumatic arms within.

There wasn't just one gun; there were several.

But he knew she preferred the .40 caliber Glock. It was the one she always wore when those challenging times presented themselves.

So he fished it out of the safe, along with its shoulder holster.

Christine had long ago taught Jamie gun safety and had taught him how to shoot targets. She had even begun teaching him the rudiments of combat shooting and had promised to send him to a three-day combat shooting course he found in Gun World.

He sat on her bed and adjusted the straps of the shoulder harness.

Then he tried it on. The gun was huge beneath his skinny left arm but it would work for him because it hung above the cuff on his forearm crutch. Ever so quietly he closed the safe and slipped back down the hallway to his room, where he locked himself inside. He went to his closet, found his denim work shirt, and slipped it on, effectively hiding the gun. He wore the shirt unbuttoned and untucked, but it did its job. Even his grandmother wouldn't notice and she normally noticed everything about her grandkids.

With the gun in place and covered, he resumed his seat at the computer.

Results were coming in. Surprisingly, the car had also driven past Sevi's location six times that day.

Which set Jamie's mind to racing.

CHICAGO FBI LEARNED from its Blackguard source that Jamie Susmann was in on the theft. The teenager had evidently passed along the technical know-how that enabled Althea Berenson to hack and transfer Blackguard's sacred documents.

Two agents were dispatched to Jamie's house to question him. Their names were Sims and Ferlinghetti. Both were agents with ten-plus years of field investigative experience in the area of computer and financial crimes. Both knew the questions to ask and the computer systems to comb through.

When they left the Arlington Heights FBI field office they took Sims' government-issued Chevrolet.

A black Impala. Then they located Jamie's home and began watching. They needed the go-ahead from the Washington FBI's Emergency Response team. Then they would go in and identify themselves and undertake their investigation of the boy's role. Moreover, they were hopeful he knew the whereabouts of the stolen documents, that he might have actually participated in their relocation and knew how to get them back.

If frightened enough.

They drove back and forth on the street running parallel to Jamie's house as they awaited clearance from Washington.

Then they decided to kill time by driving to South Chicago. Sims, who had been in touch with the FBI plant in Washington, thought he knew where the Muslim woman was holed up, as he put it.

They drove east and south and located the garage with the walkup unit above. They drove around it three times. On the fourth pass their radio crackled.

Washington. They were cleared to contact the Susmann kid.

Pedal to the metal, they headed for Christine's home--the kid's home--on the North Side.

42

He was shot because of his own gun. FBI identified themselves to XFBI guards and the latter stood down.

When the FBI agents were invited inside the house by Jamie's grandmother, they were told Jamie was upstairs and they were free to talk to him. She showed them to the stairs and nodded her okay.

Jamie had seen them approach the house on his CCTV. He had watched them park and come onto the porch. Two men in suits shooting furtive glances at their surroundings as they waited on the porch. He prayed his grandmother would send them away, but she didn't. In fact, she did the opposite: she invited them inside the house. What the hell? Wondered Jamie. Has she no good sense? And where was XFBI?

He decided to face them head-on. So he took up his position at the far end of the hall, just outside his mother's double doors. There he stood, leaning forward on his crutches, gun in hand. There was no way he was going down without a fight.

Sims was first up the stairs, followed by Ferlinghetti. Sims was a battle-hardened veteran of the First Gulf War and an expert marksman. He summited the stairs and peered around the corner. There, at the far end of the hall, was Jamie Susmann, raising the gun and pointing it directly at him. Sims immediately drew his own service Glock and fired three shots in rapid succession. The first and third shots narrowly missed their target, but the second shot caught the youngster in the face and blew him back against the double doors, where he crumpled to the floor. He was bleeding profusely and was unconscious when the two agents ran up to him.

Ferlinghetti was already on his comms, calling in the EMTs while Sims dropped to his knees and used his handkerchief to staunch the flow of blood. Jamie's head lolled to the side and his tongue protruded from his mouth as his muscles went limp throughout his body. Sims was certain the boy had died. He shook his head at Ferlinghetti, who came off his comms and dropped to his knees besides Sims.

"Wait!" cried Ferlinghetti. "He's breathing."

Sims had been feeling for a carotid pulse and, at the same moment Ferlinghetti cried out, his fingers touched the pulse.

"Quick," said Sims, cradling the boy in his arms, "check his airway."

Ferlinghetti checked the airway with his fingers and bent his head to listen. "Clear," he said, "he's definitely breathing."

"Let's get him downstairs."

With Sims lifting his shoulders and upper torso, Ferlinghetti caught Jamie around the knees and lifted him from the floor. Together the two men navigated the stairs, Ferlinghetti stepping down backwards while Sims tentatively found each step by feel.

They reached the bottom of the stairs, where they stretched Jamie out on his back.

At that moment, Christine's doctor-mother took over, again checking the airway and compressing the wound with the blood-soaked handkerchief.

"Dirty bastards," she cried at the two men. "He's a boy, a crippled little boy!"

"But he had a gun," said Sims. "He pointed a gun at me."

The doctor refocused her gaze and Jamie's shoulder holster registered in her brain.

"What were you doing with a gun?" she said to her grandson. "Stupid, poor boy!"

With sirens blazing and red lights flashing, the emergency medical crew flew up the driveway and three EMTs hit the door running. They threw open the door and banged inside with their wheeled stretcher, unfolding it and raising it as they came. The EMTs and the two agents gently lifted Jamie from the floor to the stretcher. His airway and vitals were checked. Oxygen was started and a line inserted to keep his blood pressure up. Monitors were attached and, when they had done what they could do, the EMTs wheeled and carried him to the ambulance, where he was loaded inside.

The siren wailed and lights flashed as the ambulance circled the drive and headed for the street. Jamie's grandmother grabbed up Janny and ran with her to the garage, where she fastened the little girl in her car seat and opened the garage door with a click. She was just minutes behind the ambulance as the high speed drive to the hospital ensued.

While the scramble for the hospital played out, federal agents swarmed Christine's home, taking pictures of the scene and removing Jamie's two computers: desk top and lap top. One external hard drive was also seized, along with five thumb drives they found around the room, in his book bag, and fastened to his keychain.

FIVE HOURS of surgery were required. In attendance were two doctors. The neurosurgeon went first. He tended to the bullet removal and neurologic repair. He then yielded the operating table to a maxillofacial surgeon who literally rebuilt Jamie's bony structures in his face. Tubes were inserted; screws were placed in face and skull plates. Jamie survived the long hours under the knife and drills.

CT scans were taken before and after. When the surgeons had

conferred and were satisfied they'd done all they could, Jamie was released to the ICU.

They wheeled him out of the OR and into the ICU.

He remained unconscious and unresponsive to verbal commands long after the anesthesia had worn off. His grandmother sat beside his bed with his sister.

Five hours later, his grandfather arrived from Orbit. He took over the bedside watch while Janny's grandmother carried the sleeping child to the elevator and down to the vehicle she had driven to the hospital eleven hours earlier.

They headed home.

~

A JAILER TOOK her into a conference room, notified Christine and explained what had happened. She was sorry to say she had no details beyond the fact there had been a shooting and surgery and that Jamie was now in ICU.

As would be expected, Christine became animated and demanding. She insisted on seeing a judge and having bail set without further delay. After an hour of wrangling and wheedling with her jailers she was allowed to call Ed Mitchell. Ed was away in Ann Arbor for the holiday, where he was said to be visiting his mother in her nursing home. He said he could be in Chicago in less than five hours; he was leaving immediately. They would find a magistrate and drag him out of bed, Ed promised, so Christine could make bail and get to the hospital.

At two o'clock in the morning, Ed finally tracked down the Honorable Boyd Werbler, who was spending the holiday at Lake Geneva in Wisconsin. Ed scrambled to track down the jurist. The deputy explained the situation to the judge, who groggily absorbed it all and started reading the order Ed had prepared.

Thirty minutes later, Ed had a signed order. Bail was set for both Althea and Christine at $450,000 apiece and passports were ordered surrendered. Three hours later bail bonds were posted and Ed rushed Christine to the University of Chicago Hospital, where Jamie remained unconscious and unresponsive. Althea grabbed a cab and rushed home.

Christine and Ed ran through the hospital to the ICU. The charge nurse delivered them to Jamie's bedside. Christine's father was already at Jamie's beside. He turned to Christine and shook his head.

Christine took Jamie's hand in her own and pressed it against her face.

"Jamie, open those eyes!"

Ed touched Christine's shoulder and allowed his hand to remain there, gently rubbing and trying to soothe her grief and tears.

Jamie's head and the left side of his face were swathed in bandages. Drainage tubes snaked down into suction bags as the swelling produced fluids that needed to be carried away. His left eye was swollen shut; the bullet had entered his face just beneath the eye and two centimeters to the left.

Dr. James Roanoke, the neurosurgeon, appeared behind Christine.

"You're the mother?"

"Yes."

"We don't know the extent of neurologic damage. A portion of the brain was destroyed."

"What--what about his vision?"

"My guess is that the vision is going to be unaffected. The bullet was grossly near the optic nerve but anatomically a mile away. It should be okay."

"Tell me the truth, doc. Is he going to regain consciousness?"

"You know, I have to say this in these cases again and again, and I hate it. But I'll say it anyway. In cases of trauma to the skull and brain, only time will tell. Once he's awake we can make some assessments. But for now I'm managing brain swelling, pressure, and intracranial bleeding. I think I have everything repaired but surgery is essentially 2-D while injuries are 3-D. So we'll just have to see."

Ed said, "Doc, we know you've seen this injury before in your practice. What's your best guess?"

The doctor nodded and looked up at the ceiling. "Best guess is there's going to be some degree of neurologic damage. Certainly there's anatomic damage. But you're going to need to talk to one of our neurologists about that. Remember, I don't assess neurologic deficits, my job is to repair."

"Thank you, doctor."

"Yes, thanks, doc."

"I'll be back here in the morning when I do rounds. In the meantime, if he needs me again, I'll be in the hospital and just a page away. So...say your prayers and talk to him. It all matters."

"Will do," said Christine.

The doctor moved on to his next stop.

"Jamie, can you hear me?"

43

For a crisp new hundred-dollar bill the mechanic downstairs allowed Hussein and Sevi to pull the white van into the garage for parking over the holiday weekend. They moved it in Friday night at closing time and the mechanic punched the button that lowered the articulating door of the service area.

On Sunday night, they began the process of assembling the bomb. First, Sevi taped Hefty trash bags over the windows in the garage door. She checked and re-checked until she was certain no light was escaping. Now they could work under the service bay lights.

The six fifty-pound bags of explosive ammonia nitrate fertilizer were arranged two behind the back seat of the van and two on either side, creating a U-shaped compartment within which to work.

Four fifty-gallon barrels of fuel oil were then loaded in between the bags of fertilizer. Great care was taken not to throw off a spark or do anything that would prematurely set off a holocaust right there in the garage.

Then came a helping of nitro-methane inside three barrels. They were smaller barrels, but space was now at a premium.

Once the barrels and bags were all onboard, Hussein tested the closure of the van's rear doors. They snugged in perfectly, with less than inch to spare between the inner door metal and the nitro barrels.

Hussein raised his hand.

"Time for a break. Let's think about this next part."

Sevi went inside the station to the soft drink machine and returned with two frosty cans of Coke. "Here," she said, and handed a can to Hussein, who raised it to her in a toast. She ignored him and popped the top on hers.

"When do we drive it to the school?"

"Monday morning. But one week? Why did you move it up?"

"One week. I moved it up because of you. I don't want to have to watch you until we explode it. Get it done now."

"What time Friday?"

"Ten o'clock that morning. On the button."

"How will you set it off?"

"Tonight we're going to run the fuse in the van. That part is dangerous. Then I will connect a battery and a cell phone. All I'll have to do is dial the cell phone and boom!"

"You've thought it all out."

He smiled. "We learned all this in Pakistan. There are some good bombers there."

"I know."

He leaned against the rear deck of the van, one arm hoisted up over a barrel of nitro-methane. "Well."

"You know, it was my family that was murdered," she said.

"Yes, and my wife," he retorted, for he knew what was coming.

"I am to the point where I just want to call it off. Murdering innocent school children solves nothing."

"You thought it did when we first met."

"But I've changed since then."

"I have not. My resolve is stronger than ever. This must be done."

"I don't want to go with you."

"But you are going. We will be three blocks away. I already have our corner picked out."

"Why would we be there?"

"We need to see the destruction. Anyway, I do."

"Please don't make me go."

"Oh, yes. You cannot be trusted now. You are fortunate I have lied to the other men. They would kill you without question if they knew."

"Well, why haven't you reported me? And why haven't you killed me?"

"The truth? I plan to marry you. I am going to take you with me to back to Syria and we will be wed there."

"That isn't going to happen."

"Oh, but it will."

"What if I refuse?"

"Simple. You will be killed. Your friend the lawyer will be killed. Your friend the lawyer's son will be killed. And the little girl. I am serious about this."

"I know you are."

"You will be my wife. You will bear my children."

"I cannot imagine anything worse than having your children."

"Then your imagination is lacking. We can work on that, beginning Monday at ten a.m. You will see something worse, much worse. And you will know how serious I am about you and me."

He then uncoiled the fuse and ran it between all the barrels. Primadet is a flexible detonation cord and he had no trouble wrapping the greater circumference of the rear area of the van and then running a length of the cord in and out of the interior of all bags and barrels.

"Now," he said. "That's it for tonight."

"What about the battery?"

"The battery is upstairs. We will bring it down Tuesday morning when we leave here. Along with the cell phones."

"All right. I'm very tired. Can I go to bed now?"

"You can sleep with me tonight. It will be good preparation for our wedding."

"You said it was impure. You said it was unclean."

"Like you, I have changed. Allah will forgive this one lapse."

He held out his hand.

She closed her eyes and held out her hand.

His grasp was firm and dry.

She allowed herself to be taken back upstairs.

Her eyes remained closed the remainder of the night.

The next morning the mechanic was seen backing the van out of the garage and then driving off.

Across the street the XFBI agents watched as the van departed. The mechanic had brought it there the day before and he was leaving in it now.

Nothing unusual.

A block away Hussein sat up in the back of the van.

"Back to the storage garage."

The mechanic caught his eye in the rearview. "Same place we picked it up?"

"Yes. And drive carefully. Drive carefully."

"Hands at ten and two, both eyes open. Careful as she goes."

"Good."

44

Tuesday

THE DINNER WAS CATERED on Tuesday night. The location was Christine's Conference Room A, where the table itself was covered in linen tablecloths and the caterer had provided three candelabras so neon wasn't necessary.

"Neon wrecks the mood," Christine told the caterer. "I'm looking for soft and soothing. It's been a rough holiday and we're ready to come together and have a good cry. By candlelight."

"First," Christine told her guests, "a Jamie update. He is still in the hospital but out of ICU. He's in a private room and you can stop by and talk to him but he's unconscious and hasn't been responding. Still, who knows? His doctor says the more we talk to him the better the odds are he'll respond. So please, if you get a chance, he knows everyone. Familiar voices are welcome."

"I'll stop by later tonight," said Winona. Her eyes were red from crying. She had spent the day in divorce mediation with Gorman. Just the two of them; no lawyers, and a mediator. She had much to say and was anxious to get it all out. She would get her chance.

"So will I," said Althea. "When I got bailed out of jail I went home to my kiddies. Their dad had been staying with them at my place but he needed to get to work. So I spent the holiday with them, thank God. We played video games and cooked a turkey. Turkey for Labor Day? Hey, it worked for us."

"Sevi won't be here tonight," Christine told them. "Much has happened and there's another update for you."

"Is she okay?" said Althea.

"Tell, tell," said Winona. "We miss our girl."

"Sevi has moved out. Jaime said TRAC was creating a video on her."

"TRAC?"

"New software. It takes video feeds and creates a virtual video of a subject's movements inside the city. So far it's just Chicago."

"God, what a kid," said Winona. "If I'd had a boy--"

"Same here," said Althea. "I make mine spend all their time on science and math. They all have computers and tablets and smart phones. One of them is actually getting interested in how they make software. So who knows? There's still hope."

Salads were served--small dinner salads with piñon nut bits. Everyone opted for the bleu cheese dressing.

"So, Win," said Christine, her salad fork paused, "tell us about the mediation. You get the condo?"

Winona shook her head. "The mediator says we have to split it. Which means I have to sell it. So that little bitch can get her hands on Gorman's half and buy a condo or a boat or a--I don't know."

"It's all right, girl," said Althea, "she'll get what's coming. It's karma."

"Sounds to me like the mediator is trying to push an agenda I don't think your judge would push. Judge Stanton is friendly to the wives. She has to be, since she's been divorced twice herself."

"Where's Ed been?" said Winona. "I was hoping I'd get a chance to bend his ear tonight. He needs to know what they're trying to do."

"Ed's in Ann Arbor, Michigan," said Christine. "His mother's not doing all that well. Or something. He had to run up there and see her. But he'll be back tomorrow. You can see him at work."

They finished their salads and the wait staff cleared the small crystal plates away. Then came the entree: poached salmon, steamed vegetables, and a huge baked potato served with sour cream and chives on the side. Hot rolls appeared with butter and strawberry jam available. Wine glasses were refilled; Christine opted for coffee and ice water with lemon, saying that she was driving--no alcohol for her.

"How goes it with this Ed guy?" asked Althea, who knew Ed well herself. "Is he going to be trainable?"

Everyone laughed.

"The question is, am I going to be able to keep up with him," Christine jokingly lamented. "He certainly knows his way around." There, she'd given them something to mull over. Exactly what the occasion needed.

"What about us?" Althea said to Christine. "We've got a preliminary hearing tomorrow in D.C. What time are we leaving?"

"In ten hours," Christine replied. "But don't worry. We have blankets and pillows and we can make the cabin very dark. Sleep will be possible."

"What are they going to do, exactly?" Althea asked.

"A preliminary hearing is where they put on evidence so the judge can decide whether there's probable cause to continue with the case."

"What's probable cause? We're not going to be put back in jail, are we?"

"No, no, no. The conditions of release are set. I've posted bail for both of us and that will hold until the case is finally adjudicated. Then we'll get the bail back. Assuming it turns out the way I'm pushing for."

"What are you pushing for?"

"I've got a trick or two up my sleeve."

"Such as?"

"Let's just say a little bird perched on the shoulder of the

Chairman of the Senate Judiciary Committee today. A gabby little bird."

"Oh, a mystery!" cried Althea. "I loves me some mysteries."

"Well, a certain document found its way to the Senate. That's all I can say right now."

"That document wouldn't be about the Hellfire attack on Sevi's wedding, would it?"

Christine was caught with a forkful of salmon between plate and mouth.

"My, we're certainly clairvoyant tonight, aren't we?"

Althea smiled. "Let's just say I'm making some good guesses. Am I?"

"I wouldn't deny it," said Christine. "But more will be revealed tomorrow. I just don't want to say too much in case, for some strange reason, I might want to put you on the witness stand. I already know that's not going to happen in a million years, but as the lawyer, I have to keep all options open. So let's drop the subject, can we?"

"As you wish," said Althea. "But now I think I'll be able to sleep tonight. Unlike the last two nights."

"Good. You need your rest."

"Don't we all?" said Winona. She buttered a roll and shook her head. "So what's with Ed and his mother in Ann Arbor? She's in a nursing home?" As she spoke, Win remembered with a slight shiver how Ed had squeezed her hand after their workout. She remained convinced the gesture had been more than simply a friendly squeeze. But she couldn't be sure, and so she was fishing for more. After all, he was human. And if the guy wasn't playing square with Christine, Winona wanted to tip her off.

"That's what I've been told. I don't know much more."

"Seems like he goes up there a lot."

"I can't speak to that," said Christine. "How much is a lot? I certainly don't know about her so I can't judge."

"You're sure he doesn't have someone up there?" asked Winona, ever the cop. "I'd want to check it out."

Christine gave her friend a sharp look. "Does he come across as the kind of guy who would do something like that"

Winona shrugged. She placed her butter knife on her plate.

"Look, Christine, maybe I'm talking about Gorman. Right now I don't trust anything that wears pants and pees standing up."

Christine and Althea laughed. Then Winona joined them. Even a member of the wait staff wore a smile the rest of the night.

"Well said, old girl," said Althea. "Pees standing up. Love it!"

"That could be me," said Winona. "I mean, having to wear this stupid damn bag."

"You're still having the urethra problem?"

"You betcha. Just like always. But you know what hurts? I couldn't go out with a guy now even if I wanted to. Which I don't. But just imagine trying to get him in the sack and having to untangle this piss bag and--"

Christine reached over and patted Winona on the arm. "I know. Let me finish up with this preliminary hearing and get Jamie back home and we'll take a hard look at all that. Maybe another doctor, another approach. I'm even thinking of taking you up to the Mayo Clinic and getting the best there is to look at you."

"That would be wonderful," said Winona through tear-filled eyes. "That would be wonderful. Good. You just gave me hope." She laughed and dabbed at her eyes with her napkin. "Forgive me."

"Unnecessary, girlfriend," said Althea. "That's why we get together. Sometimes we laugh our fool heads off and sometimes we might need to shed a tear or two. That's what friends are for."

"Exactly," said Christine. "Well, all that being said, I have to dash back over to the hospital. Jamie's alone without Ed here. Except for my mom. She's with him but she's old and needs to get back to my place. Dad is home taking his heart meds."

"You're pulling another all-nighter?"

"I am. But we'll meet at Midway at five a.m. We're flying out around five-fifteen, so try to be there on time, Alt."

"Will do," said Althea. "I'll set my alarm and my phone alarm for four. So I guess I'd better move out too."

"Me too," said Winona. "I just need to go home and have a good cry."

"I thought cops didn't cry. But I don't exactly see you as the strong silent type," said Althea, "now that I've got to know you."

"Hey, I'm human just like you," said Winona.

"Aren't we all?"

"Aren't we all? Exactly."

45

T uesday 2

SENATOR JOSEPH ROBERTSON III from Massachusetts ran the Senate Judiciary Committee with an iron fist on Capitol Hill. He was a three-term, no-nonsense Yankee who sailed on weekends and drank two bottles of single-malt during the week--keeping conversations well-oiled so pending legislation and compromises could be pushed through. He was six-two, silver hair worn in a brush over, stylish black eyeglass frames and gray lenses, with a strong jaw and pearly teeth that always seemed to be involved in a friendly smile when the cameras rolled and equally capable of snarling when a recalcitrant colleague needed buttonholing.

Harvard Law, Yale economics, meritorious Air Force service in Bosnia-Serbia during that civil war. Everything about him was coming up roses for the life-affirming New Englander.

He was also forty-four years old and single. His wife of twenty years had passed away from a sudden stroke and Washington's glitziest and most winsome women hadn't yet been able to sweep him away, no matter how hard they tried. Women were off his radar anymore, he told his best friend Sam Sonsuch, his administrative assistant.

Senator Robertson had thus turned to the affairs of state rather than those of the boudoir.

So when he received the courier in his office and opened the packet of documents from the attorney in Chicago, he was immediately offended and smelled blood in the water that he would use. Robertson was a democrat and for far too long the republicans had dumped billions of dollars into the Blackguards of the country with their bottomless funding of American imperialism and war making around the globe. Robertson was a fellow of Bill Gates and would rather see American treasure spent in Zimbabwe helping cure malaria and AIDS than see American treasure poured into the never-ending civil wars in the Middle East. So here, in a packet from Chicago, had arrived the opportunity to embarrass the sons of bitches where they stood. He had caught them, as he was wont to say, with their pants down around their ankles.

For the documents--Blackguard's documents--offered undeniable proof that Blackguard had called in a drone strike on a wedding party without regard to collateral damage in an effort to derail the possible sale of Syrian oil to the Chinese instead of to the Texas oilmen Edlund and Wilfred DuMont.

Now it appeared the Department of Justice was prosecuting the women who had obtained those documents. By whatever means they had obtained it, right or wrong, the senator felt the women should be treated like national heroes, not prosecuted.

A call was placed to the U.S. Attorney in charge of the case. Her name was Racquel MacAdams and she was about to get an earful. Then he was going to call the Attorney General himself and give him a good reaming. It was early that Wednesday morning, but already the day was shaping up beautifully.

Senator Joseph Robertson III always enjoyed a good plate of intrigue and a big bowl of slap down.

Now he had both placed before him, ready to wade into.

46

Wednesday

THEY TOUCHED down at Reagan National Airport and were hurried to a waiting limousine. Christine entered the back seat first, followed by Althea. Althea was just a little groggy, having slept all the way from two hundred miles east of Chicago into Maryland airspace. But she was coming to and adjusted her lipstick in the mirror on the seat-back before her.

Christine poured coffee out of the silver service in the center console.

"Not for me, darling," said Althea. "I want to remain on the planet."

Christine doctored her coffee and took a large mouthful.

"Ah," she exclaimed, "hot and black."

"Don't tell me. Just like you like your men. Am I right?" laughed Althea.

"Hey, you said it. Don't push that off on me, lady."

"So here we are in Washington, home to more white-collar crime than any other sixty-eight square miles on God's green earth."

"You could say that. You could definitely say that. I'm just glad I don't live here."

"You and me both."

Twenty-five minutes later they were dropped off at the U.S. Attorney's office. Passing through building security, Althea read the hand-out:

The United States Attorney's Office for the District of Columbia is unique among U.S. Attorney's Offices in the size and scope of its work. It serves as both the local and the federal prosecutor for the nation's capital. On the local side, these prosecutions extend from misdemeanor drug possession cases to murders. On the federal side, these prosecutions extend from child pornography to gangs to financial fraud to terrorism. In both roles, the Office is committed to being responsive and accountable to the citizens of the District of Columbia.

The Office also enforces the law and defends the interests of the United States in civil suits brought in the district. Its location in the seat of the federal government gives it responsibility for many cases of national importance, including far-reaching challenges to federal policies and employment practices.

Althea snorted and tossed the handout into a trash bin. "I'll just bet you're all that and more," she said to no one.

They passed through the security line, delayed twenty minutes by the huge influx of citizens coming to see justice done in the District of Columbia.

At long last they reached the imposing double doors with gold lettering that said U.S. ATTORNEY DISTRICT OF COLUMBIA.

The two women entered and waited at the counter.

A woman turned to them and Christine stated their business.

The U.S. Attorney was expecting them and they were to be shown right in.

Except it wasn't Racquel MacAdams, who was back in Chicago, explained the man behind the desk.

"I'm Norris Basilone," he told them, and shook their hands. "I'm an Assistant USA and I'll be handling your case from here on out. Obviously the venue has been moved to D.C. I'm sure you understand why, Ms. Susmann."

"So what's the plan for today?" asked Christine. "Is the preliminary hearing still set for ten o'clock?"

Norris Basilone, it turned out, was a man of few words. And he wasted none in bringing them up date.

"We've received a call from Capitol Hill. Apparently someone there has received a document pertaining to our case."

"Oh," said Christine, all innocence. "What's that mean?"

"It means that the Chairman of the Senate Judiciary Committee is looking at the two of you as heroes. God forbid. But that's a whole other matter. Anyway, politics being politics, we've been politely asked--adamantly ordered, actually--to back off all prosecutions until the Senate Judiciary Committee can hold hearings."

"Hearings," said Christine.

"Yes, hearings. Evidently there is an initial impression that a certain government contractor was playing outside the rules when the missile strike against your client was ordered. Something about collateral damage assessment requirements being ignored."

"So my client lost her entire family because someone in the States didn't play by the rules, that's what you're saying?"

"Well, that's the initial impression. Time will tell, of course."

"Where does that leave us with the conspiracy charges?"

The USA removed his glasses and spun them by the stem. "Yes, yes. Well. As you're definitely aware, prosecutions happen when the interests of the public are brought into play."

"Yes."

"The initial thinking here--just initial, mind you--is that more needs to be known about the underlying facts before the overlying facts--your facts--are hauled into court."

"So maybe we stole documents, is what you're saying, but maybe public policy is going to end up saying we did the right thing when we did it. Kind of like Ed Snowden?"

The USA scowled. "Definitely not like Edward Snowden. That's a whole other can--well, let's not go there since that's still perhaps an active prosecution. Investigation, at least."

"So what about our case? Will it be dismissed? Held in abeyance? You and I both know the Federal Rules of Criminal Procedure guarantee us a preliminary hearing within certain time limits."

"It's my case now. My initial inclination is to dismiss the case without prejudice."

"Without prejudice means the case could be refiled," Christine told Althea.

"Oh. That's not right."

"I agree. I don't think we want to agree to that. If it's dismissed it should be with prejudice. Neither of us wants to go through this again."

"Really, I'm up against it. If you don't agree--"

"If we don't agree, then we go to our preliminary hearing, which calls down the fires of hell on you from the Judiciary Committee now that you've been told to back off. Looks to me like you have no choice but to dismiss with prejudice."

"I'll dismiss with prejudice. Is there anything else?" His demeanor had turned glum. Christine saw it was time to gracefully and graciously back off.

"I can't thank you enough for your forthrightness and willingness to allow justice to be done, Mr. Basilone."

Which perked him up just a hair.

"Well...we do our best."

"I know you do."

They shook hands.

"Oh, before I forget," said Basilone. "Senator Robertson has asked that you stop by. He'd like to brief you on his upcoming hearings."

"I'll make arrangements," Christine said. "It won't be today, but I'll swing back soon. Please give him my regards, tell him my son is in the hospital, and that I'll be in touch soon."

"Will do," USA Basilone said with a warm smile. "And sorry to make you come all the way back here. You were in the air when I got the order--the news."

"Not to worry."

Neither woman burst into gleeful laughing until they were alone on the elevator.

The plane ride home included a glass of champagne and okra fried with crookneck squash, don't spare the ground pepper--one of Althea's favorites. Christine felt like she owed her friend for what she had put her through. So the summer treat was a peace offering.

Althea had earned no less.

47

Thursday 1

JAMIE'S CONDITION remained unchanged by Thursday morning. It had now been five days since the last CT scan had shown no change. Christine was panicked.

"I cannot tell you how hard this is to watch your child languish in a hospital bed," she tearfully told Ed by phone. He had called the room to check in and see if there was any change.

"I don't have children so I can only imagine," he said. "It must be horrible."

"I just feel so helpless. He lies there and doesn't move. He doesn't swallow, doesn't blink, and doesn't respond to my touch. They come in and suction him every half hour and he doesn't flinch. Nothing affects him. Nothing."

"Are you eating anything?"

"No. My mom is coming at noon and I can run downstairs and eat then."

"Maybe I'll come join you."

"That would be wonderful. It would be good to see you, Ed. I have missed our times together."

"Me too."

"And how is your mom? Are you going to Ann Arbor this weekend to see her?"

"Probably. It depends on whether there's any change with Jamie. And on whether you need me or not."

"I always need you. Don't ever think otherwise. Uh-oh, they're here now. They're going to do another CT scan and draw blood. Call me back before you leave the office, okay?"

"You've got it."

She hung up and stood to the side while they moved Jamie out of the room and down to radiology. She wasn't allowed along, so she sat back down in the comfortable visitors' chair where she had been spending her nights all week. She had to admit the hospital was thoughtful in that regard: the chair fully reclined and provided a comfortable footrest. Staff appeared with blanket and pillow in the evening so she could be made as comfortable as possible while she kept her vigil at her son's side. She had no complaints.

As she sat staring at nothing, a thought occurred.

She lifted the receiver on the room phone and pressed 0.

"How do I get an outside line?"

"Dial nine."

"And information?"

"I'll transfer you. Local or other."

"Ann Arbor, Michigan."

"Wait one."

The line went silent then beeped three times over a space of perhaps thirty seconds. Then a female voice answered.

"City and state, please."

"Ann Arbor, Michigan."

"What listing?"

"For Edward Mitchell."

"On Holtzman Way?"

"Yes."

She had no clue; she just decided to try the first one given.

"I can dial that for you."

"Please."

The phone began ringing. Then a girl's voice came on.

"Mitchell residence."

"Hello, is your dad there?"

"Nope."

"Is his name Ed?"

"Yep."

"Where does he work?"

"Chicago."

"Is your dad a lawyer?"

"Mom, it's for you!"

"Wait, please. Is your daddy a lawyer?"

"Yep."

She pressed the end call button.

Her hand shook as she replaced the receiver.

So. New information. She sat back in the chair and closed her eyes.

Now what? She asked herself.

Now exactly what?

48
———

T hursday 2

THE DOCUMENTS WEREN'T FORTHCOMING. So the DuMonts went behind the curtain and pulled strings.

Randall C. Maxwelle, the Naval Academy graduate and navy commander (retired), who headed up Blackguard's military-commercial liaison team, would occasionally task an ex-special forces officer to resolve domestic problems. His name was Alduous McIlhenny and he was from Rockland, New Jersey, just twenty miles west of the George Washington Bridge. Maxwelle made arrangements to meet McIlhenny at Battery Park outside the Ellis Island ferry docks. There was an eatery there, Maxwelle told the Special Forces man, where fried clams were served with large glasses of iced tea in the summertime. They would meet and talk.

Alduous McIlhenny was a survivor of Iraq and Afghanistan, two tours each. He had been discharged from the Army medically and Blackguard had immediately offered him a position. Officially his designation was Logistics Manager II, but his real work involved public relations that were neither public nor relational. In point of fact he was a shootist, an artist with small arms, whose sudden and blind attacks on unsuspecting corporate officers in competition with Blackguard were well known.

McIlhenny was short--five-four--but built like a small bull with huge, muscled shoulders and legs and back that could jerk lift four hundred pounds without a drop of sweat. Multiple times. He was a Sentinel Military Academy graduate with honors and remembered fondly by his teachers there as "a little guy with huge potential."

McIlhenny entered Battery Park from the east side and walked to his meet with Maxwelle. Along the way he bought a Styrofoam cup of black coffee and stood--his back against the counter, surveying the faces around him--while his cup was filled. Satisfied he wasn't being watched, he closed the final one hundred yards to the outside table and sat down across from the ex-navy commander.

"Mac," said Maxwelle, "thanks for coming."

McIlhenny turned the Styrofoam cup and took a sip out of the opposite side. "You pay me for it. What can I do for you, Mr. Maxwelle?"

"Randall, please."

"All right. What can I do for you, Randall?"

"There's a young man in Chicago. We want to exchange him for some documents."

"Can do. Who and where?"

"Well, the where part is difficult. We've received word he was wounded by the FBI and is now at the UC Hospital."

"How serious?"

"He hasn't regained consciousness."

"Well, what the hell? What do you want me to do, carry him out?"

"That's exactly what we want you to do. We've looked it over. His health won't be severely compromised if he's removed from the hospital. Besides, it likely will be only for an hour or two while we get what we want from his mother."

"What is it you want?"

"Mama has documents. She stole them from us. We want them back."

"Why not just call in the cops?"

"The FBI has the case. In typical FBI-fashion they're playing by the rules and so far haven't managed to do jackshit. We need some muscle."

"Let me see if I have this. You're telling me I should go to the hospital and carry a patient out. Kidnap a patient. Where was he shot?"

"In the head. There are drainage tubes attached but even that's not critical now."

"How do I sneak him out of the hospital?"

"That depends on your imagination. Maybe a wheelchair, maybe wrapped in something, maybe in one of those waste carts they push up and down hospital floors. We leave the details up to you. You've never let us down."

"There have been close calls. I don't have to remind you. Randall."

"Yes, there have been. But the brothers believe in you. I believe in you."

"How much?"

"Fifty. Plus expenses, of course."

"Of course."

"You will take him to an address we'll give you. You will hold him there until we have what we want. Follow me?"

"Yes. Can you give me part now?"

"Yes. Twenty-five now, twenty-five when we're done."

"What if he dies? Do I still get paid?"

"Of course. You've done your job. It isn't your fault if he dies. We'd only ask that you leave his body off."

"Where?"

"Any convenient alley will do. You know the drill on fingerprints and DNA. None of that. So dress appropriately."

"You're talking scrubs and hair net."

"I'm talking scrubs and surgical cap like the docs wear. Get yourself an ID badge and you'll fit right in."

"I think I'm seeing how this just might work."

"Of course it will work. Doctor."

"I'm helping transfer a patient. I'm using a wheelchair. I steal a transport van and load him in. With the help of an orderly or two."

"Now we're talking. See how easy it was?"

McIlhenny scowled. "Brother, all we've done so far is talk. Leave the twenty-five on the table and leave the park. Now."

Maxwelle pulled a fat pack of Benjamins from his pants pocket and plopped it down. Without another word, he then turned and left the park.

McIlhenny waited behind. Fried clams sounded like just what the doctor ordered.

Dr. McIlhenny, that's who.

He smiled and pocketed the fat envelope.

Six hours later he woke up a thousand feet off the O'Hare runway when the cabin lights blinked on with a tone, indicating seat belts should be fastened for landing.

Groggy, he looked out his window. Raindrops blew past at 180 knots.

Ninety minutes later he pulled the American United Healthcare transport van into the queue of transport vehicles alongside UCH's west side loading zone.

Simple.

He slipped inside, found laundry services, and helped himself to a doctor's outfit: scrubs, footies, and cap. Hospital green. The ID badge was one he had found inside the stolen transport van. Someone had conveniently left it dangling from the rearview mirror. It wasn't UCH-issue, of course, but what the hell? Who was ever checking these things anyway?

A friendly orderly directed him to the trauma center's ICU. He knew he would find his boy there.

Jamie Susmann, said the inked words on the palm of his left hand.

"Susmann," he whispered to himself as he rode the up elevator.

It was almost midnight but the place was crawling with attendants and nurses when McIlhenny made it to the Sixth Floor. He decided to wait several hours until the crowd died down.

It was a simple matter, finding a physicians' break room to lie down and catch some shuteye. He would need to be sharp.

What of his transport van? he thought.

He went to the phone on the desk and buzzed Security. He explained his situation. They agreed to watch the transport van. No one would touch it; no one would move it.

McIlhenny laid down and closed his eyes.

He was out two minutes later, but not before setting his watch alarm for seven a.m.

49

F riday

IT WAS eight o'clock Friday morning and Christine still wouldn't leave Jamie's side.

Neither did she want to confront Ed about her call to Ann Arbor. At least not yet, not while the office was underwater and she had no other attorney to call on for help. It had occurred to her more than once that she might call on Thaddeus Murfee, who had already stopped by twice to check on mother and son. But not yet.

Ed brought coffee. Then he brought a chicken salad sandwich. An hour later he brought coffee again. In the interim he went outside by the parking lot and managed several pressing legal cases by cell phone. Christine's calendar would have to be cleared for the week, and Ed was already on it.

The office was fully staffed due to Christine's emergency and would continue to be, 24/7, until some resolution was reached. Secretaries were given orders, Billy A. Tattinger--Christine's key paralegal--

was notified, and the wheels were put in motion. The law firm was busy and the attorneys' calendars were packed. It was reminiscent of a small military maneuver to clear a week's worth of court hearings, depositions, client appointments, and re-set case contacts to a later date. But Ed was all over it. Then he would return to Christine, they would speak again while she held Jamie's hand, then he would return to the sidewalk where he would issue more orders and directives to staff.

He returned a third time with a perplexed, frustrated look on his face.

"It's the District Attorney. I've got her home phone. She won't agree to a continuance of Monday's preliminary hearing in State versus Brewster."

"Let me call her," said Christine. "Wait here with Jamie."

"Roger."

Christine found her own cell phone and headed downstairs.

Outside on the sidewalk, she punched in the District Attorney's number and waited to be put through.

"Regarding what?" came the female voice.

"Regarding my case. This is Christine Susmann. I'm the lawyer."

"Why are you people calling me at home? And this early! Seriously?"

UPSTAIRS IN JAMIE'S room a radiology tech came for him.

"CT scan," the tech told Ed. "You'll need to wait here."

Ed nodded. "Will do. I'll tell his mom you'll be back in how long?"

"Thirty minutes, give or take. The scanner is free now."

"Roger that. Thanks."

Ed sat back in the hospital room chair--overstuffed for sleeping-- and reclined. He pulled his smart phone from his shirt pocket and opened iBooks, where he began reading the latest thriller. Soon his eyes grew heavy. He'd been up all night and was tired. He dozed off.

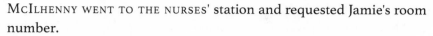

McIlhenny went to the nurses' station and requested Jamie's room number.

"Thank you, doctor," the charge nurse said to the man in green scrubs. "Are you here for a procedure?"

"I need to examine him. ASAP. Where is he now?"

"They just took him to radio. CT scan."

"Which way is that?"

"Follow the black footprints. Take you right there."

McIlhenny found the CT scan suite and walked by the desk operator.

"Doctor?" she called after him. "Doctor?"

He ignored her and opened the door to the scanner room. As he did, the patient was being inserted into the circular ring by means of the sliding table.

"Put that patient back on the gurney immediately," McIlhenny ordered the two orderlies who were assisting. "He's being transferred STAT!"

The orderlies looked at each, shrugged, and withdrew Jamie from the CT ring. He was unceremoniously plopped back onto the gurney he had come in on. The orderlies wheeled him out, following McIlhenny's instruction.

McIlhenny stopped the orderlies in the hospital hallway.

"Gentlemen, this is my patient and I need help loading him for transfer."

"Where to?" asked the redheaded orderly.

"We need orders," said the black orderly. "I don't see no orders."

"Sir," said McIlhenny, "do you question all the physicians who request help with their patients?"

"No, sir. I'm just saying."

"Well please step on it. We're taking him back to the elevator. Hurry!"

"We can go as far as the elevator," said the redheaded orderly. "But we're assigned to Sixth Floor. We can't leave here."

"Fine. Just get him on the elevator. I'll get help downstairs."

They wheeled Jamie onto the elevator and watched the door close behind McIlhenny.

"Asshole. I hate every one of them."

"Me three."

RETURNING from her most recent sidewalk phone call, Christine was shocked to see Jamie on the gurney when her elevator door opened on the ground floor.

"What?" she said to the man in green scrubs.

"My patient," said McIlhenny. "Move back, please!"

"My son!" said Christine and she pushed back against the gurney McIlhenny was trying to force by her.

"What the hell, lady? I'm a doctor and I'm transferring my patient!"

"Oh, then," said Christine, "excuse me."

She stepped aside and allowed the man in the green scrubs to pass by with her son. Then, when his back was to her, she hammered the side of his head with a sweeping kick. She was wearing hiking boots and the blow staggered the man, dropping him to his knees, where she could kick at him again, knocking him face down onto the floor.

Security came running.

"This man is impersonating a doctor!" she cried, and pushed Jamie's gurney back onto the elevator. "Arrest him and send someone to help me with my son!"

The door closed behind her and she was suddenly moving on an up elevator to the Sixth Floor.

When the doors opened again, the same two orderlies as before were waiting to help.

They took over the gurney and quickly moved Jamie back into his room. Ed was waiting there.

"What? What happened?" he asked.

"Did you even bother to stay with him?" Christine cried.

"The radiology tech said I should wait here, Chris! They wouldn't let me in there."

"Dial Security, Ed. We need detectives from CPD and we need protection for Jamie. I think I know who just tried to kidnap him."

"Blackguard."

"Certainly. They want their records back. They thought Jamie would make a quick trade."

"Assholes!"

"Ed, think about it. They were going to jeopardize Jamie's life for a bunch of paper."

"It's more than that, Chris. Your documents hold the key to freedom or prison for them. Calm down and think about that."

"I don't know how I've been so blind. Of course they would try something."

She stabbed in the number for XFBI, her security service.

"Gerald, is Janny okay? Everything at home okay?"

"Yeah, Chris. What's up?"

"Double down today. More boots on the ground. Blackguard just made a play for Jamie. I'm worried for Janny. And my parents."

"I'm inside your house now, in my office," Gerald said. "It's quiet here."

"Well, double-down anyway. That's an order."

"Yes, ma'am."

"Keep everyone out today. Trust no one."

"Yes, ma'am."

"And get a second crew on the perimeter immediately as well. I'm bringing Jamie home and I want it safe."

"Should I send someone to the hospital?"

"Yes. No. Ed's arranging for a transport service right now." She covered the phone. "Ed?"

Ed waved. "I'm on it."

"Gerry, we'll be arriving in about two hours. Watch for us."

"Roger that, Chris. I'm all over it."

She clicked off.

"We're outta here," she told Ed.

He held up one finger. "On the line with Hartz Medical Transport. They're sending a crew."

"Excellent. The sooner the better."

"Okay," said Ed. "While you were downstairs they called about my mom.""You have to go to Ann Arbor. Right?"

"Yes. And I'm sorry. But she needs me."

"Of course she does."

"We each have a sick one to care for this weekend."

"Sure we do. It's tough on both of us."

"Goodbye Chris," he said, and leaned to kiss her.

She pulled back.

"What?" he said and held out his hands. She took another step back.

"Not now, Ed. We'll talk."

50

S unday

ED MITCHELL and a young woman entered the First Methodist Church of Ann Arbor for the 9 a.m. service. Accompanying them were three young girls, ranging in age from three to seven. All three were dressed alike and even similarly to the young woman. Pastels and hair ribbons were the order of the day. The three-year-old was taken to the end of the hall outside the entrance to the sanctuary and deposited in daycare where she would remain for the next hour or so. The five-year-old and seven-year-old accompanied the two adults into the church.

The procession journeyed to the front of the church, second pew, right hand side, where, young woman first, they slid in. The five-year-old, then the seven-year-old and then Ed himself followed the young woman. The two girls immediately pulled hymnals from the wooden pouches screwed to the back of the first pew before them. They then took deposit envelopes from the same pouch, short wooden pencils, and began writing and drawing on the envelopes. Ed Mitchell seemed to be praying, as he sat with his eyes closed, lips moving, a look of deep reverence on his face. At the other end of the small group, the young woman plucked a compact from her straw purse and checked her makeup--eyes, forehead, nose, cheeks, and then quickly smiled and checked her teeth. A daub of lipstick was applied with a brush and spread evenly across her lips.

Slowly the sanctuary filled up behind them as parishioners found their usual seats--unreserved except by common assent, as everyone had a favorite location in the church. Then a white-robed choir filed into the choir benches and a first chord from a piano was struck, sending the pitch of the first note fluttering across the still air.

A hymn erupted as the choir began singing about clouds of gold, mighty horses in the sky, and strong hearts committed to a heavenly army. Visions and images were called down and hearts soared among the congregants as the timeworn hymn launched the traditional service.

As the last notes died away, Reverend Helen Paulsen emerged from offstage and took her place behind the pulpit. She raised her arms to indicate the attendees should remain standing while she prayed. Which she did. Ninety seconds later the prayer ended with a bold "Amen!" and "In Jesus' name!" and the reverend indicated all should sit. Which, with a sigh of relief, they did. Launching into a twenty-minute sermon, the reverend reminded the congregation what mankind had experienced on 9/11/2001. She spoke of the creation of a country designed to accept those who were persecuted for their beliefs elsewhere. A safe nation where people could worship, as they believed. And she spoke of forgiveness, and the redemptive powers of the shed blood. Ten minutes into the oratory, chins were dropping onto chests, eyes were fluttering and closing, and the five- and seven-year-old were fighting below the surface of the pew to see which of them would have both handouts they had received upon entering the sanctuary. The object was to control them both and the silent dispute raged until the young woman boldly reached between them and jerked away both handouts. The five year old's bottom lip projected in a flat line and tears coursed through her eyes as she wept silently, her hands palm down on the plank beneath her as she struggled to remain silent. On her right her sister glared at her mother and soundlessly moved her lips. To the casual observer it looked like she might have said, "Dumb damn bitch," or "Why did you do that?"--one couldn't be sure exactly what the words were. Maybe she even said both phrases, thought an old man with white hair and an ebony cane with a brass handle. A small smile flitted across his face as he agreed with the daughter. The woman was a dumb damn bitch for ruining their fun. Why did she have to go and do that?

Ignoring all this and straining to remain engrossed in the sermon, Ed Mitchell twiddled his left thumb against his left ring finger. There was a gold band there--a wedding band--that his probing thumb obviously found stimulating by its presence. Clearly, said the thumb, he wasn't accustomed to having the ring there and anyway it was bothersome.

As for Ed, it took great effort to remember when the ring and when not the ring. In Ann Arbor, Michigan, the ring appeared. In Chicago, Illinois, the ring went unseen.

At the end of the sermon there was another prayer, an out-loud reading and response, two more hymns about this redemption and that blessed re-birth, a rousing rendition of "God Bless America" and a fond farewell from the reverend. Plus there was a "drive safely on the way home."

"Dismissed," said the reverend, who then hurried back up the sanctuary's center aisle so she could arrange herself at the sanctuary entrance and begin shaking hands as her flock swept outside and away.

The young woman retrieved the three-year-old. She rejoined the others. First in but last out came Ed and the four females.

"Mr. and Mrs. Mitchell," said the reverend. "Thank you for coming."

"We'd be here more often, but Ed spends so much time in Chicago anymore," explained the woman called Mrs. Mitchell.

Ed, for his part, nodded shyly at the young woman.

Yes, he indicated, it was true. He was away an awful lot and yes, they would be seen around the church many more Sundays if his work weren't so demanding.

"Well, you take care, Ed and Genevieve. And you darling girls, don't you look breathtaking today?"

Said the middle girl, "We're going to Chuck E. Cheese. Finally!"

"Ed, honey," said the young woman, "Why don't you bring around the car and I'll wait with the girls. I'm afraid we'll lose someone if we try walking through all the traffic in the lot."

Ed had to admit, there was a lot of traffic that morning.

The young woman leaned and kissed him quickly on the cheek as he nodded and moved away.

"Daddy," cried the three-year-old. "Daddy, we love you!"

Without turning around, Ed nodded.

He was loved, that much he was sure about.

He was definitely loved.

When he was pulling out of the lot with his family, Ed might have noticed the Nissan behind him. Its license plates were Illinois and its driver wore sunglasses and a ball cap pulled snug over his head.

The man nodded to himself and picked up his cell phone.

"Christine?"

"Go ahead, Andrus."

"Wife and daughters, three cute little girls."

"Did they arrive together at church?"

"Yes."

"Did they leave together?"

"Yes."

"Are you following them now?"

"Yes. We're headed back to where I fell in behind them this morning."

"At the lake front home?"

"Yes."

"Where he evidently stayed overnight?"

"I'm sorry, Christine. Yes, he stayed overnight there. He's been there all weekend. He's come and gone with the girls. He's barbecued outside for them. He and the wife went out Saturday night."

"Went where?"

"Dinner and dancing. Restaurant called The Flame.

"And you personally witnessed them dancing together."

"Chris, I wasn't three feet from them. They danced right past my table."

"Okay."

"I'm sorry."

"Okay. Come home. You're finished."

"So is he?"

"So is he."

51

M onday 7 A.M

ON MONDAY MORNING the buses loaded up and moved out. Headed for Windsor School in one bus was a collection of just under fifty grade school students.

It was 7:10 a.m.

Samantha Evans was ten years old, taller than all the boys in her fourth grade class, a girl who rescued guinea pigs from laboratories, and loved doing art on her Nintendo Pokémon Art Academy. She thought biology class wonderful and played center front on her grade's champion volleyball team because of her height. Samantha's long blonde hair was most often arranged into two tight pigtails that bounced on her shoulders whenever she leapt to spike the ball or ran from the school bus to the classrooms where most mornings she arrived just after the final bell, thanks to "our dopey bus driver." The girl's report card was usually filled with two's and three's--average and a bit above--and the social comments indicated she was quite a handful in class, never cowed from arguing with anyone, including her homeroom teacher.

Her mother and father were teachers at her school. Jameson Evans, her father, taught physical education; Madison Evans, her mother, taught math and science. Thus the threesome spent their days together--yet apart--at Windsor School District's Elementary School Number 9. The school was a unified school in the northern end of Cook County where the rolling hills had lured Hussein with their promise of a reflected bomb blast.

On Monday, September 14, Samantha carried her Pet Taxi with her onto the school bus. Loaded inside with hay and a small water bottle were Gus and Andy, two guinea pig boars who, in the pink of life, weighed in excess of a pound each, and who wheeked nosily when Samantha stuck lettuce through the door of the small cage as the bus bounced along. The extra lettuce was a thoughtful inclusion from her mother, a welcome addition to the lunch Samantha carried in her backpack.

"It's Show and Tell in Miss Maroney's class today," Samantha told her seatmate and best friend Aine Rautherson. "So I brought Gus and Andy. I'm going to show how they know their names. Plus they know tricks."

Aine poked her finger through the door. Gus immediately ambled up to the door to investigate and nibbled curiously at the digit. Aine shrieked and jerked her hand away. "He bit me!" she cried.

"Don't be stupid," said Samantha. "He was only tasting you. Guinea pigs don't bite but they do taste when they think it's food. Next time ask me before you stick your finger in."

"What tricks do they know?"

"Oh, you'll see. They're a-ma-zing!"

"Oh, I'm sure. Now I'm going to feel stupid showing how to make a cake. Guinea pigs are a thousand times better to show off."

"Hey, do you get to cook the cake?"

"Your mom said she'd help me get it cooked in the cafeteria. It only takes a half hour. So if I go before you I can take my cake over there and have it back before class ends. Cool?"

"Yeah, cool."

Two seats forward on the bus sat Rashad Nidal, a Muslim student born and raised in Chicago. He was thirteen years old and a seventh grader and a huge fan of World Soccer. He frequently played soccer and was often the fastest kid on the field. Rashad--Rash, to his buddies--had grown up without a father and his closest adult male influence was Jameson Evans, Samantha's father. Mr. Evans had promised Rash that if he trained hard and studied hard he would one day be good enough to play for the Chicago Fire. He said Rash would get a chance to tryout his junior year because Mr. Evans knew the Fire coach. Rash sat facing forward, his knees close together, balancing a ball on his lap. He spun the ball in his hands as the bus accelerated and decelerated, always mindful that it must be kept moving all the way to school so he got in a full workout in ball handling. A goalie, Rash was the only player on his entire team to ever actually touch the ball with a hand during the games, and he was working hard to get all the hand-eye workout time he could manage.

Next to Rash was Jimmy L. Johnson, a classmate of Rash's whose glory in life was the trumpet. Jimmy blew high and blew low and he played "Lady of Spain" during the school's talent contest and came in second. Balanced on Jimmy's lap was his trumpet case, complete with a bumper sticker that said Obama-Biden 2008. Jimmy regretted defacing his trumpet case with anything--his regret wasn't political-- and he had tried many times to peel away the sticker but it had embedded itself in the pebble grain of the cowhide cover. So Jimmy L. Johnson rode along tapping the fingers of his right hand against the trumpet case as he closed his eyes and practiced several songs he was going to tryout with at this year's contest. At those moments, hearing music with his eyes closed, regret was the farthest thing from his mind. Like Rash, Jimmy's goal was to one day go pro too. Only he wanted to play for Chicago, the rock band.

There were forty-eight other kids on the bus that day, most of them similar in likes, hopes, and dreams to Samantha, Aine, Rash, and Jimmy.

The last thing any of them expected was to die before their next birthday.

But then they didn't know about the white van that would seek them out.

No one did.

52

M onday 9 A.M.

HE BACKED the van out of the storage garage. Sevi was riding in the front seat, both hands pressed up against the headliner to her right.

He pulled into traffic on Washington Street and headed northwest.

There was no parking in front of Windsor School so Hussein considered his options. A suggestion from one of the cell members had stuck with him.

As he passed a telephone company truck with its orange cones and pedestrian guard, he decided to give it a try.

He pulled over, stole up to the phone company truck, and removed eight orange warning cones from its bed. Quickly he laid these in the back of the van.

Sevi turned to see what he was doing in the back, but her head wouldn't swivel that far. She was handcuffed to the passenger seat panic bar. Both hands were cuffed and pressed above the window glass. She was all but immobilized.

"What will we do?" she asked Hussein when he returned to the driver's seat and they were again moving with traffic.

"We? I will park the van. You will wait in the van."

"Wait in the van? With you?"

He smiled into the rearview mirror. "Time will tell, dear Sevi. Please try to be patient."

In the console between them were two unregistered cell phones. "Burners," he had told her when he brought them home. One of them would remain behind in the van, wired to a twelve-volt battery. The other would accompany the twosome when they left the scene some ten minutes before the bomb would detonate and level the school.

Traffic was heavy and Hussein was extremely alert. They were riding on enough explosive to propel a moon shot, as she had heard him tell someone on the phone that morning. He maneuvered through downtown Chicago, keeping as far from other vehicles as possible. It was difficult. Soon the usual honking and tailgating and cutting in and out by taxicabs was overrunning the private automobiles and trucks that were frantically trying to find a parking spot or simply trying to escape the downtown and get back out to the freeway they wished they'd never left.

At the Circle Interchange they waited four lights to cross back and head westbound on the Kennedy. Traffic was a snarl all the way and they found themselves stopping and starting, starting and stopping. Hussein became frustrated and pounded the steering wheel at one point. Sevi watched traffic flowing around a stalled vehicle in the third lane. "Poor guy," she said as they managed to cut into the right lane and pull around. Hussein merely shook his head.

"Abu will pick us up two hundred meters east of Windsor School," Hussein announced. "You will call him when I say. He is speed dial one. Under no circumstances are you to make any other calls on the phone. If you do, you run the risk of blowing us all up by setting off the cell on the battery. Do you understand me?"

"Yes."

"Say it!"

"Abu is speed dial one. I am to make no other calls. Who would I call anyway? I know no one in Chicago. Or even in America. It's ridiculous, what you tell me."

He raised his hand as if to backhand her and she winced. It wouldn't have been the first time he had hit her, if one could judge by her response. Then he slowly lowered his hand, shaking his head.

"It is that mouth that I have come to despise. You are venom, woman."

"Please, I'm only trying to help us do this and get away."

He looked across at her for one second. "I thought you wanted us to abort. You have changed your mind?"

"I think only of my family, gone. And I think the infidels must be stopped."

Four miles west they took their exit and rolled down the ramp in the right lane. Waiting no more than ten seconds, they turned right.

It was 9:20 a.m.

Windsor School was less than a mile down a heavily congested road.

53

M onday 9 A.M

IT WAS ONLY FITTING that his little sister would play the music so loud and so many times that he literally had to wake up to make it stop.

It was so.

During the tenth evolution of the *Veggie Tales: Minnesota Cuke and the Search for Samson's Hairbrush* he had evidently had all he could stand.

At least, that's how they would tell it later, when everyone was older and more settled.

His hospital bed was in the family room, where he was guaranteed the most stimulation. Janny had replayed her video into the tenth opening credits when--

He opened his eyes.

Opened his eyes and moved his head to the side.

"Son ob bitch shot me," he muttered.

"Mommy!" shrieked Janny. "Jamie's swearing!"

The home health nurse leapt to her feet and went to his bedside.

"There, there, just relax," the nurse was saying in her most soothing voice. "We're all here with you and everything is going to be fine."

"Son ob bitch shot me!"

Christine ran into the room.

"He did shoot you, Jamie. But you're going to be okay," his mother said. Waves of relief washed over her body and through her mind and touched her soul. She had been dreading--oh, how she'd been dreading! After all, she felt one hundred percent responsible for the shooting. If she hadn't hidden documents, if the FBI hadn't--

She stopped herself. That all could wait.

For now, there was Jamie.

"Mom, can I please have some water?" he said, and he simultaneously drew his finger across the angry suture site on his face. "Ow!"

The nurse was already inserting the straw between his lips and pulling his shoulders more upright. "Drink, please."

"Jamie, you're swearing," said Janny.

"Janny, please turn that video off," said Christine. "We need to talk to Jamie right now."

"Crap. It's always about Jamie!"

The little girl stalked from the room, carrying her iPad and scuffing her shoes as she went.

"How is your vision, honey?" said Christine. "Do you see all right?"

"Mom, I see fine. What's this thing?" he asked, and weakly pulled the sheet aside. "They've got a tube in my dick!"

"It's a catheter," said the nurse. "If you're feeling better I can take it out. But for now let's just wait a little while. That okay?"

"Okay. More water, please."

Additional water was administered through the straw.

Jamie pushed himself up on his pillows.

"Oh my God," he said. "Sevi!"

"What about Sevi, honey?" said Christine. "We don't need to talk about all that. I've got it all under control."

"No! They have Sevi and we need to find her! What day is it?"

"Monday."

"How long have I been out?"

"Just over a week."

"Have you heard from Sevi?"

"No."

"Have you tried to find her?"

"Yes. No. We've all been focused on you, Jamie. You came first."

"Quick, mom, bring me my laptop."

"The FBI took your laptop."

"Then bring me your laptop. Please!"

Christine retrieved her laptop and placed it on Jamie's crossed legs.

"Look, my site's still up."

He browsed Chrome to his website and searched on Sevi's picture. The uploaded videos were scanned, then--

"Look here! She's in a room of some kind and they're putting big drums in the back of that van. What the hell?"

Christine leaned across his shoulder. "Run that again, please."

Jamie replayed the sequence.

"I can't see exactly what he's doing, but those bags are ammonium nitrate. Oh my God," said Christine. "OKC."

"What's OKC?"

"That's what they used in the OKC bomb! Ammonium nitrate! We have to find that van immediately."

Christine got on line with XFBI, who got on line with Chicago Police and Illinois State Police. They had a license number--thanks to Jamie's video--and within ten minutes several thousand eyes of Chicago's finest were looking for the van.

But eyes alone weren't enough. It was going to take more.

Jamie's TRAC software continued its search. He changed the parameters of the search to look not for Sevi but for the van. Immediately there were hits--lots of hits. The van on the Kennedy Expressway, the van westbound, the van taking the off-ramp, the van approaching Windsor Elementary School.

Outside CCTV had it all the way.

Jamie threw up a live shot of the van.

Outside the school.

Parked within eight orange road cones, it appeared the van's occupant was working on a fire hydrant nearby. He had a wrench and he was bent to his work.

Jamie froze the man's face and enlarged the shot.

"Mom, look at this!"

She looked once and a chill shot up her spine.

"Hussein. That's Hussein. And the van. Surely that's Sevi in the passenger seat, too."

"Gerry," Christine said to the XFBI agent in the doorway. "Windsor Elementary. Approach with great care. It's a bomb. A huge bomb!"

Gerry nodded and left without a word. He had a direct line to the authorities and he used it.

Within minutes the CPD's bomb disposal unit was underway on the Kennedy.

54

M onday 9:55 A.M

HUSSEIN BENT to the fire hydrant and carefully surveyed his surroundings. Abu would be circling a block away. Hussein nodded to Sevi. Still cuffed to the panic bar, she pressed speed dial on the phone between her palms.

"Hussein says now."

A voice came back. "We're one block east. We'll begin to close right now."

"What are you driving?"

"Red Volvo. Wagon."

"I can see you now. You just came around our corner. Wait. Go back, there are police on the way!"

"Police?" said the voice. "We see no police. There are no sirens. What are you saying, woman?"

Sevi screamed into the phone. "Get away! Now! Now! Go!"

She watched as the Volvo Wagon spun a U-turn and disappeared back the way it had come.

At just that moment, Hussein came into the driver's seat.

"The phone. Give me the phone."

"No."

He reached and backhanded her across the face. Her nose spurted blood. But still she kept her grip on the phone.

"You are not going to hurt these little kids! I won't allow it!"

"Woman, the phone!"

He reached across and jerked it away from her. He immediately hit speed dial one.

"Abu? What the hell, man? Where did you go?"

"The woman. She said the police were there!"

"There are no police here. Return at once."

"You're sure?"

And at that moment the first of dozens of police vehicles squealed off the highway and came rolling up the street at high speed.

Hussein had the ingredients wired with Primadet and had added the Tovex explosive at indicated points in the back of the van. It was ready to explode.

All except for one thing. Hussein wasn't ready to explode with it. He didn't give a damn if Sevi went up with it, but he wasn't going to.

He calmly and matter-of-factly began walking away on the sidewalk, his finger poised on speed dial two. One click of the finger and the entire school and student body would be leveled. Gone, dust.

But Jamie had been busy. He had cropped Hussein's face out of the video feeds and now all CPD cars and officers had a picture of the prime suspect. Hussein, of course, wasn't aware of this. He simply kept walking.

The bomb disposal unit rolled up, jumped out headed for the van, took a look inside, and carefully detached the switch from the phone. "No spark, no boom," said Sergeant Davis.

"No spark, no boom," said his partner, Helene Montgomery.

Both were Iraq war veterans of IUD disposal warfare. The fertilizer bomb was overwhelmingly simple for them.

Within seconds its fangs were pulled.

Minutes later, Hussein was facedown on the sidewalk, hands yanked into the air and cuffs wrapping him up. Sevi was freed and removed from the front seat of the bomb.

Then it was done.

55

Visitors came in increasing numbers to congratulate Jamie.

The first visitor Christine allowed into Jamie's room was Diana Apersain, his first love. They touched hands and tears came to Diana's eyes. Christine backed out of Jamie's room and closed the door.

"I came to see you at the hospital. I was so scared."

"I knew you were there. Or else I dreamed it."

"I talked to you for a half hour. Then I kissed you when no one was looking."

Jamie smiled. "Damn, I missed that? Well, how about we try that again?"

She leaned down and kissed him fully on the mouth.

"You're my first love," she said. "And I'm so proud of you. You saved all those little kids."

"*We* did. Remember, you and I worked on TRAC together."

"But you were the brains behind it."

"Anyway, I'm lying here thinking we should form a company and be partners in it. We can license our software around the world."

She smiled. "I'm supposed to go to college next year. At least according to my mom."

Jamie took her by the hand and pulled her close. He kissed her again.

"Let me handle your mom," he said. "We can make her an offer that makes more sense than college."

"I'm in. Let's move ahead."

"As soon as they let me get up, we're moving."

Jamie was also visited by the FBI representatives who came to apologize for the shooting. Their shooting panel had ruled the shooting justified, but, in the aftermath, they had also decided the young man was a hero and deserved special recognition. So they brought him a plaque with a brief inscription and presented it to him.

Jamie accepted the plaque and accepted the apology. Then he made one of his own.

"I'm not really a gun guy," he told the Regional Special Agent. "I shouldn't have been touching my mom's gun. It was really stupid of me."

They agreed but didn't push it. He shouldn't have touched the gun, especially given the circumstances of XFBI agents on duty protecting him.

Then they dropped it and left. Jamie felt better and told everyone he wouldn't ever so much as touch a gun again. He had better ways to spend his time.

The police officials came to say thanks. They wanted to move ahead with full installations of TRAC. Their attorneys were ready to talk to Jamie's attorneys about licensing the software.

The principal of the Windsor School dropped in and cried when she saw the young man who'd saved her students. Two of the students from Windsor presented him with letters from every student. All with smiling suns and happy faces. Jamie was embarrassed but accepted the accolades as best he could.

By the Friday of that week Jamie was back up and moving around on his crutches. Diana came by several more times and they sat at their laptops, coding and laughing.

56

M onday 12:00 P.M.

HEADED BACK TO CHICAGO.

He stopped for gas at the Exxon on the southern edge of Ann Arbor. The pump refused his company credit card. He tried it again, pulling it out and slowly sliding it back in.

Refused.

He tried again, moving it in and out of the slot as fast as possible. Refused.

A prickly feeling played across his abdomen. No, try Amex.

He pushed the platinum Amex into the slot. Refused.

Once again. Refused again.

He hurried inside the station and pushed a hundred dollar bill across the counter.

"I need a hundred bucks on six, please."

"A whole hundred?"

"Just a fill. Whatever. I'm in a hurry, here. Whatever it takes."

"All right." The clerk pressed the button on six and nodded. "Good to go. But your car just left, buddy. You want I should call the cops?"

But he knew. He knew all too well.

"No. No need. But can you call me a cab?"

"Pay phone's outside. You need change?"

"I've got my cell."

Then he thought about the cell phone, realized it was a phone she paid for, and he smiled. "I need change. Cell won't work, I'm positive."

"Somebody must have clipped your wings, buddy."

"Something like that."

He went outside to the pay phone. He was certain none of his credit cards would work in the phone, including the AT&T card. She controlled them and he had the picture. He did have his own bank debit card, a Visa, but the phone refused it. It wanted a credit card, which he didn't have. Not anymore.

He fed quarters into the silver slot.

Then he dialed. "Jennifer, Ed. Put Christine on, please."

Moments later the line clicked on. "Yes?"

"I'm sorry."

"I know you are."

"I love you."

"I know you do."

"Can you at least hear me out?"

"Goodbye, Ed. Enjoy your family."

"Goodbye, Chris."

"Senator Robertson? My name is Christine Susmann. I'm calling from Chicago."

"Christine," the Senator effused. "How kind of you to call."

"Thank you."

"You did call me. Thanks for that, Christine.

"Sure."

"Listen, you and I should meet. Would you have time if I flew into Chicago?"

"Sure. I'll make time. When?"

"Does this Saturday work?"

"It works just fine."

"Fine. What do you say we plan on Ditka's for that big steak Saturday night. Interested?"

"I can always find something at Ditka's. I'm in."

"Wonderful. I'll call you when I touch down."

"Okay."

"And don't worry about dress. I'm a blue jeans guy on weekends."

"That will work well, then, I'm a blue jeans girl."

"Hell, we might even want to dance a dance or two before the night's over."

"You know, we just might at that."

57

T he jury awarded her forty million dollars from each
defendant, which could be said to represent one million
dollars for each family member she lost to the DuMont
brothers and the United States Air Force.

Althea still had the DuMonts' trainload of documents; the
DuMonts still knew better than to harm her. If they did--as she had
made it abundantly clear--the documents she would release would
make Edward Snowden's efforts look trivial.

Sevi's satisfaction was short-lived.

By the time she and Christine stepped out of the federal building
onto Dearborn Street, the young computer professional felt an over-
whelming sense of grief. She checked both ways on the sidewalk.

"You riding home with me?" Christine asked.

Sevi shook her head.

"It's time I found my own place."

"Well you certainly have the money to do that now."

"I do. I will, thanks to you."

"Look, please come home with me and let me help pack your
things."

"No, I just want to walk."

"Understand. Grab a cab later?"

"Yes."

"Got cab fare?"

Sevi touched her shoulder bag. She nodded.

"I'm okay, Chris. I just need to be alone."

"Well, hey. The Sisters in Law will be meeting at Durant's at noon. What do you say?"

"Noon today?"

"Yep."

"That's on the Loop somewhere?"

"Yep. Durant's."

"Me and you and Althea and Winona?"

"Yep."

"That's all? No men?"

"Do you mean is Senator Robertson still in town? No, he's back in D.C."

"So maybe I'll come there. I think I will."

"We all love you, Sevi. We're your family now, you know."

Sevi's eyes brightened. "That was it. I was feeling lonely."

"Come on, jump in my car. We can go there now."

Sevi tapped her foot on the sidewalk. She patted her purse and glanced around.

"Okay. I'm in."

"Yes, you are."

58

The Kin-Tooka proprietors of the Hong Kong flower giant hadn't noticed anything odd about their server farm. As the seller of forty-six percent of all flowers sold in China the daily traffic on the servers numbered in the millions of transactions. Each transaction consisted of a product, a receipt for the sale, a delivery time and place, and the common data surrounding commercial transactions. Each transaction required no more than a few bytes of storage on the servers.

The computers were serviced in house. Kin-Tooka's IT department consisted of eighty-eight dedicated Chinese citizens, each of whom had no less than a bachelor's degree in computer science or software engineering. How, then, it would be asked, could such an exemplary group of coders, database administrators, and systems engineers have missed the millions upon millions of documents that arrived on the network and were distributed among the machines that made up the server farm almost randomly? The answer was simple: the owner of the documents had simply disguised each document as a flower sale. The document itself was disguised as product, the date on the document was disguised as the date of sale, the recipient of the document was disguised as the purchaser in the flower transaction, and the seller of the flowers was none other than Blackguard itself. Genius, it would be said in the years to come. But who could have concocted such an intelligent scheme that passed through firewalls and data integrity scans without notice and without a single failure?

The answer to that inquiry was found inside the bedroom of a sixteen year old computer geek in Chicago, Illinois. His name: Jamie Susmann. Only two people would ever know about his role in the greatest theft of military-industrial documents in the history of the United States. One of these was his own mother. The second was the woman who had gone to work for Blackguard and tapped into its own databases and uploaded the code that transferred the company's documents first to Ireland, then to Peru, then to Haiti, and then on to Hong Kong. Neither woman was talking and neither was the sixteen year-old.

With the documents in place in Hong Kong, Christine Susmann then went on the offensive.

It was time to ruin the DuMont brothers.

But how would she do that? Physical attacks would be too empty and wouldn't accomplish the purpose of destroying their company, their worldwide vigilante and oil procurer: Blackguard. So physical was crossed off the list.

Next, a lawsuit was considered. But that had already been done and had conferred a huge sum of money on Sevi al-Assad. Another lawsuit—predicated on an extant theory of action—would not destroy the company. Using its thousands of contracts with the United States government the company would quickly bounce back from any economic loss a lawsuit might incur. So a lawsuit was crossed off the list.

How do we ruin the company? Thought Christine as she was driven into her office in Chicago one icy morning in January. The answer materialized before her eyes when she saw a street musician blowing a saxophone on the Madison Street Bridge over the Chicago River. He was bundled up against the icy temperatures but wore fingerless gloves to allow his skin to contact the keys on his sax. She realized then and there that the lowest common denominator of the DuMont brothers was the same as the saxophone: their stock in trade. And what was their stock in trade? Why, stock, of course.

She would attack their stock.

She would cause their stock to plummet in price to the point where it became worthless. Worthless as the ink that composed the stock certificates. Made worthless by the scheme that came together in her head that freezing January morning.

"Stop the car!" she told her driver.

He did. He put on his hazard lights and ignored the angry honking that erupted from behind.

Christine jumped from the black Mercedes and walked back up the sidewalk to the street musician. She pulled a bundle of bills from her shoulder satchel and paid them into the musician's open instrument case.

"Enjoy your week," she told him with a smile. "And thanks."

"Lady, thanks for what. But you ain't even heard me play."

"I'm donating for what you're *going* to play. It's going to be sweet and it's going to give respite to people from this cheerless city."

"I don't even know what you saying."

She did a quick curtsey and began walking back to her car.

"And I don't play the saxophone. So we're even. Thanks again!"

CHRISTINE and her staff reviewed Blackguard's SEC filings. The filings were self-disclosures about Blackguard's fiscal doings. She was able to assess the size of the company in dollars and the value of the company in stock shares and the bottom line: Assets Minus Liabilities = Net Value. The DuMonts' ownership in Blackguard amounted to 95% of the brothers' personal net worth. Christine was elated, because she now knew that if she ruined Blackguard she would break the brothers. They wouldn't have enough assets left over to pay off other liabilities such as mortgages, commercial paper, and private loans from private corporations and associations.

Where to begin to break them?

Christine hired a team of CPAs and lawyers to locate and analyze all contracts between the United States military and Blackguard. Reports came in thirty days later. One-hundred and thirty-three thousand such contracts had been located and analyzed and future profits projected and summed. Then the same thing was done with contracts between Blackguard and agencies of the United States. Forty-six thousand contracts were located and analyzed and future profits projected and summed. At this point, Christine knew Blackguard's projected gross profits over the next sixty months.

The bottom line became clear: if she could de-value the stock of Blackguard to the point where it was worthless on paper and obtained that worthless paper for herself, she would be left with a small warehouse full of contracts that stood to net in excess of one-hundred billion dollars over the next five years.

So the question became: how do we gain control of a super corporation's stock? She had nowhere near enough resources to do that by herself. She would need help.

So she turned to Pilcher, Rasmussen, Damon, Escard'a and Floe, the world's largest stock brokerage.

"I want to short Blackguard's stock," she told her broker.

"What does that mean, short their stock?" Jamie asked her as he overheard Christine's phone call with the broker.

So when she got off the phone she explained it to her son.

"Read this," she told him, and handed him a one page strategy sheet created by her CPA team:

TO: CHRISTINE SUSMANN
FROM: STRATEGY TEAM RE BLACKGUARD INC.

Ordinarily when you invest in stocks, you hope to profit from a company's good times and rising profits. But there's a whole other class of investors, called shorts, who do just the opposite. They search the Internet for news stories about diners getting food poisoning at a restaurant, for instance, and look for ways to cash in on the stock falling.

To sell a stock short, you follow four steps:

*1.**Borrow the stock you want to bet against.** Contact your broker to find shares of the stock you think will go down and request to borrow the shares. The broker loans you the shares. Sometimes outside lenders will be needed as well.*

*2.**You immediately sell the shares you have borrowed.** You pocket the cash from the sale.*

*3.**You wait for the stock to fall and then buy the shares back at the new, lower price.***

*4.**You return the shares to the brokerage you borrowed them from and pocket the difference.***

Here's an example: Shares of ABC Company are trading for $40 a share, which you think is way too high. You contact your broker, who lets you borrow 100 shares. You sell the shares and pocket $4,000. Two weeks later, the company reports its CEO has been stealing money and the stock falls to $25 a share. You buy 100 shares of ABC Company for $2,500, give the shares back to the brokerage you borrowed them from and pocket a $1,500 profit.

"So you are going to short the stock of Blackguard?" Jamie asked.

"Yes, I am."

"Do you know the CEO of Blackguard has been stealing? Is that how you're going to depress the price and make it fall through the floor?"

Christine smiled at her son.

"I can do much better than embezzlement," she said. "I've got murder, torture, theft, rape, pillaging, country-building, anarchy, genocide, and on and on. The list of crimes committed by Blackguard is endless."

"But how can you prove it?"

"You know the documents you transferred to Hong Kong?"

"Sure, mom."

"They have been scanned and data-mined. We now have a data-base for armed conflicts, for infrastructure building, for petroleum mining, refining, and sales, for electric power plants, and—"

"Okay, mom, I get it. Blackguard is into everything that can earn it a dollar. So how does it go broke?"

Christine nodded and closed her eyes.

"Imagine this. Imagine millions of shares of Blackguard stock being dumped on the stock market. All owned shares are sold at a loss. A huge loss."

"What makes that happen?"

"CNN makes that happen."

"By doing what?"

"By reporting on Blackguard's abuses and crimes beginning with the fall of Saigon at the end of the Vietnam War up to and including its interference and war-making and petroleum theft in Baghdad, Pakistan, Afghanistan, and now Syria."

"Flower sales. Hong Kong flower sales," Jamie said. His face lit up. "Holy shit, mom. That's brilliant."

"CNN has the files as of twelve midnight tonight. At that exact moment they are uploaded to WikiLeaks. At nine in the morning Althea Berenson will be interviewed live on CNN and tell the world about the threat Blackguard has made against her life if the files go up on WikiLeaks. She names names, Edlund and Wilfred DuMont. If anything happens to me, she says, go after these two men."

"Genius."

"When the stock prices go through the floor we buy and then return the borrowed shares. With interest, of course. The difference between what we sold the shares for and what we bought them for will be astronomical."

FORTY-EIGHT HOURS LATER, after a massive sell-off of its stock, Blackguard lay smoldering, burned to the ground. The run on its stock had been instantaneous following the WikiLeaks/CNN disclosure. Where the DuMont brothers had once owned stock worth in excess of $400 a share, their stock was now virtually worthless. They could not borrow enough to keep their company operating with short-term cash while the government contracts paid off like the slot machines they were. The government contracts then went into default when Blackguard could no longer perform on them. All work under the contracts came to a sudden and full stop. Government payments dried up. Blackguard officers went unpaid and walked off. Blackguard workers went home without paychecks and didn't return.

∾

THIRTY DAYS LATER, Blackguard filed a Chapter 11 bankruptcy case in New York's bankruptcy court in Manhattan. Liabilities far exceeded Assets. The DuMont brothers were finished. The bright spot: the Blackguard employees had priority claims against the remaining assets of the company and their wages were paid before all other claims. Families were fed and clothed and life continued as usual for that group made special according to the bankruptcy laws that grant priorities to certain creditors. Christine exulted when the bankruptcy trustee paid the workers.

All was well with the people who had actually earned the money for their employer.

And she exulted because Blackguard, along with the DuMont brothers, had gone out of business.

∾

SO...THE sisters in law threw a party. A dinner party. It began at eight o'clock on April 15 in Scottsdale at the Branding Iron. Christine had flown her friends to Scottsdale for a shopping spree and makeovers paid for by the DuMont brothers.

During the dinner, Sevi al-Assad announced that she was funding a girls' school in her home town of Deir ez-Zor in Syria. The DuMonts were paying for that out of her share of the short sale.

Then it was Althea's turn. She announced that she was funding a mini-Pulitzer annual prize for the best military-industrial reporting of the year. It would be awarded to five deserving writers on an annual basis, available anywhere in the world, and would include cash prizes of $100,000 per winner. The DuMonts were paying for that.

Winona's turn came around when the main course was done and cleared away.

"I'm investing in stem-cell research for victims of violent crimes who need organ and tissue repair. I will be the first patient and it will go out from there. Hopefully I can quit wearing this bag that I've been married to under my clothes. Oh, and thank you Ed and Will DuMont. Your contribution to our medical quest is applauded."

During after-dinner coffee it came to be Christine's turn.

"I am turning over my share of the short sale to Infinite Water. IW is a company I've created that is going to begin digging and capping clear water wells in Ethiopia and spread worldwide from there. The technology is also being created to purify black water."

The party went on for three more days before ending in Chicago with a Cubs game and box seats along the first base line.

The Cubbies lost.

Unfortunately.

But predictably, blowing a six run lead in the top of the ninth and failing to score in the bottom of the inning.

From his home on the banks of the Potomac River, Edlund DuMont turned off the TV.

"Nationals beat the Cubbies," he said to his wife, Ginny. "We won one."

"We did?" said Ginny. "We got a letter today says the bankruptcy court wants to sell our house."

"We'll find another house," growled Edlund.

"With what?" said Ginny. "We have nothing left but the little bit I inherited from my Dad thirty years ago."

"So we'll rent."

"How so? You need good credit. We're bankrupt."

"I'll think of something."

"Not watching the baseball games all day and all night you won't."

"That's when I do my best thinking."

"Then do this. Every time one of your players crosses home plate, think 'home.'"

"Home."

"As in, we need one or I'm moving in my sister."

"We could always do that."

"Who said anything about 'we'?"

"Well, then."

"Home, Edlund. Home."

He would never watch baseball again, not with the same enthusiasm. For every time a run scored he was reminded.

He had no place else to go.

THE END

ALSO BY JOHN ELLSWORTH

HARLEY ELLIS SERIES

No Trivial Pursuit - Detective Noir

Hollywood Division (preorder)

HISTORICAL FICTION

The Point of Light

Unspeakable Prayers

Lies She Never Told Me

THADDEUS MURFEE SERIES

A Young Lawyer's Story

The Defendants

Beyond a Reasonable Death

Attorney at Large

Chase, the Bad Baby

Defending Turquoise

The Mental Case

The Girl Who Wrote The New York Times Bestseller

The Trial Lawyer

The Near Death Experience

Flagstaff Station

The Crime

La Jolla Law

The Postoffice (Preorder)

SISTERS IN LAW SERIES

Frat Party: Sisters In Law

Hellfire: Sisters In Law

MICHAEL GRESHAM SERIES

The Lawyer

Secrets Girls Keep

The Law Partners

Carlos the Ant

Sakharov the Bear

Annie's Verdict

Dead Lawyer on Aisle 11

30 Days of Justis

The Fifth Justice

PSYCHOLOGICAL THRILLERS

The Empty Place at the Table

ABOUT THE AUTHORS

John Ellsworth lives in Mexico with his wife and dogs and guinea pigs. The Pacific Ocean is out the front door and the mountains of La Mision out the back.

John writes books and music. He plays guitar, and his favorite musician is Naudo Rodrigues of Tenerife, Spain.

His favorite book is yet to be written.

Jode Ellsworth is the sister of John Ellsworth. She lives in Mexico with John and his wife, dogs and guinea pigs. In a prior life Jode was an editor at one of the Big Five publishing houses until she decided to put her own words on the page and see if anybody wanted to read them. They did.

Jode also teaches creative writing over by Skype and she presently counts a dozen writers among her students, many of whom you may have heard of if you read romantic suspense.

ellsworthbooks.com
johnellsworthbooks@gmail.com

For Our Family

Made in the USA
Middletown, DE
21 September 2020